INFANTS OF THE BRUSH
A CHIMNEY SWEEP'S STORY

A. M. Watson

Red Acre Press
CASTLE ROCK, COLORADO

Red Acre Press
Castle Rock, CO
www.redacrepress.com
enquires@redacrepress.com

Infants of the Brush: A Chimney Sweep's Story is a work of fiction. Names, characters, places, and incidents are a product of the author's imagination. Locales and public names are sometimes used for atmospheric purposes. Any resemblance to actual people, living or dead, or to businesses, companies, events, institutions, or locales is completely coincidental.

Cover design by Carrie Knoles
Cover images: A. M. Watson (boy), iStock.com (rooftops and chimney)
Book Layout ©2017 BookDesignTemplates.com

Infants of the Brush: A Chimney Sweep's Story / A. M. Watson. -- 1st ed.

ISBN 978-0-9995122-0-3, 978-0-9995122-2-7

eBook ISBN 978-0-9995122-1-0, 978-0-9995122-3-4

Library of Congress Control Number: 2017957288

For Caleb, Seth, Malachi, Titus, and Lydia
May you seek adventure beyond the familiar
and find what makes your heart soar.

Part One
London, 1720

"We come now to burning little chimney sweepers. A large party is invited to dinner – a great display is to be made; and about an hour before dinner, there is an alarm that the kitchen chimney is on fire! It is impossible to put off the distinguished personages who are expected. It gets very late for the soup and fish – the cook is frantic – all eyes are turned upon the sable consolation of the master chimney sweeper – and up into the midst of the burning chimney is sent one of the miserable little infants of the brush."

-Edinburgh Review, 1819

CHAPTER I

Reeves grasped the haypennies in his pocket and counted each one as it slid through his fingertips. Four coppers. He needed eight pence before returning to Distaff Lane, twelve if he wanted to earn Master Armory's goodwill.

In the early hours of the morning, Reeves had scoured a chimney clogged with soot thick enough to catch fire. He scraped away at the sticky grime until the lingering smoke was drawn up the flue into the cool autumn air. The work was worth far more than four coins.

His stomach rumbled as he fingered the coins again. Some days he found work that paid a few coins as well as a scrap of food. No such luck today.

"Sweep, sweep," Reeves yelled up at closed shutters.

No one responded. London was on holiday.

The lower classes observed Gunpowder Treason Day with disorder and revelry while respectable society waited out the lecherous festivities locked inside their homes. Opening the backdoor for a chimney sweep's boy was ordinary enough, but opening your door for any reason on Gunpowder Treason Day was like inviting Guy Fawkes to Parliament and offering him flint and steel to ignite the explosives.

Not many were that foolish. Even constables patrolled in groups, avoiding certain streets unless their services were necessary to prevent London from burning to the ground again. London was a tinderbox. The sheriff's bucket boys patrolled the streets to extinguish destructive fires while illegal behavior thrived unnoticed.

The dregs of society, those too poor to belong to the lower classes, had only one choice on holiday: seek charity or engage in crime.

Reeves was considering the latter when several men rolled a flaming barrel of tar down the street, yelling vulgarities between pulls on flagons of liquor. Reeves backed away.

The men steered the barrel with long poles away from the piles of wood, rotten clothing, broken furniture, and other debris that dotted the streets. The rubbish would be lit when the sky darkened, lighting up the city with the glow of bonfires. The embers would burn long into the night, turn to ash, and add to the filth on London's streets.

Reeves wandered through the commotion, looking to rooflines for chimneys smoking too much or too little. There must be work somewhere. Although, if he could not earn enough to face Master Armory tonight at least he could sleep warm on the streets.

A group of peasants marched down the street holding a tall figure in dirty white robes; orange flames consumed its head. Onlookers jeered and spat at the effigy. The peasants replied with smiles and cheers. Reeves squeezed through the crowd to get a better look.

"Who is that?" he tugged on the skirt of a woman standing next to him.

"Why that be a figure of Pope Clement hisself."

"Wot's they burnin' him for?"

"He plots to assassinate King George. Wicked like Guy Fawkes he is."

"And the Stuarts too."

"Yer a smart lad." The woman smiled, revealing rows of brown, decaying teeth. "Wot's yer name, child?"

"Reeves."

"That yer birth name?"

"Don't know."

"And who be yer parents?"

"Never had any."

"We all had parents."

"Not me."

The woman reached out to the sweeping mask Reeves wore on his head. She tucked a frayed piece of yarn into the folds.

"There now. It's out of yer eyes."

"Thank ye," Reeves mumbled.

"A mum prayed for you, of that I'm sure." Her eyes betrayed loss, long past but always new.

Reeves dropped his head to look at his bare feet.

"Come child, help us build." She picked up a bundle of refuse and walked toward a small pyre in the middle of the street.

Reeves started to follow her and then froze when he saw the image of the Devil fixed on a wood pole. Its black eyes stared down at Reeves from beneath a brown cloak held up by long twisted horns. The stare dug into his soul.

Reeves shuddered.

He imagined the figure descending the pyre, grabbing him, and dragging him to the depths of Hell. He staggered around the side of a stone building and ran. The heat of the Devil's eyes followed him.

The streets had taught Reeves four absolute truths: respect King George or lose your head, be wary of Stuart conspirators, obey God and the church, and, most importantly, flee from the Devil.

Reeves ran down two streets before he slowed his pace and looked about. No demons haunted his view. He fingered the coins in his pockets again.

"Sweep," Reeves yelled. It was futile. No more doors would open to him today.

Reeves found an empty spot on the street corner and sat on his sack of ashes. Careful to avoid the charred skin along his cheek, Reeves rubbed at the soot in his red, swollen eyes. His dirty knuckles aggravated the inflammation, releasing a bit of pus.

"Away with you!"

Reeves looked up at a rotund man gesturing aggressively at him with his arms.

"No beggars on my corner!"

"I be a sweep, sir, not a beggar. Mightn't yer chimney need a brush, sir? Only a fourpence. There's no other sweep betta than me."

"No whelp! Off with you!"

"You there!" A man stripped down to his small clothes yelled and stumbled towards the merchant's door. "A drink my good man!" he slurred.

The merchant ran inside and slammed the door. A bolt slid into place.

"Jackeen," the man mumbled as he slumped down against the closed door.

Reeves picked up his brush and sack and headed towards Thames Street. Business was always happening there. With a bit of luck, he would find an odd job in exchange for a boiled potato.

Thames Street boomed with excitement. People dashed across the wide cobblestone street with fuel to build their fires.

"Thief! That's our wood, you bloody thief!"

A group of angry pursuers tackled a man running down the street with an armful of kindling. Fists pummeled the accused while new thieves snatched up the scattered wood and disappeared.

Bystanders knocked Reeves aside to jump into the fray. Fists walloped friend, foe, and stranger. Blood and rotten teeth sprinkled the pavement as constables blew whistles from the sidelines.

Across the street, boys were setting squibs on fire and tossing them into the air to explode. Reeves watched wee sparks of light erupt from each firecracker. The white flames flickered and disappeared as if they had never been.

The sounds of fighting, revelry, and firecrackers intensified as the sky darkened. Bonfires illuminated the streets with crackling flames. A stream of alcohol ignited into a line of fire leading to an effigy of Guy Fawkes. Reeves watched as flames devoured the traitorous wretch.

A group of children skipped around another fire, singing between squealing peals of laughter:

"The fifth of November, since I can remember,
Was Guy Fawkes, poke him in the eye,
Shove him up the chimney-pot, and there let him die.

A stick and a stake, for King George's sake,
If you don't give me one, I'll take two.

The better for me, and the worse for you,
Ricket-a-racket your hedges shall go."

Reeves watched the children. He crept closer to hear their lyrics and laughter. The fire began to warm his skin when the children noticed his blackened face and inflamed eyes.

"Demon!" yelled a girl.

"Changling!"

The children's laughter turned to screams of delight as they hurled insults at Reeves and ran about in mock terror.

"Troll!"

"Get back you demon!"

"Devil boy!"

When the children began chanting "burn the troll, burn the troll," Reeves covered his ears and backed away.

"I'm no troll," he screamed.

He was a parish orphan, without parents or a real name, but he was not a changling – a troll left in the cradle to replace a baby stolen from careless parents.

Finding an empty spot away from the bonfires, Reeves sat on his ashes, drew his knees up, and wrapped his bony arms around himself. He watched the spectacle as tears stung his eyes and flowed down his cheeks.

Reeves could smell meat roasting somewhere nearby. His mouth watered. He watched the celebration decline into drunkenness and decided not to go hungry again tonight. He put his sweeping brush into the burlap sack of ash and hid the sack in a darkened corner.

Reeves milled through the inebriated crowds.

"To King George!" a man bellowed.

"To King George!" the crowd echoed.

"Long live the king!"

"Long live the king!"

When heads tipped back and liquor flowed down, Reeves' wee hands darted in and out of unattended pockets. He relocated coins to his own pocket and limped away by dragging his left foot along the cobblestones.

No one noticed a cripple, and every street urchin could fake a good malady.

Reeves circled the bonfires, careful not to spend too much time in any one place along the street. Feeling the weight in his pocket, he retreated into a dark alley off Thames Street.

He studied the coins in his hands.

"Maybe I do be a demon," he choked. Stealing was the Devil's work.

Reeves untied the empty drawstring purse around his waist and put the coins inside. He added the haypennies from his pocket before hiding the pouch under his britches and walking back to the street.

"A bit more and I will never pinch again," Reeves whispered to himself.

Tears traced fresh charcoal lines down his cheeks. Reeves took a deep breath and wiped the shame from his eyes.

More than one thief worked the crowded streets. The next two unattended pockets were already empty.

Reeves picked up a discarded purse. He opened it and, finding it empty, dropped it back on the ground. Reeves wandered, reassuring himself that he could make his soul right again in the morning.

At the edge of the firelight, Reeves saw something flicker from the folds of discarded cloth. Like the spark of a squib, only lasting.

Reeves picked up the cloth. It was a discarded women's blouse. The collar ruffle was torn and stained. Underneath a slit in the fabric, there was a jeweled pendant. Three rows of seed pearls surrounded the round cut stone. Reeves held it up to the firelight. The edges of the jewel flashed a brilliant red. Mesmerized, he traced the edge of the pendant with his finger. It was beautiful.

"Long live the king!"

The words startled him. Reeves clutched his fist around the blouse and held it to his chest. He caught his breath and looked around.

Did anyone see him pick up the blouse? Was the jewel real? The stone was clear and brilliant; it could not be colored plaster. Why had it been thrown away with the rubbish to burn in the streets? It had to be worth at least five guineas. He needed five guineas.

Reeves ripped the pendant from the fabric and threw the ruined blouse into the closest bonfire. He rushed through the crowd, taking the jewel far from where he found it. People flew by unnoticed as he hurried to retrieve his tools and sack of ash.

At the edge of Thames Street, voices began jeering at him.

"What you running for wretch?"

"Stop, you bloody broomer!"

Reeves looked over his shoulder. The hooligans of Cheapside had spotted him. They were a gang of boys who had escaped their masters and survived by stealing from working children.

Reeves continued to run until he reached the corner where his sack remained hidden. In the darkness, he buried the pendant beneath handfuls of ash.

"Filthy little jacke."

Reeves turned to face his pursuers. His chest heaved from exertion. Dirty ash sifted through his hands.

The boys sauntered towards him, eyes gleaming in the darkness.

Reeves groped for the drawstring purse tied around his waist and held it out to the boys.

"Take me coins and leave me be," Reeves pleaded.

"We've been watching you tonight, stealing from honest folk." The largest of the boys sauntered through the others to face Reeves. "Hey, ain't you the one that stole our coppers?"

"I never stole nuffink from you," Reeves stammered.

"I think it was you."

"It was him, Scot, I know it," said one of the other boys.

"What shall we do to him, Scot? Can we rough him up?" The boys circled Reeves.

"Please just take me coins," Reeves cried.

Scot tore the bag of coins from Reeves' hand and pulled at the strings. "Not bad, not bad. At least two bobs. Check his sack."

Two of the boys unfolded the burlap material and looked inside.

"Nuffink but ash and an old brush."

"Don't need that. I ain't never sweeping another brick. What more do you got?" Scot asked.

"Nuffink. I got nuffink more," Reeves said.

"A thief always has sumfink more."

"But I don't."

"Then you owe us a bit of fun."

Scot's fist slammed into Reeves' face, followed by a punch to his empty gut.

"Have at him, boys!" Scot yelled.

Reeves crumpled to the ground as hits came from all directions. His eyes went dark.

CHAPTER II

"**E**gan."
   The sound was in Mum's voice today, the sound that Egan had been waiting to hear.

"Take Kerrin down to the dock to see if yer Da's ship has anchored. We can't let the ship arrive with no one waiting for him."

Egan's face lit with anticipation.

Live every day as if I am coming home tomorrow, Da had said. *Think about wot you say and how you act. Obey yer Mum. If I come home tomorrow, next week, or even next year, I want to be proud of you and know you are doing yer best.*

When Egan was old enough to go outside by himself, he wanted to go to the dock every day to watch for Da. Mum would not consent until the time of Da's return was close. He sometimes went anyway. When Da's ship, the Earnest Vesper, came down the River Thames, he and Kerrin would be waiting by the dock.

Egan wished that Da never had to leave. His visits home were much too short, and his time away was far too long.

An Irishman called by the sea can never be happy on dry land, Da had said.

Wot does that sound like, when the sea calls? Egan had asked.

It's a sound that the heart hears. The sound that tells you yer home among the waters. Yer Irish, me boy, and the sea will be calling you.

It will?

To be sure. Then you'll meet a lass with such beauty that yer heart will split in two, between the sea and yer lass. Da's free hand had circled Mum's waist.

Pretty talk for a sailor, Mum had replied.

You know I love thee more than the sea.

Then turn yer back on the water and return to me. Mum always told Da that before he left.

Near eight weeks had passed since Egan had watched Da's ship depart. Egan did not want to be left behind any longer. He had heard the sea's call as surely as he had been born with saltwater in his veins.

Da had promised to sign him on as a ship's boy when he was old enough. Egan was determined to convince Da he was ready.

"Tis there!" Egan exclaimed. "Can you see the mast, Kerrin?"

Egan pulled Kerrin up to hold her on his hip and pointed to the merchant ship traveling down the River Thames into the slow waters of the Pool of London. The vessel's progress was slow as ships competed for space along the bank.

"Da!" Kerrin yelled although the ship was further away than her squeaky little voice could travel.

"That's right, Kerrin. Da is on that ship!"

By nightfall, Egan would be singing Irish songs with his father following a dinner of mutton stew Mum had simmering back home.

Egan was different when Da was at sea. Each time Da left, Egan had to figure out anew how to keep going. Mum and Kerrin were different too. It was not living. It was surviving; a mere passing of each day to preserve the present so that Da would not miss anything. As Da's ship drew near, Egan's whole body began to tremble in excitement. Egan slid Kerrin to the ground, grabbed her tiny hand, and ran with her down the embankment laughing and waving their free hands at the approaching ship.

Egan looked for Da on the deck. He would be there to wave.

A ghrá mo chroí, he would call out. *Tell Mum I have returned.*

It would be a while before Da was free to leave the ship; it would anchor as the crew brought the goods from below deck to negotiate sales with the merchants, but still, Da was home.

Egan and Kerrin waited on the bank, searching for Da as the crew unloaded the goods. Da did not appear.

"Not Da's ship," Kerrin whined as she tugged at Egan's sleeve.

"But it tis." Egan recognized the letters on the hull, the frame of its masts, the tarnished color of the tied down sails.

At dusk, when the crew was released from duty aboard the vessel, Egan approached a departing sailor.

"Sir, could you fetch me Da?" Egan requested. "He hasn't come above deck yet."

"Would you be Whit's boy?" the sailor asked.

"Aye, sir."

The sailor gripped Egan's shoulder with a calloused hand, "Son, the sea claims those she loves."

CHAPTER III

The world was as dead as Da. Clouds darkened the sky while autumn stripped leaves from the trees and slowly surrendered to winter's bleak hoarfrost. The light in Mum's eyes was gone. The daily activities of work and play subsided as Mum spent hours staring into the fireplace. It was not the flames or hot coals that held her attention; the fire remained unlit.

The captain visited Mum the day after arriving in port. He described the accident aboard ship and the prayers said over Da before surrendering his body to the sea. He gave Da's share of the sale of goods to Mum and included an extra stipend. A captain does his duty to the departed's family. The money would not last long, but it absolved the captain's responsibility for their loss.

Mum accepted the news with vacant recognition. She thanked the captain, placed the money on the table, and resumed her place by the cold fireplace.

Mum was gone too. She moved and breathed, but callousness weighed down her mind and crushed her spirit. Mum forgot how to live. She did not remember to eat or prepare food for Egan and Kerrin. She did not wash or tidy their small home. She abandoned her position of stitching for the tailor. The extra wages were not much but always filled the gaps in expenses while Da was away. When payment was due on their tenancy, Mum did not acknowledge the debt or arrange for a late payment.

Egan set about conquering the impossible task laid before him. He sought after every job he could find, but paid work for a child was scarce, and he wasn't strong enough for larger tasks. For a wee sum, Mister Carrington paid Egan to make deliveries, carry crates, and keep the street in front of the dry goods store clear of dung. Neighbors and friends came by with food, candles, and coal. Still, the charity of others only stretched so far.

In the bitter cold of January, Kerrin caught the fever. Her reddish-brown curls clung to her damp forehead. Her eyes were teary and red. She coughed until her throat bled. On the fifth day of the fever, thousands of red bumps erupted from her skin. Kerrin thrashed in her sleep and scratched the blisters until they bled. Egan tied her hands together with scraps of cloth to keep her from opening fresh wounds, but nothing he did eased her suffering.

Kerrin's illness awakened Mum to their desperate situation. She stayed close by Kerrin's side, soothing her skin with cool water Egan brought from the cistern. Mister Carrington sent Egan home with potatoes, but the coal and money were gone. The dreadful cold seeped in from the night.

Egan tucked a blanket around Kerrin's feverish wee body.

"Yer me bestest brother," Kerrin whispered.

"I'm yer only brother," Egan responded.

"Me bestest brother." Kerrin attempted to smile.

Egan found it difficult to comprehend that his cheery, four-year-old sister, just two years younger than him, was marked for death.

"She needs the apothecary," Mum muttered. "But there is no money for theriac."

"How much is it?" Egan asked.

Mum ignored his question. She knelt in silence, watching Kerrin. Then Mum fixed her eyes upon Egan. She studied him as if seeing him for the first time. He started to ask his question again but was silenced with a slight shake of her head.

"There's no choice," Mum murmured, pushing a stray hair back towards her loose bun. "Kerrin won't survive the workhouse. You know that, Egan. Don't you?"

"Yes, Mum."

"Would you help her?" Mum asked.

"Yes, Mum."

"Will you do wot I ask, Egan?"

"Yes, Mum."

He had never heard this sound in her voice before.

Mum grasped her arms around him. Egan tried to pull away, but she held him and broke into a sorrowful cry. Mum wept as if Da had just died.

Egan surrendered to Mum's embrace. He choked on his grief and allowed Mum to comfort him. He understood then. He understood the paralysis of pain. He let the ache wash over him and released the confines of his sorrow. In Mum's arms, he was safe again.

Life had been restored, and tomorrow they would find their way.

CHAPTER IV

The hired carriage stopped in front of Goldsmith's Hall where a red brick building stood on the corner of Maiden and Foster Lanes. Its Doric columns extended upwards towards the arms of the Worshipful Company of Goldsmiths – a shield bearing leopards, cups, and buckles between two unicorns.

Paul de Lamerie stepped down from the carriage and looked up at the imposing building. "A plague on my pocketbook," he muttered.

Lamerie had been admitted into the livery at the Company three years earlier – a great accomplishment for a man of only 29. He admitted to his wife, Louisa, that it was quite a surprise considering he had not yet paid the £20 fine for not having his work hallmarked the year before. Since his admission to the livery, Lamerie walked a fine line between hallmarking his work for society clients and making ends meet by selling silver on the unregistered market. To his wealthy clients, he appeared to be an upstanding member of the Company. To the French Huguenot community, he was the master of illegal trade.

"I shan't be long," Lamerie called up to the coachman.

"Yes, sir. Thomas, get the crate for Mister de Lamerie."

The footman retrieved a large wooden crate from the floor of the carriage and followed Lamerie to the assay office inside Goldsmith's Hall.

A spindly clerk greeted them. "Ah, Mister de Lamerie. Welcome. What fine piece do you have for us today?"

"A cup and cover, commissioned by the Honorable George Treby. Do you know him?"

"Never had the pleasure," the clerk answered as he pulled the silver cup from the crate by one of the two handles. "Nice, very nice. It will be a beauty when polished."

"It will indeed."

"It's sterling silver I assume?"

"No. It's Britannia standard – 95.84% pure. Only the best for my patrons."

"Of course, sir," the clerk said.

"Has the tray I brought last week been assayed and hallmarked?"

"I believe so. I'll just check in the back."

"I'm to indenture two apprentices this morning and must go. I'll be back in a bit to sign for the tray."

"Very well, sir. I'll have it ready for you," the clerk said.

Lamerie turned towards the footman. "Wait by the coach," he instructed.

"Yes, sir," the footman nodded and left.

Lamerie walked to the commissioning office in the back of the building. He was hesitant to take on an apprentice, much less two, but he needed the premiums to pay the duty on the silver cup and cover, not to mention his recent order for silver bullion. They would be indentured for ten pounds each, a paltry sum for the burden he would assume for the lads' education.

Master Beaufort, the prime warden of the Company, was waiting for Lamerie in a small office with two other men and two ashen-faced boys.

"Ah, here he is. Mister de Lamerie, may I introduce you to Mister Bradshaw and Mister Cargill. Mister de Lamerie is one of the Company's most esteemed members."

"Mister de Lamerie, how nice to meet you. I am Phillip Cargill. This is my nephew, Charles Greville. He turned fifteen just last week. I am responsible to my sister for his education."

"And I am Bennett Bradshaw. This is my son, also named Bennett Bradshaw. He will be fifteen next month."

"Two fine lads. I am happy to see to their education in the trade." Lamerie responded. "Thank ye, Master Beaufort, for arranging these apprenticeships. Have the preliminaries been addressed?"

"All but payment and signatures. Gentlemen." Master Beaufort held out his hand and collected £10 from each man. He handed the sum to Lamerie.

"Thank ye, sir," Lamerie said.

"Very well," Master Beaufort continued, "Now the young men and their fathers must sign the Roll of Denizations before they are legally qualified to apprentice. Mr. Cargill may sign on his nephew's behalf. Gentlemen, sign here."

The men signed the register.

"And now the young men."

Each lad scrawled a signature on the line opposite their guardian.

"Bennett. Charles. Welcome to the Worshipful Company of Goldsmiths. You are now apprentices, indentured to Mister Paul de Lamerie for a term of seven years, after which you may receive your freedom by service and enter your own maker's mark, provided, of course, that your skills qualify you for membership in the Company."

"Thank ye, sir," Bennett and Charles responded.

"Mister de Lamerie, your apprentices." Master Beaufort flourished his hand towards the young men.

"Thank ye. Lads, report to my workshop on Great Windmill Street near the Haymarket on Monday next," Lamerie ordered.

"Yes, sir."

"Gentlemen, Master Beaufort, good afternoon." Lamerie gave a slight bow and left to return to the assay office.

The Goldsmith's Hall was quiet, just as he had hoped. His footsteps echoed as he reentered the assay office.

"Is it clear?" the clerk asked.

"Yes. What news is there?" Lamerie asked.

"Beaufort started a new investigation of ingot and bullion sales on the London Bridge. A man named Pinotte was arrested yesterday for failure to pay the duty on a silver plate, not that he had a choice. You can't very well pay taxes on illegal sales. Do you know him?"

"He's an acquaintance. Where is he?"

"Newgate Prison. His plate was stamped with a counterfeit hallmark. I told Beaufort that I hadn't seen anything like it, but it looked similar to the one you have registered."

"How so?"

"The crown, the initials "LAM" above a fleur-de-lis."

"It isn't mine," Lamerie snapped.

"I know, but Beaufort will be round to inspect yer shop. Best hide any unregistered stamps."

"The Company should just register foreigners. It would collect more in taxes and put an end to these ridiculous investigations." Lamerie reached for the wooden crate on the desk. "Is this my plate?"

"Inspected and hallmarked. That will be £3.80."

"Did taxes go up again?"

"No, the price of silver did though."

"A plague on my pocketbook," Lamerie muttered as he handed the clerk the coins.

"What? Not a coin for the information?" the clerk asked.
"Call it a payment against the debt you owe me."

Part Two
London, 1721

"He offered me also sixty pieces of eight more for my boy Xury, which I was loth to take...I was very loth to sell the poor boy's liberty, who had assisted me so faithfully in procuring my own."

-Robinson Crusoe by Daniel Dafoe

CHAPTER V

In the early hours of the morning, Mum and Egan left the flat where Kerrin slept blistering with fever. Egan knew Mum would not want to be gone long, so he hurried to keep up with her pace as they walked over the uneven cobblestones. Mum held his hand too tightly. The tenderness of her embrace the evening before was replaced with a forceful persistence. Her disposition tormented Egan more than the wounding grip, but he kept silent.

Mum led Egan towards the wharf and down Tooley Street where they approached a broad, mulish-looking man. His features were scrunched together on his face when compared to the wide balding stretch across his head, which was bright red from the blustery cold. Egan wondered why he didn't wear a hat; the man looked prosperous enough to afford one. A fine beaver hat would keep his forehead safe from frostbite.

The man did not speak, he just glared at Egan. Egan bowed his head and waited.

"Are you Daniel Armory, the sweep?" Mum inquired.

"Aye."

"This is me son," Mum introduced Egan by nudging him forward.

"How old?" the man asked.

"Six last April."

"He is tiny," the man said, looking Egan over. "I need little boys. Chimneys are getting smaller and smaller. Has he been sick this year?"

"No, sir," Mum answered.

"Two crowns," he offered.

Egan's mouth gaped in horror. Mum tightened her harsh grasp on his hand.

"Surely a boy as fine as me son warrants a higher sum," Mum bargained.

"Madam, I'll be teaching yer son, giving him a trade, taking care of him as you have not the means. Surely his welfare is of greater value to you than silver."

"It tis, but I have another child that is also in need," Mum replied.

"A boy?" he asked.

"No sir, a girl."

"Three crowns, me final price," he dug into his pocket and pulled out three large silver coins. He held out the coins in the palm of his hand.

Mum nodded and took the coins.

Struggling to keep from grieving, Mum steadied her voice, "Egan, you are to apprentice with this man. His name is Master Armory. When things get better, I'll come for you."

"I don't want to." Egan shook his head as tears filled his eyes.

"When Kerrin is better, I will come for you," she said as she held his face in her hands. "Take care, me love. Don't you become a highwayman like Jack Hall," she whispered with a teary smile. She kissed his forehead, turned him around, and prodded him towards his new master.

"No," Egan whimpered, turning back to Mum.

She backed away, tears streaming from her eyes.

"Mum, no!" Egan pleaded.

Picking up her skirts, she turned and ran into the crowd of merchants bargaining for the latest wares arriving on the river.

"NO! MUM! NO!" Egan screamed and ran to catch her disappearing form, only to be detained by Master Armory's hefty arm about his waist. Egan flailed his limbs and screamed.

With his free fist, Master Armory grabbed Egan's hair, heaved his head back, and spat in his ear. "Boy, you have three seconds to quiet yerself before I give you sumfink to cry about."

Egan's body went limp with fear, but he whimpered through streaming tears. Master Armory unwrapped his arm from Egan's waist and held him up off the ground by his hair. Egan's cry grew louder, but he did not lash out.

"That's right boy. You won't live long if you fight me." Master Armory chuckled as he backhanded Egan down across the face and threw the boy to the ground.

The milling crowds observed the incident but did not react. Pauper children inundated the city streets in abundance; this one drew no special interest.

"Get up boy," Master Armory commanded.

Egan tasted the salty blood that flowed from his upper lip and struggled to lift his body into a sitting position.

"You belong to me. I don't tolerate deviant behavior. Do you hear me?"

Egan nodded.

"Pitt, ready him for work," Master Armory ordered. Egan had not noticed the boy standing a few yards away observing the scene.

"Yes, sir." Pitt pulled Egan up by the arm and then retrieved a large burlap sack, long pole, and brush.

Pitt hastily pulled Egan down the adjacent street. Egan glanced back to find Mum but instead met Master Armory's cruel sneer following his every movement. The boys rounded a corner and Pitt's formality broke.

"Thomas Pitt is me name. Call me Pitt. Wots yers?"

Egan broke into a run. He heard the clash of Pitt's brush and pole on the cobblestones only a second before a hand gripped his shirt collar and pulled him to a stop.

"Yer not going anywhere. Unless you want another beating, you'd better stick with me. Now...wots yer name?" Pitt asked again.

"Let go," Egan yelled.

"Not going to happen. You run, and I's the one who gets whipped. Then I gets whipped every day till I chase you down. Me backside is none too fond of whipping."

"Let me go," Egan repeated meekly.

"Tell me yer name," Pitt asked again.

"Egan Whitcombe," he yielded, shrugging awkwardly from the pressure Pitt's hand applied to his neck.

"Promise not to run, Egan Whitcombe?"

Egan shook his head.

Pitt asked again, tightening his grip.

"I promise," Egan relented.

"How much do you promise?"

"I just do."

"Not good enough."

"I swears on the Bible then."

"That'll do," Pitt said. "Wot shall I call you? Whit?"

"No, that was me Da's name," Egan replied angrily, fresh tears ran down his face. He could not take Da's name.

"Just Egan then?" Pitt asked, ignoring Egan's foul expression.

"Aye," Egan gritted his teeth.

"Well Egan," Pitt said as he released Egan's collar, "I'm to teach you to be a broomer, meaning you'll follow me around and do wot I says until yer right smart enough to be on yer own. Twig?"

"Twig," Egan relented in a meek voice.

"To the undertakers then," Pitt responded.

Egan froze in place, and his eyes widened in fear.

"Relax, you git," Pitt laughed. "I ain't taking you to be buried or killed. You need a head shave, and we can sell yer hair for a proper sweeping cap. The undertaker offers the best deals in London on formerly owned effects, if you know wots I mean."

"Wot?" Egan asked, grabbing hold of the mess of hair that Mum had neatly fastened at the nape of his neck that morning.

"You have enough of it, should get a fair price."

"Why for?"

"You don't know wot yer bought for?"

"No."

"Yer one of Master Armory's little boys now. Little boys for little flues."

"Wot's that mean?"

"They call us human brooms, climbing boys, or as proper folks say, 'chimney sweep's boys.' But us, we call ourselves broomers. We climb and clean chimneys. Coal creates a mean soot that sticks to the bricks. We climb and clean cloggers that fill houses with smoke."

Egan looked up at Pitt with a blank expression.

"Are you listening, kid? We clean the holes, collect the ash, and make Master Armory coin. It's simple."

"I want to go home," Egan whined.

"Five guineas pays yer debt to Master Armory; then you go home," Pitt said. "Catch is, all the quid you makes is Master Armory's because he owns you. Still, the only way out is to pay yer debt or be bought, sold, or dead. Twig?"

Fresh tears welled up in Egan's eyes.

"Cheer up. We're not as bad off as the yobs at the lime foundry or workhouse. Most days Master Armory lets us work on our own, and when we earn extra, we eat wot we want without telling him. Just like kings, we are. It works out right nice when we're on our own, like the castaway Robinson Crusoe."

"I know about Robinson Crusoe. Da told me about him. He was a sailor."

"See? We'll get along just fine. We'll just get you the proper cap, shave yer hair, and you'll be ready. It can catch fire hair can; you need to shave it off and protect yer face the best you can. Yer no good to Master Armory if you get blinded or burnt too badly."

Egan looked up at Pitt. "Is that how you got that?" he pointed to a long, thin scar running across Pitt's eye and down his left cheek.

"Naw, that's not from burning." Pitt unknotted the end of his shirt sleeve and pulled it up, "This is from burning."

The thumb and two fingers were missing on Pitt's left hand; the remaining piece was a wrinkled mass of scarred flesh that curled inward. His flesh was stained black, with splotches of violently red flesh peering through charred skin that ran along the edge of his two amalgamated fingers. Egan reached to touch the damaged skin, but Pitt pulled away and retied his sleeve over the deformity.

"The scar on me face be from Master Armory's whip," Pitt said.

"Wot happened?"

"I ran away," Pitt responded, "Only not far enough. Master Armory spotted me late that night near a pub, thought I'd been pick-pocketing the crowd instead of sweeping."

"Were you? Pick-pocketing?"

"Spot on," Pitt admitted with a smirk, "but only enough for a boiled potato that I had already ate. I spent the whole day wandering not earning a copper, and I have this scar to prove it."

Pitt led Egan through the carts, carriages, and merchants that weaved amid the shops and houses on the London Bridge. The bridge was its own city, crowded and busy. A disorienting hour later, the boys exited through the guardhouse on the London side of the bridge.

Growing up in a wee section of Jacob's Island, everything and everyone had been familiar to Egan. As Pitt led him down two narrow streets and a wide avenue, Egan was overwhelmed with buildings and people, the likes of which he had never seen. The boys turned down a back alley, which was littered with filth and plagued with a gruesome stench.

"Gardy-loo!" someone yelled from a second-story window. Both boys quickly backed to the side of the building as the contents of a chamber pot were hurled into the alley.

"Here we be. Mister Bixby takes care of the living poor by taking care of the rich dead. We knock around back so as to not disturb the fancy folks."

"Ain't they dead?"

"The dead don't walk in by theirselves, now do they? I'm talking about the folks that bring the bodies here. Wouldn't be good for Mister Bixby's business if the likes of us are seen in there." Pitt knocked on the back door. "He and the missus be classes up but are still noticing of us broomers."

Egan gasped as a woman opened the door. She looked like Mum, a bit older, but almost the graven image. Her dark black hair was pulled back with unruly escaping curls. She was small and thin, but quick with a pointed gaze. The lines around her mouth formed a permanent smile.

"Pitt dear, here for another head shave, love?" she asked. It was not Mum's voice.

"Just him, Missus Bixby. He's got a bit, and I was hoping it be enough to trade for a sweeping cap."

"Come in, and we'll see. I don't have a sweeping cap, but have something that might work for a bit." She guided the boys in and pointed to two sturdy chairs along the back wall of the room. "Have a seat; I'll be right back." She walked at a running pace down the hall to another room and disappeared.

A long table stretched almost the length of the room. Pitt seemed at ease and ignored the covered bodies that lay on the table and the uncovered one in the hefty wooden box underneath. Egan stared at the forms until he could no longer contain his curiosity. He stood, reached out, and slowly lifted one of the sheets.

Pitt grabbed Egan's shoulders and pushed him back into the chair. Egan yelped.

"No, you don't," Pitt reprimanded. "The soul lingers for three days. If you disturb a spirit, it might be tempted to follow you instead of moving on. Don't need a haunting spirit in our bin."

Egan tucked his hands underneath his legs so they would not be tempted to reach out again.

"Why is there a person in that box?" Egan asked.

"It's not a box. It's a coffin."

"It looks like a box. Wot is he in there for?"

"Rich people get buried in a coffin or put in a crypt to just lay there. The likes of us get put right in the ground."

"Not me Da, he was buried at sea."

"I'd like that. I'd rather have fish than worms eating me bones."

"Me too," Egan agreed as his eyes remained fixed on the table, watching for movement under the sheets until the spry woman returned. She set a razor, a bowl of water, and some rags down on the table. She pulled Egan's chair quickly around, so he was facing the wall and went about work without another breath.

"Wot will you do with me hair?" Egan asked.

"Sell it to a master peruke maker, of course. It will be woven into a wig for a fancy lady or maybe a gentleman. Folks can't grow enough of their own hair for the styles these days. Excepting me that is, I have more hair than I can deal with most days. I sold me own hair once. Used the coin for a new dress so that I could leave the convent. I was scolded terrible by Mother Rachel. She could have saved her breath because I cut me hair too short and had to wear a cap every day near a year and remain hidden at the convent until me hair grew enough to leave wearing that silly dress. That was punishment enough for me. I didn't belong in the convent. Every day was a trial from the good Lord."

Missus Bixby combed and plaited Egan's hair and then began shearing the locks clean off at his scalp.

"Then I left and married me mister and realized that there are the same comings and goings here as in the church. Me life is meant for the dead and the poor, but I wouldn't have it another way. Here I dress as I want without the need to sell me hair again. Boys can go bald without hassle, but not women. There now, how's that feel?"

Egan felt his shorn head. "Cold and prickly."

"It will take some getting used to, but tis the safest in a flue." Missus Bixby handed Egan some rags. "Until you get a proper climbing cap, wrap these tightly about yer face when you sweep. If it gets hard to breathe you get out of the hole as fast as you can, hear me? No matter wot yer master says, take care of yerself."

Egan nodded.

"Try this," she said, placing a cap on his head. "It may be a bit itchy with yer shorn head, but it's a fine cap of good wool bought through Blackwell Hall. Snipped it off a gent last week as there was no use in it going to waste."

The cap was too big and fell past Egan's ears, but it instantly warmed his head.

"Me mister always says a person has no right doing a job when he don't know wot he is doing or don't have the right tools. There's lots of foolish people out there with no smarts about things. You know where they end up?" Missus Bixby asked and then continued without waiting for a response, "In me front parlor, stiff as a board. Don't you two be following them to an early grave."

The woman pulled a rag from the bowl of water, lifted the rim of Egan's cap, and proceeded to scrub his face. "Tears wash away, love. Not much good they'll do you anyhow." Missus Bixby carefully dabbed at the blood clot mending Egan's split lip.

"I'd like to take a whack at who gave you this!" She pursed her lips as she patted the cloth around the bruise forming on Egan's cheek.

"Now, let me look at that hand," she beckoned to Pitt.

Pitt unknotted his shirt cuff.

"When did this happen?" she asked, pointing to some freshly singed skin.

"Two days past," Pitt responded. "I've tried to keep it free from the hot bricks, but needs it to climb."

Missus Bixby rinsed the rag in the water bowl and proceeded to clean the burned area. She then retrieved a bottle from the shelf and poured the clear liquid onto the rag to dab on the wound. Pitt winced.

"Stop that," she ordered. "Doesn't hurt worse than when you burned yer hand near off." She wrapped the wound with fresh bandages then retied the shirtsleeve down over Pitt's hand. "You need to keep it clean and wear a thick covering over it when you sweep."

"Yes, Ma'am."

"Now you two, let me see yer elbows and knees," she commanded, producing a brown bottle. With a rag, she washed down each arm and leg. The liquid stung Egan's scrapes.

"The brine will toughen yer skin, make it harder to burn through. And both of you remember to wash yer eyes of soot every day, even in the cold."

"Don't that much washing make you sick?" Egan questioned.

"You would rather be blind than sick now, would you?" the woman retorted with a sarcastic smirk.

"No," Egan answered.

"Off with you now," she placed the bottle back on the shelf and opened the door for the boys. "I have others to attend to, even though they don't be complaining about the service."

"Thank ye," Pitt said.

"Thank ye," Egan echoed.

"Take care dearies, and come to see me next month for another douse of brine," Missus Bixby instructed before shutting the door.

The boys exited into the putrid alley and made their way to the main street.

"You almost look the part. Here, carry me sack and brush and let's have a look at you," Pitt took two steps back and studied Egan. "Aye, just a little coal smudge and you'll be a regular broomer." Pitt tugged his cap down on his brow, "It's time we were finding some business," he said.

CHAPTER VI

"Sweep!" Pitt called out into the main street. "Sweep!"

Egan trailed behind, taking in his surroundings. He did not remember this street. He desperately looked for a familiar building, person, or anything that would point the way home.

"Pitt, which way is it to the River Thames?"

"Not a chance I'll tell. Right as rain you can find yer way home from the river."

Egan scowled and continued to plod along. He studied the cobblestones and tried to avoid the excrement that littered the street. Looking down, Egan noticed that Pitt was wearing sturdy, expensive shoes. Egan wore socks Mum had knitted that were crudely wrapped in thick burlap.

"Cheer up, broomer. I'll take you sweeping near the river when I can trust you not to run."

"Where did you get them shoes?"

"Nice, eh? Missus Bixby gave them to me after me hand burned. Said it was too late for me hand, but she could protect me feet. Nicest things I own. Rory tried to steal them once, so I wear them all night too."

"Sweep!" Pitt yelled again and then continued, "Egan, look to the chimneys when yer calling for business."

Egan looked up. "Wot?"

Pitt backed Egan against a building and pointed up at a chimney across the street. "See the white smoke?"

"Sure."

"That is a clean chimney to let out that much smoke. No work for us there. But down there," Pitt pointed and began to jog down the street, "smoke is hardly coming out the hole. Tis right wispy. Either there ain't much of a fire in the hearth or the chimney is blocked. If it blocks all the way, the servants will go find a sweep. But if they hadn't left yet, they will hire us. Follow me."

"Sweep!" Pitt yelled, walking by the house. "Yell it too, Egan," Pitt ordered in a low voice.

"Sweep!" Egan obeyed. "Sweep!"

No one came to the door, so Pitt and Egan continued yelling down the street.

"Give them some time," Pitt paused. Egan imitated Pitt, studying the tops of the chimneys for signs of constrained smoke.

After a minute, Pitt started walking back down the street yelling his advertisement with Egan close on his heels.

The boys' efforts were rewarded with an open door.

"How much?" called out a servant.

"Fourpence a flue for a tip-top clean," Pitt responded.

"I'll pay a tuppence, nothing more," she countered.

"How about a tuppence and a bite to eat for both of us?"

"Very well, come 'round the back."

The woman ushered the boys in the back entrance, led them through the kitchen, and into the front parlor where the air hung with smoke while failing coals smoldered in the hearth.

"It's still a bit warm, but it has been going out for hours. Shouldn't be a problem for cleaning."

"We'll clean it proper," Pitt assured the woman.

"Don't make a mess," she ordered and left the room.

Pitt opened his sack to remove a few tools and an empty sack.

"Egan, remove the screen and look up the hole," Pitt instructed. Egan stuck his head into the fireplace. The warm air was heavy with smoke that pressed upon his lungs. Egan withdrew his head with a fit of coughing and choked until his lungs cleared.

"You get used to it," Pitt said. "A cloth across yer face helps filter the smoke. Where are the rags Missus Bixby give you?"

Egan removed the rags from his waistband. Pitt grabbed one and proceeded to tie it around Egan's nose and mouth.

"Did you look up into the chimney?"

"No."

"Then stick yer head in again."

Egan stuck his head back in the chimney and twisted his neck to look up. The chimney flue was narrow and dark with a wee crack of daylight shining through near the top.

"It's dark."

"It's blocked up with soot. This is a scraper," Pitt held out a tool with a handle and wide flat edge for Egan's inspection. "You climb up and scrape away the soot by starting in the middle where the light is and chipping away to the walls. When you can get through, you climb up to the top and brush it down with this," Pitt picked up a long-handled bristle brush. "Watch me climb then hold the extra bag over the hole to keep the dust inside the hearth. Twig?"

"Twig," Egan agreed, although his face betrayed fear.

Much to Egan's dismay, Pitt stripped his shirt and trousers off right down to only his skivvies and fancy shoes.

Pitt chuckled at Egan's reaction. "Clothes get stuck and hung up on the walls. Most broomers don't even wear shoes, but I got these nice ones, and I never take them off." Pitt pulled a climbing cap down to cover his head and face. The cap near covered his eyes with two crude holes to see through on either side of his nose.

"You sweep nekkid?" Egan asked incredulously.

"Not quite, but I can wriggle out of me underwear if I need to."

"Missus Bixby said to keep that hand covered," Egan pointed at Pitt's wrinkled skin.

"I know it," Pitt responded sharply. "Toss me one of yer rags."

Pitt wrapped the rag around his hand and arm, tucking in the ends. He grabbed the scraper, bit down on it through the sweeping mask, entered the chimney, and started to climb. Egan looked in after Pitt but withdrew quickly as bits of debris fell into his eyes.

"Cover the hole," Pitt's voiced sounded hollow and far away.

Egan picked up the bag and stretched his arms over the fireplace as far as he could reach. A scraping sound echoed through the chimney as Pitt began to chip away at the soot. Egan heard pieces of the grime fall and bounce off the hearthstone.

Egan thought about how dark it must be in the chimney. He shivered as he imagined the shadows that lurked in the darkness.

Egan removed the sack upon hearing Pitt descend.

Pitt emerged, drew the rag down, and gasped for breath.

"All right, Pitt?"

"It's blocked up good. I couldn't last long enough to break through. Give me a moment," Pitt choked. He held himself up with his hands on his knees and wheezed for fresh air. His breathing slowly returned to normal. Pitt grabbed his long pole and hoisted himself back up the chimney.

Egan covered the hole again and listened for sounds of progress. The thumping sound soon became methodic, and Egan leaned his head against the fireplace to rest. He was so weary and tired, just like the day after Da died.

"All up!" Pitt yelled.

Egan let the bag drop and looked up into the hole. Pitt was climbing down from the very top of the chimney. He started to brush his way down, and Egan quickly covered the hearth again. Pitt emerged in a cloud of dust that filled the room.

"Feel this," Pitt instructed as he held out the end of the scraper to Egan, who just glared suspiciously at it. "Go on. It's not hot."

The pitchy black substance on the end looked gooey and hot but was surprisingly hard.

"I'll scrape it down outside," Pitt explained, putting his shirt and trousers back on as he left. "Sweep out the hearth and shovel the ashes into me sack."

Egan scooped the ashes into the sack and then swept the hearth clean. He could do this job, Egan decided. He cleaned the hearth out at home for Mum.

Pitt came back in and inspected Egan's work. "Right good, let's get paid!"

In the kitchen, the woman produced a tuppence, a boiled potato that was still warm, and a slice of brown bread cut in half. The boys took the loot and escaped into the alley. Egan ate his piece of bread and watched as Pitt ate the potato. A little over halfway through, Pitt gave the rest to Egan. Egan devoured the remaining bites.

"Let's look for another job," Pitt stated. "Master Armory tells us how much we need to earn each day, usually a shilling or more depending on the time of year."

"How much is that?" Egan asked.

"Twelve pence is a shilling. Two shillings is like sweeping chimneys in 'bout twelve houses, ten if we're lucky."

The boys walked up and down the streets, yelling an advertisement when little or no smoke emerged from a nearby chimney. They were offered five pence to clean two chimneys in one house and another tuppence to break up a difficult clogger in another. Egan covered the holes to keep the dust from spreading and dutifully cleaned the hearths when Pitt was finished.

"The best way to clean a hole is to smack the soot off with the handle of yer brush then brush the sides down," Pitt instructed.

Egan nodded, but he was worn out. "I'm hungry."

"There's no extra coin today. We was supposed to get a shilling, but Master Armory should go easy as you was with me to train. We'll earn and eat tomorrow." The two walked in silence for a bit. Egan watched the merchants closing up shop, earnestly seeking a familiar face.

"Do you like sweeping chimneys?" Egan broke the silence.

"No, but it's wot we do. Come summer we have choices, but during the year we sweep or starve. Twig?"

"Twig," Egan exhaled.

"It's not so bad as the workhouse. We get by if we do wot we're told and bring in coins."

Pitt led Egan down a narrow alley along the back side of row houses that appeared piled atop each other. Unlike the cleaner, maintained facades of the houses, the alley revealed the decaying reality of the structures. The street had been elegantly built following the great fire of 1666. However, the lower class of people, mostly tradesmen and merchants, moved in when the wealthy sought more opulent homes in the latest fashionable district. It was nicer than Jacob's Island and anywhere Egan had ever lived.

Egan looked up at the three stories in awe.

"How many live here?" Egan asked.

"Upstairs just Master Armory and his wife. Don't set yer sights too high, Egan. The likes of us don't go upstairs. But we got a roof over our heads and that's sumfink."

Pitt drew open the back door and guided Egan into an empty kitchen. The air smelled deliciously of roasted bird, but there was no evidence of food on the long wooden table.

"Don't say nuffink," Pitt warned in a low voice.

Egan gaped at the luxury of the house as they walked through an elegant hallway and into the formal parlor in the front corner of the house.

Master Armory sat in a large wingback chair by the fireplace reading a paper pamphlet. The shapes of letters and drawings danced across the page in the firelight. Egan wished he could read.

"Well?" Master Armory looked annoyed.

"Ninepence, sir," Pitt handed Master Armory the coins, "a bit short for training the new boy and all."

Master Armory slipped the coins into his pocket and dismissed the boys with a slight nod.

Pitt grinned and led Egan back through the kitchen to a short hallway that stopped abruptly at a door. Egan followed Pitt through the door and down a set of stairs leading into a dark coal cellar.

"Egan, welcome to our bin."

CHAPTER VII

Trailing behind Pitt, Egan descended the murky stairs. The rotting boards creaked with each step. The damp chill made Egan shudder even more than the moldy stench. A single candle in a tin holder mounted on the wall flickered light around the edges of the room. The flaming wick crackled, spattering wax onto the wood slab walls and dirt floor. Piles of bulging burlap sacks covered the floor. A small path ran down the middle of the sacks, dividing the room.

"This is our bin. You sleeps on wot ash you collect."

Pitt crossed to the back corner and kicked a thin sack of soot. "We sold most of Reeves' ash to a farmer visiting the city, but kept this sack for the new broomer, which be you. Use the pot before you come down. Armory locks the doors at night, and we don't like the stink when someone can't hold it 'til morning."

"Introductions be in order, Pitt."

"Shut it, Rory. I was getting there." Pitt turned to Egan. "The redhead is Rory."

Rory nodded in Egan's direction. Egan wondered how Pitt knew Rory had red hair; his head and face were black with soot.

"The tall one is Will." Will gave Egan a slight smile with the corner of his mouth.

"That's Ignacio; he hates his name, so we call him Iggy. He don't like that either," Pitt pointed to the wiry boy on the sacks next to Egan's sack at the far end of the room. Iggy was feigning sleep, but his eyelids fluttered when Pitt mentioned his name. "He doesn't talk much."

"Who's taking Reeves' place?" said a voice descending the creaky stairs.

"Andrew, about time you finished for the day. Andrew, this is Egan."

"Pleased to meet you," said Andrew. "You working with this rogue?" he smacked Pitt lightly on the chest with the back of his hand.

"I'm no more of a rogue than you are," Pitt smirked, grasping hands with Andrew in a firm shake that made them look like grown men.

"Adam is coming down the steps. He's Andrew's little brother," Pitt continued.

"I'm not little," Adam said in a squeaky, high-pitched voice.

"That's right baby face," Andrew started, "Yer such a big boy that Master Armory won't let you sweep by yerself, baby brother. He still makes me watch after you."

"He does not. I'll show you." From the third stair, Adam jumped on Andrew's back, swung his arms round his neck, and wrestled him to the ground. Andrew rolled over onto his back, pinning Adam to the dirt floor. Adam whimpered as he tried to hit Andrew with his free fist.

"They like each other more than you'd think," groaned Pitt. "Andrew, let him go so we can get some peace."

Andrew rolled over and stood up quickly, not giving Adam a second chance for attack.

"You got me dirty," Adam pouted as he brushed the dust off his soot-stained shirt. He was filthy from head to toe. If anything, rolling around on the ground had shaken off some of the grime.

"You know, Adam, yer the perfect height for sumfink," Andrew baited.

"For wot?"

"Me fist in yer face."

Adam launched at Andrew, who defended the attack by gripping Adam's forehead and keeping him at arm's length. Adam leaned into Andrew's hand and flung his fists violently forward; his target was well out of reach.

"Cut it out," Pitt demanded.

"Did you see Tick out there?" asked Will.

"Naw, but he will be back soon," Andrew assured, "Master Armory wouldn't send him too far on his first day brushing alone."

"Listen up brooms, Egan is pairing with me until he learns the way of the brush. No one gives him any trouble," Pitt warned, "not even you, Adam."

Adam halted his attack and stood up. "I don't give anyone trouble. You all give me trouble. All the time trouble."

"You are trouble," Andrew said.

"I am going to find Tick," Will announced. "He don't know one street from another. He'll be out wandering all night and then get lashed for being late."

"Tick has to learn. You keep watching out for him and he never will," Rory yelled up the stairs at Will. Rory turned around, "If Tick listened half as well as Iggy did, Will would have been rid of him weeks ago."

Iggy snorted a little. His gaunt face glowed in the shadows like skin stretched across a flickering lantern.

Egan dropped to his knees and flattened his sack of ash. The other boys had piled several sacks to make a full bed. Each makeshift bed was indented in the middle to fit a body snuggly into the ash. The beds looked quite comfortable, but Egan's sack was short and thin. His heels scraped the dirt cellar floor when he stretched out. Wee rocks poked into his back.

"So Egan, are you scratch from the orphanage or the workhouse?" Rory asked.

Egan glared an angry silent response.

"Leave him alone, Rory," Pitt warned.

"Just want to know wot we are dealing with."

"His mum sold him. So leave him be for a bit."

"How much did she get for you? No more than a farthing, right?" Rory pestered. "You don't look worth more than that to me."

Egan pulled his knees to his chest and shrunk closer to the floor.

"Shut it you arse," Pitt pushed Rory against the wall.

"Just want to see how long it takes him to cry," Rory smirked.

"Why? Trying to prove that yer a rake?"

"We already know that, don't we Pitt?" Andrew joined in. "Yer just like yer father, Rory. Remind me where he is again?"

"He's in prison!" Adam squeaked.

Andrew cuffed Adam's ear.

"Ow! You told me that's where he was!"

Rory fumed with anger, and then two sets of feet descended into the cellar breaking up the argument.

"Lost again?" Rory changed the direction of his malevolence towards the boy trailing behind Will.

"Yeah," Will answered, "I found him near the Little Conduit. Armory hasn't checked yet?"

"Naw, yer in time," Pitt assured.

The boys found their ash beds quickly and settled in. Egan considered the seniority of their places. The older boys were located near the staircase, Pitt being the closest, while Adam, Iggy, and Tick were situated at the far end. As the last to arrive, Egan was in the furthest corner from the stairs.

"Look at the wee thing, he's frightened," Rory sneered at Egan.

"Shut it," Pitt warned.

Pitt snuffed the candle just before Master Armory opened the door at the top of the staircase. He took a few steps down. Holding up a polished silver candlestick, he looked about the room then climbed back up the steps and closed the door. Egan heard the lock turn.

The boy that arrived with Will looked over at Egan. "So yer the new one now?"

"Suppose so," Egan responded.

"I'm Thomas; the broomers call me Tick."

"I'm Egan."

"Where are you from?"

"Talk can wait until tomorrow, Tick."

The room fell silent upon Pitt's command.

Egan shifted on the ashes trying to push the wee rocks into the ash. One larger stone would not flatten beneath him. After a few attempts to move it aside through the burlap, Egan stood, shook the bag sideways, and relocated the stone to the edge of the sack.

Egan stretched out and stared into the darkness. The pain in his chest was exhausting, but images of that morning kept his mind awake.

Soon the noises of the room occupied his thoughts. Out of the common snorting and wheezing, there were three distinct snores. One was a nasal whistle, while another thundered in rhythmic spurts. The third was troublesome. The boy was trapped inside a nightmare, half-wheezing and half-mumbling. His snore was uneven and fitful; Egan could hear his body toss about in the dark.

Cold crept into Egan's feet as they dangled onto the dirt floor. The chill spread up his body, and he shivered. He should not be here. He should be at home wrapped in blankets beside Kerrin, dreaming about Da's ship on the horizon.

Before Da left the last time, he had given Egan strict instruction. *While I am away, yer the man of the family. Be strong for Mum and yer sister, and take care of them.*

Da would have been so disappointed in him. Kerrin got sick. There was no money for medicine. Mum sold him. Egan had failed.

"Thinking 'bout yer family?" The voice startled Egan. "I know yer not sleeping. I can tell by yer breathing. So, you must be thinking about sumfink," the voice said.

The voice was close and unfamiliar. It had a crackly, shrill tone, like a creaky wheel on a carriage.

"Iggy?" Egan guessed aloud.

"Yeah."

"Why aren't you sleeping?"

"I can't sleep when Pitt has nightmares."

"That's Pitt?"

"Yeah. I think he's dreaming 'bout the day he got that scar on his face. Sometimes he wakes up in the morning with new scratches down his cheek. Don't say nuffink to him about it. Is it true how Pitt said you got here?"

"Aye, me Mum needed money and..."

"You knew yer mum?"

"Aye, and when things get better..."

"Things never get better," Iggy interrupted again.

After a long silence, Egan asked, "You don't know yer mum?"

"No. Master Armory took me from a parish orphanage. Me and Reeves and Will."

Across the darkness, Egan heard Pitt thrash about with a hoarse, throaty whimper that betrayed unconscious fear. Then Pitt fell silent, either surrendering to his fate or escaping the delusive turmoil.

"Iggy?"

"Yeah."

"Wot happened to Reeves?"

"He died."

"When?"

"November last."

"Me Da died last December at sea. How did Reeves die?"

"You don't need to know. Just go to sleep."

Egan's heartache succumbed to an overwhelming emptiness that seeped through his body. His tears dried up. The numbness took everything, everything but the knowledge that he did not know the way home.

CHAPTER VIII

"**U**p you. We got work to do and a debt to pay." Pitt nudged Egan with his foot.

Egan opened his eyes. The cellar was still dark, except for the light flickering down through the slats of the kitchen's floorboards.

"Tis morning already?"

"Will be in a few hours. We gets up before servants do. Cold flues are easier to sweep."

"Yer arm and face can get burnt off in a hot hole," Rory leered. "Better hope yer lucky not to get stuffed up one of them holes like Pitt was."

"Shut it, Rory. Why do you have to make everything worse?" Will grumbled.

"Cause I doesn't care nuffink for nobody."

"Sumfink is wrong with yer head."

"Least I says the truth."

"Egan, those are yers now," Pitt pointed in the corner by the staircase. "There's an empty sack and brush in the pail that you can use. You sleep on the ashes you collect."

Egan stumbled to the corner and retrieved the brush and rough burlap sack protruding from the pail. The empty sack was as tall as he was and twice as wide. It was large enough to make a proper bed.

Sacks and tools in hand, the boys lined up at the bottom of the stairs, Pitt first followed by Rory, then Will, Iggy, Andrew, Adam, and Tick. Instinctively, Egan joined the line behind Tick. The other boys carried long wooden poles. Egan looked around but did not see an extra pole for him. The boys waited quietly in their place until the door at the top of the stairs opened, and soft candlelight fell down the steps.

The broomers ascended, set their tools down in the short hallway, and leaned their poles against the corner of the wall.

"Are you the new boy then?" a young woman asked in a soft voice as Egan entered the kitchen. She did not wait for an answer. "I'm Miss Clara, the kitchen maid," she said, handing him a bowl of gruel.

"Thank ye, Miss Clara."

Egan took the bowl and joined the other brooms standing and eating around the stove at the far end of the kitchen.

"Master Armory was late getting home from the pub." Miss Clara said. "You are on yer own, but no dawdling. We know how he gets when the profits suffer. Try to bring in a bob and tanner each. Eat up now."

The gruel was bland and watery, and bits of hard grain floated upon the filmy substance. Even so, the boys eagerly slurped the gray substance until the wooden bowls were empty. The food disappeared too quickly, and half-empty tummies exited through the back door into the icy darkness of the morning. With buckets, bags, poles, and brushes in hand, they started down the alley towards the main street.

"A free mornin' you blimey broomers! Ain't we lucky!" Andrew exclaimed in a loud whisper.

"We don't got to sweep?" Egan asked. Excitement teasing at his veins, he thought about retracing yesterday's steps back to Jacob's Island.

"No, we still sweep," Pitt said. "It's just nice when Master Armory's not around. If we get lucky, we can sweep a whole day's wages in the morning and then earn extra this afternoon for a full belly."

"I'm hungry. I could eat a whole pig by meself," Adam whined.

"I'd share the pig with you," Tick said.

"Sure, you can have an ear."

"And I'd eat it."

"How do you get a pig?" Adam asked.

"Yer not stealing a pig, Adam," Andrew said.

"Never steal sumfink you have to cook," Rory said.

"I'll eat it raw," Adam said.

"Me too," said Tick.

The boys stopped in the middle of an intersection, which was still quiet in the early morning.

"Split up and sweep broomers," Pitt ordered.

The boys formed a semicircle facing outward and then took off in the various directions they were facing. Egan was facing the alleyway the broomers had just walked down. He looked towards Master Armory's house.

"It doesn't work that way ya eejit," Pitt smirked. "Yer with me. This way."

Egan looked up at Pitt and smiled. All he wanted was to go home, but he owed a debt. Da would want him to pay the debt. You always pay yer debt, or you end up swinging from a tree.

"Yer watching over me?"

"Aye, until you learn the trade. You good with that?"

Egan nodded.

Egan attempted to match Pitt's stride down the dark cobblestone street. Streetlamps flickered, casting eerie shadows across their path. Egan drew the wool cap further down to warm his ears.

"You gets used to the cold," Pitt remarked. "Going back and forth from fiery holes to winter outside, you soon forget how hot or how cold it tis. Me, I's perfectly grand even though it be cold out here. I didn't remember the cold until you said so."

"I didn't say nuffink."

"You pulled at yer cap, and that's just as good as saying."

"Oh."

"Are you learned?"

"No."

"Me neither, but I can count coins, and that's wot's important for broomers."

"Me Mum wanted me to go to school, but Da said I should learn a man's trade. He was going to take me aboard as a ship's boy."

"Is yer da a pirate?"

"No! He's a sailor, but he died last November."

"How?"

"Don't know, Mum wouldn't let Kerrin and me hear when the captain came to talk to her."

"Maybe he died fighting pirates."

"Maybe. He was strong, and he could fight," Egan imitated a swordsman by thrashing his arm through the air. "Someday I'll be just like him. Wot's yer father like?"

Pitt hesitated.

"You don't have to say anything if he's in prison like Rory's da."

"Naw, he was a good man."

"Me Da was a good man too. Me Mum will come for me when Kerrin gets better."

"Is Kerrin yer sister?"

"Aye, she is sick with the fever and bumps."

"I've seen that sickness."

"Where?"

Pitt ignored Egan's question. "Here's me corner," he announced. "Most sweeps' gather at the Little Conduit near the new St. Paul's and we sometimes do too, but we get more morning business spreading out and getting to folks before they can walk there."

"Sweep!" Egan yelled into the darkness.

Pitt immediately clamped his palm against Egan's mouth. "Trying to wake the dead? We can't be yelling in the morning. Folks will chase us off. I'm just establishing this corner as me mornin' spot. Folks find us in the morning; we don't go shouting for work yet. Twig?"

Egan nodded, and Pitt removed his hand. "I'm sorry. I want to help."

"Help by keeping yer mouth shut."

Egan pressed his lips together.

The boys sat and leaned against a frigid lamppost crowned with a dark glass globe; the flame had long since been extinguished by the wind. Egan tucked his legs up to his chest and wrapped his arms around his knees to get warm. Pitt sat sprawled out as if it was mid-summer.

"Would you rather be a pirate or a highwayman?" Pitt asked in a low voice, breaking through the silent darkness.

"Neither, Da said honest work is best."

"But if you had to choose which would it be?"

"I wouldn't choose neither."

"But wot if you were captured and put to work with no choice, except not by a sweep, would you rather work for pirates or highwaymen?"

"Well…probably pirates."

"Why?"

"Because I want to be a ship's boy. Do pirates have those?"

"Maybe. But wot about the Royal Navy running down all the pirate ships? A cannonball could blow you out of the water."

"Then I'd die on the sea like me Da. Wot 'bout you?"

"I think I choose highwayman. It would be easier to hide and not get caught."

"Wot about Jack Hall? He was a highwayman, and he got caught." Egan was wide-eyed. "Me Mum told me the king strung him up to do the Tyburn jig!"

"Maybe, but Jack Hall got rich before being caught. He was a chimney sweep just like us once, you know. Somedays I want to be that rich, even if it ends real bad." Pitt admitted.

"Me too. I'd sail to the Americas. Mum and Kerrin would come with me and I would grow tobacco."

"Tobacco?"

"Yup, me Da said tobacco makes folks rich in the Americas. He traded for it on his ship."

"Have you smoked it?"

"No, but I bet I can grow it and get rich."

"That's a good plan."

Silence settled over the boys as they watched a candle flicker in a nearby window. Someone had either stayed awake most the night or, like them, had awoken far too early.

"Pitt?"

"Yeah?"

"Master Armory owns me."

"Yeah, he owns me too."

"And if I pay Master Armory five guineas, me debt will be paid and I'll go free."

"Yeah, that's the way of it."

"How do I get five guineas?"

"We gots our ways."

"Wot ways? Highwayman ways?"

Just then, the boys heard the clapping of shoes on empty cobblestones. A young woman appeared around the corner and hailed the boys.

Pitt elbowed Egan. "Sometimes we broomers see a pretty poppet."

"Chimney sweeps, yes?"

Pitt nodded.

"Wot's yer price?"

"Tuppence a flue milady," Pitt answered with a slight bow.

"Never you mind the pretty talk. Just come quickly."

She turned back the way she had come. Pitt and Egan collected their things and ran to catch up as she was already halfway to the next corner. She led them down two streets and through an alley to a door, which was wafting gray smoke into the dark walkway.

Through the door, a spindly old man was poking a broomstick up the kitchen chimney. He jabbed the end up at the same time he tightly closed his eyes and turned his head aside.

"I think it's about opened up," the old man said as they entered the room. He opened his eyes to reveal clean wrinkle lines protected by his squint from the falling soot.

"Grandfather, you can stop now. The sweeps are here."

"I suppose I will, but this old broom did clear some of the smoke."

Pitt approached the fireplace and set out his tools. He started to strip down.

"Dear me!" the young woman exclaimed.

Pitt froze with his arms in the air and his shirt gathered above his head.

"I'll excuse myself," she said and hurried out of the room.

"Guess she's never seen a chimney cleaned before. No matter, carry on, carry on," the old man said.

The boys joined the old man in a chuckle as Pitt finished skimming down. He wrapped his arm and covered his face with the climbing cap. Pitt ducked into the hearth and started to climb. Without being asked, Egan draped the fireplace the best he could with the burlap tarp as Pitt's feet disappeared. The old man grabbed a corner of the tarp and held it up, leaving Egan free to hold the other corner.

"Thank ye," Egan said.

"There's nothing like a fine sweep when the chimney smokes," the old man said.

Clumps of coal pitch started to fall into the hearth, making random sounds like wee pebbles bouncing across a stone floor. Egan could hear Pitt grunt in exertion as he chipped away at the dense blockage.

"How long you been sweeping?"

"Since yesterday."

"You like it?"

"No, I want to go home."

"Can you?"

"No." Egan blinked back the tears that had dried up the night before. He fixed his eyes on the bricks in front of him and remained silent.

The old man did not seem to notice. "That's a shame. I didn't leave home until I was ten. Then I apprenticed for a builder and became one myself. I've laid more bricks than I can count, but it was good work that made me strong. That is until me body plum wore out. Seems all I'm good for now is trying to unblock a kitchen chimney before the sweeps arrive."

Egan looked at the old man.

"Getting old ain't easy. Then again, life ain't easy either."

"No, it ain't," Egan agreed.

Shuffling noises signaled Pitt's descent into the hearth. Egan pulled back a corner to see how close he was to the bottom.

"Mind letting me out?" Pitt was standing in the ashes.

"You slid down fast!"

"Naw, just been done is all. You had a right good clog about halfway, but tis cored and swept out now, and you'll breathe good air again soon."

As Pitt talked, the opaque smoke in the room appeared to drift towards the fireplace and seep upwards into the flue.

"Any more work for us?"

"Not today, young sweep. Although, I'll send for you earlier next time."

The old man handed Pitt a tuppence.

"Thank ye, sir."

Pitt dressed as Egan swept out the hearth. It wasn't much ash, but every bit would make for a better sleep that night. Pitt and Egan gathered their things and exited onto the street.

While still dark and cold outside, light began casting shadows through the morning fog. Egan followed Pitt back to his established corner where a footman stood waiting.

"This do be a lucky day," Pitt whispered to Egan. "May we be of service, sir?"

The footman grimaced. "From your attire, I assume you provide chimney sweeping services?"

"Certainly, muh lord. We do be the very best broomers in all of London," Pitt gave a slight bow with a smile.

The footman's demeanor remained firm. "Follow me. You shall settle terms of service with my employer if he finds you suitable."

Pitt acknowledged the backhanded offer with a nod. The boys followed the footman across several streets and down a lane to an impressive house across from a garden, which lay open and fraught with winter's desolation.

Egan looked up at the grand house.

"You live here?"

"Yes, the house includes quarters for those of us essential to the family."

The footman steered the boys through a side door.

The footman found his employer in the hallway adjacent to the entry door. The employer was a solid man in a smart black suit with a starched white collar. He had one long black eyebrow that extended across his forehead, hovering slightly above large, wideset blue eyes and slightly below slicked, iron-gray hair.

"The sweeps have arrived, sir." The footman snapped his feet together, lifted his head, and waited for further instruction.

"Who are these urchins?"

"The sweeps you requested, sir."

"These are sweep's boys, apprentices at best. I requested a master sweep."

"My apologies, sir. The master sweep was not about."

"Very well, I suppose you will do considering our timetable. Who is your employer?"

"Master Daniel Armory," Pitt handed the man a dusty card from his pocket. The card read:

Little Boys for Little Flues
Mister Daniel Armory, Master Chimney Sweep
Distaff Lane, London

The man studied the card, placed it in his pocket, and proceeded in a deep, commanding voice. "I am the head butler responsible for this property and its chattels. If necessary, you may refer to me as Mister Hollings. The family is on a brief holiday, and all the chimneys must be swept and cleaned. What is your charge?"

"A tuppence a hearth, sir," Pitt answered.

"There are fourteen fireplaces, but only eight main flues as certain rooms share a chimney. I'll pay two shillings and a meal in the kitchen when you finish. Do you accept?"

"Yes, sir. That's a right good price, sir."

"If you do a good job, I'll schedule your master on a regular basis."

Pitt's face lighted up with a wide grin. "You won't be disappointed, sir. Master Armory is the best sweep in London, and he would be honored to serve this great house."

"We shall see. Get to it now. Franklin will take you through the house and remain with you." The butler nodded to the footman and departed.

"Wot did he mean saying he might schedule Master Armory?" Egan asked Pitt.

"Grand houses like this don't wait for a flue to smoke, they gets regular sweeping. Master Armory likes getting new regulars and favors the broomer that gets them."

"How so?"

"When I goes with him to sweep the other grand house I brought in, he gives me the rest of the day off to do as I wishes, but not any of the other broomers, just me. Maybe he will reward us both for this house."

"There will be no future business if you don't meet my expectations," the footman stated, reassuming an air of superiority.

"Yes, sir," Pitt said.

"Yes, sir," Egan echoed.

"You shall start in the family bedrooms. Follow me."

The footman led the broomers up a back staircase where they entered a long exquisite hallway. Egan's head fell back as he gaped at the sight. A large chandelier dominated the ceiling over a grand staircase in the middle of a great hall. Even though the candles stood unlit in the fixture's golden leaves, the grandeur was unlike anything Egan had ever seen. Its immense structure was reflected in the highly polished wooden floor beneath their feet.

"Start in the far rooms and work your way back to the servants' stairway. Most of the furniture is draped against your filth, but the family is not away long enough for a full draping and cleaning. I will not hesitate to toss you out if you make a mess."

The broomers nodded, and the footman led them down the hallway. Egan studied the portraits of distinguished men, gentile ladies, and well-favored children that adorned the walls. A man stared down at Egan from one portrait with a severe, angry expression that matched the thin scar down his cheek. He had only one arm and was dressed in black.

"Was he a pirate?" Egan whispered to Pitt, pointing to the picture.

"How dare you say such a thing! The Jamesons are a respectful family," the footman snapped."

"How did he lose his arm?"

"Shut it, Egan." Pitt quickly stepped close to Egan and pinched him.

"And get that scar? Was he fightin a pirate?"

"Sir William Jameson, the elder, was a man of great stature. He lost his arm nobly fighting for king and country."

"But why is he so angry?"

"Perhaps I shall remove your arm and take a saber to your face just to see if it makes you angry," the footman answered.

"That would make me angry."

Pitt pinched Egan again.

"Ow!"

"Shut it!"

Egan clenched his lips together.

The footman led the boys through a door into a fine bedroom, dominated by a canopy bed covered in old muslin sheets in the center of the room. A table and two chairs were placed by a large window framed with delicate lace. Towards the wall on the side through which they had entered, stood a large polished wood wardrobe delicately carved with a leaf design. The ceiling was painted with cherubs carrying ribbons and fruit around a large open circle. The fruit was the expensive kind from the summer markets that Egan had never tasted. His mouth watered.

The footman cleared his throat, reminding Egan of his purpose. Pitt had already skinned down to his underclothes and shoes and had laid out a tarp and brushes.

"Egan, skin down. You need to learn to climb."

CHAPTER IX

Egan's muscles became stiff. His heart pounded in his chest, and he began to tremble.

Pitt placed his hands on Egan's shoulders. "The flues are cold. This is a perfect time to learn to climb."

Pitt's eyes were full of calm assurance.

Egan clenched the fabric of his breeches in his fists.

"Skin down," Pitt repeated.

Egan nodded and removed his outer clothing. He unwrapped the burlap from his feet and pulled off his socks, wriggling his bare toes. He wrapped the rags around his nose and mouth as Missus Bixby had instructed. He drew in cool air through the cloth, but the steam of his breath clung to the fabric as he exhaled. He gasped, getting used to the restrictive material.

The footman, uninterested in the boys' work, untucked a newspaper that had been secured in his waistband and settled on a chair by the window to read.

Pitt slid the fire screen from the hearth and shook the grate, trying to keep the ashes contained in the hearth.

"Start climbing," he instructed, placing the grate on Egan's near empty sack and handing Egan the brush.

Egan nodded and ducked into the grate. The hearth was little more than half his height, but he had room to stand up inside the chimney.

The cold air was heavy with stale smoke. The haze pressed on his lungs. The soot-stained bricks extended far above him. The chimney was narrow. Too close. Too dark. No space. No air.

Egan's body began to quiver with fear. Tears stung his eyes. His trembling fingers dropped the brush as his knees gave way. He crawled out of the dirty hearth and ripped at the cloth covering his face.

"I can't…just can't, no…me throat."

Pitt knelt and held Egan's face steadily in his hands. "Take a deep breath."

Egan forced air into his lungs.

"Good. Close yer eyes. Breathe. Yer just fine."

"Here now, what are you playing at?" The footman's voice was harsh.

"He's been feeling skittish. I'll take this hole while he gathers his wits."

Pitt turned back to Egan. "I'll sweep the hole and be back down for you."

Egan squinted back his tears and watched Pitt disappear into the hole.

He took deep breaths until he regained control of his body. Moments later Pitt descended.

"There's one hole for both rooms. I'll sweep out the hearth in the other room while you get this one and two will be finished," Pitt told Egan.

Egan stood up and began cleaning out the hearth. He had cleaned the hearth at his home. He cleaned hearths yesterday. He could do this. He swept the hearth walls and floor meticulously, depositing the ash into his sack and replacing the fireplace fixtures.

Egan collected their tools as Pitt rejoined him.

"These two rooms are finished sir," Pitt stated.

"Very well. All these rooms need to be done. I'll inspect every room when you are finished." The footman sat on a velvet chair in the hallway and unfolded the newspaper once again.

Pitt grinned and led Egan into the next room. "A bit of luck. This is hard enough without that hedge-bird watching."

Pitt began the same routine of laying out the tools, moving the fire screen, and shaking the grate.

"Egan, these are wide holes, and there are iron rungs on the walls. Look for them when you stand up. Take a deep breath and use the rungs to pull yerself up. There is fresh air at the top. Look fer the sky."

"I don't want to, Pitt."

"You need to learn with me or Master Armory will whip you again and again 'til you do learn."

"But I can't."

"It be like battle, Egan. This be a battle you must fight if you ever want to go home. Like Robinson Crusoe fighting the mutineers. Be brave like him."

Egan took the brush from Pitt's outstretched hand.

He drew in a deep breath and ducked into the hearth. His chest immediately tightened again. He began to shake and sweat.

Pitt's hand grasped his calf.

"Breathe, Egan. Breathe and look up. Do you see a metal rung?"

Egan looked up. A foot above his head was a blackened metal loop curving out from the bricks. "Aye, I sees it."

"Grab it, pull yerself up, and then search for the sky."

Egan stretched his neck back and looked towards the top of the chimney. Like the mouth of a pirate cave, the wee light beckoned him upward. He grasped the first rung and pulled himself up.

The rung was cold. Egan leaned his back against the bricks and thrust one knee up to steady his position. He rested his hands and arms for a moment while he looked for the next rung. It was only two feet further, but he could not reach it. He placed his hands on the sides and pushed up with his free foot. He leaned back and stabilized himself, not trusting his grip. The rung was in reach. He grasped the cool metal, pulled himself up, and anchored his knees on the walls of the hole. After a few more rungs, two chimneys joined together giving him more room for a few feet. Egan climbed with increasing confidence, establishing a repetitive technique. Pull up on the rung. Lean back. Anchor his knees. Push upward. Grab the next rung.

About halfway up, he noticed a thick film of soot collecting on the bricks, making the surface slick. Egan anchored himself by pulling one knee up and slouching against the wall as Pitt had instructed so that he could freely use his hands. He tested his position. He was able to pull his knee in, drop it down, and climb freely. Being able to move chipped away at the edges of his fear.

Egan reestablished his anchored position and considered his location. He was quite far up and still about ten feet from the top. He forced himself to continue the climb and was rewarded with a swift arrival at the top. He pulled himself up and hugged the outside of the chimney that rose from the roof of the grand house.

"All up!" Egan yelled.

"All up!" Pitt echoed.

Egan shifted around the flaunching until he could see Pitt poking out from a chimney across the roof.

"I did it!" Egan yelled.

"So I says you could!"

"All up!" Egan announced again to all of London as adrenaline surged through his veins.

"Now sweep the chimney out, you sot!" Pitt yelled and disappeared into the chimney stack.

"I did it!" Egan whispered to himself as he surveyed his field of victory. London's rooftops spread out before him, bathed in the full light of morning. Egan dangled at the top of the world among the birds that glided upon the wind. Specks of people trod upon the streets below. They could not reach him. They could not look down on him. For a moment, he exceeded their station.

Egan let the breeze caress his face as he breathed in the cool, fresh air through his mask. From a distance, Egan heard Pitt's voice. Reluctantly, Egan skootched his way back into the chimney.

"Are you going to start sweeping up there?" Pitt was yelling up from the hearth.

"Beautiful up here, innit, Pitt?"

"Yeah, now start sweeping! We got a job to do."

Egan tapped the black film at the top rim of bricks with the handle of the brush. Nothing happened. He smacked the handle harder against the edge, and a wee chunk of soot broke away from the brick. Egan repeated the attack all the way around the rim and down to the first metal rung with success. He then brushed the bricks up and down to remove the lingering soot and continued to the next section.

He repeated his task, finding the soot thinner the further he descended. The last three sections required only brushing.

Finally, Egan dropped down into the hearth and straightened up. His body ached. Far removed from the sun's light, the chimney stretched upwards in the vast expanse of the newly cleaned brick. It was not as formidable now. Still, he did not want to spend extra time in the confining space. Egan ducked out and met Pitt in the room.

"You scraped and brushed the entire hole?"

"I sure did!"

"Good. Sweep the hearth while I get the next room."

Egan collected the ash and cleaned the hearth. As he was replacing the grate and fire screen, he heard Pitt ask the footman for a spare rag. The footman grumbled but was exiting the hallway when Egan emerged from the room.

"Egan, take these two bedrooms and then clean the hearth in the master bedroom when you are finished. The flue in the master bedroom connects to the great room on the first floor, so I'll sweep down below. Meet me down there when yer done. Twig?"

"You won't stay with me?"

"There are lots of holes to sweep, we need to split up. That's yer next room."

"Wot if I can't?"

"Wot if you can?" Pitt smiled at Egan and scurried down the back staircase.

Egan took a deep breath and looked up at the painting of the one-armed man staring down at him.

He took a few steps down the hall and then walked the other direction. The man's harsh gaze appeared to follow him. Egan lunged down to the floor and then stretched as tall as he could. The eyes never broke contact.

Egan slowly backed away. The floor creaked beneath his step, and the noise was enough to send Egan scurrying into the next room away from the painting.

Egan removed the screen from the hearth in the room and looked up the hole. He heard Pitt talking to the footman and was just about to enter the hearth when Pitt popped into the room.

"Egan, here's a rag to wipe away our footprints in all the rooms when yer done," Pitt said, dropping the rag and leaving Egan alone once again.

Egan ducked into the hearth and looked up. The spirit of the one-armed man seemed to lurk in the bricks, waiting to smother him in the darkness. Egan suppressed the urge to cry and searched for the sky. He thought about the view waiting for him at the top and reached for each rung fixed into the mortar between the bricks. He passed the ledge where the hearths joined into one flue and gave himself a moment to stretch his legs.

Egan's muscles strained to reach the top, but he would not give up. He was strong. Da had said so.

"All up!" he yelled with less enthusiasm than his first climb. The view was still spectacular, but the sight did not surprise him as it had before. He took a moment to look about the rooftops and then lowered himself back down the hole.

Egan chipped and scraped and brushed away at the soot down the hole and cleaned out the hearth in both rooms. He headed towards the master bedroom and was immediately taken in with the lavish sight. The paintings and drapery were finer in this room than the others. There were two paintings above the fireplace – a man and a woman with opulent features and large gray wigs.

"Yer better-lookin' than the bloke in the hallway," Egan said to the paintings.

There was a small room off to the side dominated by a large white basin, big enough to fit a person inside, surrounded by shelves of all manner of soaps, brushes, powders, and towels. Egan looked at the room in wonder.

"Distracted, are we?" the footman scowled from the door.

Egan hung his head in shame and walked back to the hearth. The footman remained fixed at the doorway.

"Wot's all that?" Egan asked, pointing to the small room.

"Tis a washroom. The maids fill the large basin up with water for the master to wash in."

"Like swimmin' in the river?"

"Something like that."

"Yer master must be really dirty to need a heap of things for washin."

"Because of that heap of things, he is never dirty. Not that my master's cleanliness is any of your concern."

Egan dropped his head and diligently set about climbing and scraping the hole, sweeping the hearth, and replacing the fixtures. Egan remembered Pitt's last instruction when he saw the clean rag on the floor.

On his way to the first room, Egan noticed gray footprints on the floor. His footprints. He had made a mess in the first room; clumps of dust and smeared prints were everywhere. Pitt had left a few shoeprints, a few scarce blots compared to Egan's. The floor looked like he had danced around the room.

Egan wiped down the floor, bent in half and stepping backward out of the rooms to catch any fresh footprints he was making as he went. The process resulted in dusty stripes looping around each room and down the hall and zig-zagging in front of the painting of the one-armed man.

Despite his harsh warning, the footman seemed to find the process amusing. Egan heard him chuckle several times before the two proceeded back downstairs.

The great room was imposing and hollow. Other than tall candelabras in each corner and a few chairs, the room was empty.

"Why is nuffink in here?" Egan asked.

"Tis a ballroom for assemblies and dancing," the footman replied.

"Tis big."

Pitt was not in the great room, but his shoeprints faintly crossed the floor between the fireplaces on opposite sides of the room. Egan swept out the two large hearths. He clinked his brush on the brick and metal grate a couple of times to hear the ding echo throughout the spacious room.

Egan wiped the footprints from the floor and followed a single path of prints to the next room. Judging from the shoeprints, Pitt was up the chimney at the far end of the room.

Egan approached the hearth and listened to the melodic scrape of Pitt's brush against the brick. He sat on the floor to wait for Pitt to finish scraping the hole. Egan started singing one of the songs Mum sang on market day.

"To market, to market, to buy a fat pig,
Home again, home again, jiggety-jig.

To market, to market, to buy a penny bun,
Home again, home again, market is done."

On the way to the market, Egan and Kerrin would each hold one of Mum's hands. She swung their hands and taught them songs about cows and ships and bridges and cobblestones. After the market, Mum held onto Kerrin with one hand and carried the basket of food in her other. Mum did not have a free hand for him.

Yesterday, Mum had held his hand.

Egan wiped away tears as Pitt descended into the hearth. The saltwater smudged a layer of soot on his face.

"There's no shame in it," Pitt said.

"In wot?"

"Being sad. Crying a bit."

"I weren't crying."

"Just remembering then," Pitt conceded.

Egan cleaned the hearth in silence, and the boys proceeded to the impressive fireplace in the front hall.

"I'll do it," Egan offered.

"Yer sure?"

"Aye."

The climb did not deliver a thrill of achievement, but it did serve to distract Egan from his memories. When he returned to the hearth, his eyes were dry.

Egan and Pitt completed the servant's quarters and laundry room chimneys, where the butler observed them pushing the large black laundry pot back into the hearth on its chimney crane.

The butler raised his one long eyebrow.

"I hope your disheveled appearance is not an indication of the state of the house."

"Wot?" Egan asked.

"Franklin? How did the young sweeps perform?"

"All but the kitchen is complete. The sweeps performed satisfactory work, even though the rooms will require attention to address some dust," the footman reported.

"As to be expected, but a satisfactory job nonetheless. The kitchen will not be swept today as the flue is already hot. However, you may have your master call upon me mid-September for a thorough sweep."

The butler handed Pitt a small card and two shillings.

"I will. Thank ye, sir."

"Franklin, escort the lads to the kitchen. The cook set aside food from the midday meal for them. And then find Miss Nettle to see about tidying the house before tomorrow morning."

The footman nodded respectfully but as soon as the butler departed, he scowled, "You'd think I had nothing better to do than to deliver messages and watch children all day."

"Wot do you have to do?" Egan asked. He was immediately answered with a light smack on the back of the head from Pitt.

The footman ignored Egan's comment and walked down a narrow hall to the back of the house without checking to make sure that the boys followed. Arriving in the kitchen, the footman pointed at two table settings across from each other at the end of a long table.

"Eat quickly," he ordered.

The broomers set their tools and ashes down at the foot of the table, approached the dishes, and sat down. A piece of bread, bowl of soup, and cup of tea had been set aside for each of them.

The boys, still dressed in only their smallclothes, started to devour the feast.

"This tastes like Christmas!" Egan's eyes lit up.

"There be sausage in here. Delicious," Pitt observed after the second spoonful.

A contented silence fell upon the room as the boys consumed the meal in delight. However, the moment was fleeting, and soon the broomers were getting dressed and being ushered out of the grand house.

"No Master Armory, full stomach, and two bobs. This do be a lucky day!" Pitt tossed a coin into the air and caught it and slapped it on the back of his hand. "Good lord, it's King George's head." A roguish smile spread across Pitt's face. "I'm having a thought."

CHAPTER X

"Me Mum don't let me go into public houses."

"Yer mum is not here. And this be the Cheshire Cheese. Respectable people drink here." Pitt pulled the heavy wooden door open and headed into the public house.

Egan followed Pitt into a dark, gloomy room. Tables and chairs were scattered about, most were empty save a few working men drinking their pay between jobs. The establishment's stench was sour, smelling of sweat, ale, and urine. In the corner, a hefty man lay sprawled out on the floor in a puddle of his own vomit.

Pitt headed straight towards a scrawny barkeep that lazily wiped at a long counter.

"Change for a shilling, sir," Pitt said, showing the barkeep the coin.

"And you think I looks like a banker?" The barkeep spoke as if his nose was permanently pinched closed.

"Can you exchange the bob or not?"

"I have a full purse," the barkeep grabbed the coin and bit into it. Finding the metal solid, he counted and returned ten pence to Pitt.

Pitt counted the coins. "You gave me 10p. The bob is worth 12p."

"Wot do you intend to do about it?" the barkeep sneered.

"I'll fetch me master. He's a man of business and doesn't like to be robbed."

"I must have miscounted," the barkeep said in his nasally voice. He picked another tuppence from his purse and handed the coins to Pitt.

"Would you be needing anything else, young squire? Maybe some lager to lift yer spirits?"

"No, sir." Pitt took the additional coins. He counted all the coins again, sliding the change from one side of his scarred hand to the other. Satisfied, Pitt placed the coins in his pocket.

"Thank ye."

Pitt thanked the barkeep and led Egan outside.

"Wot are you going to do?" Egan asked.

"I'll give Master Armory a shilling and eight coppers as our earnings. I'll keep the extra coins to make up earnings on a day when work is hard to come by. Eventually, I'll have five guineas to pay me debt."

Pitt sat on the ground and removed his left shoe. He lifted a strip of stiff fabric that lined the sole and carefully placed the extra coins beneath.

"Wot if Master Armory finds out you kept coins?"

"I get whipped. You gets whipped. We gets whipped anyway. Having a stash saves yer tail when yer short coins some days. Master Armory don't know when we earn it. He only cares that we brings it in each day. And we all needs savings for our debt."

"It don't seem right."

"Wot part? Lying to Master Armory or getting whipped or paying our debt?"

"The lying part."

"Take that up with King George next time you dine with him." Pitt laced his shoe and stood up, shifting from foot to foot. "That's comfortable."

"How much you got?" Egan asked.

"I ain't telling. I'll buy me freedom in about four years. Johnny Pasey taught me to sweep. When I first came to Master Armory, Johnny, he says to me, *Stash and save, Pitt. You'll be free on yer own if you stash and save*. Johnny, he had a stash and just disappeared one day. Master Armory didn't throw a fit. He just picked up Will, Reeves, and Iggy to replace Johnny. I'll do it too one day, pay me debt and leave. Be sure to start yer own stash. A pence here and a haypenney there adds up. And don't go eating just because you have the coin. Savings is better than a full stomach."

"I'll save. I'll save some for Mum and Kerrin too."

"Here." Pitt handed Egan tuppencefF. "Put these in yer sock. We'll give Master Armory a shilling and sixpence."

"Thank ye!" Egan beamed and dropped the coins down his sock and shook his foot until the coppers sunk to the bottom. "Hope me socks don't have holes."

"Holes in the soles," Pitt said.

"Holes in the soles and me feet get cold," Egan laughed.

"Holes in the soles and yer feet get cold cause you walk like a troll," Pitt added.

"I do not!"

"I win!" Pitt claimed as he lightly smacked Egan's arm. A cloud of black dust escaped from Egan's shirt.

"I don't walk like a troll."

"Careful with yer stash, socks do get holes real easy."

"I don't walk like a troll," Egan repeated his protest.

The boys ambled down the street in silence. Egan watched Pitt for clues on what came next, but Pitt seemed to be enjoying the afternoon without a specific purpose in mind. Pitt ambled towards Stocks Market, found an empty corner, and sat down with his tools at his feet. Egan followed.

When his curiosity became uncontainable, Egan spoke up, "Wot are we doing?"

"Nuffink. It's not quite dark and with this much coin, we can go to the bin at our leisure. Hardly ever happens but when it does, I sits and looks at London."

"Oh." Egan rested his chin on his knees.

"It's quite a city."

Egan looked up and down the street and then sniffed the air. It smelled of fresh bread and sweet fruits. He watched a grocer wheel a cart of oranges into a nearby shop.

Egan had never tasted an orange. He was tempted to use his coins to try one, but Pitt's words echoed in his head. An orange might cost more than 2p anyway. Egan resolved to wait to purchase one until he was on his way home. He would share it with Mum and Kerrin. They would like that.

An empty fishmonger's cart passed, wafting the scent of rotting fish entrails. Its driver looked quite pleased; he must have finished the day with a profitable sale. The horse's hooves clopped along the cobblestones past tea, cordwainer, and wax and tallow chandler shops. Egan noted which direction the cart went, thinking that it might be going towards the River Thames.

Another wagon led a spotted cow through the street. The cow objected to the crowds and the direction it was forced to travel. Its loud moo attracted the attention of other merchants and amused onlookers. In contrast, the caged chickens in the back of the wagon seemed docile and content. Perhaps the cow understood that there would be fresh meat at the butcher's shop the next morning while the hens were only expected to deliver a new egg.

Across the street, a footman assisted a lady as she stepped down from a carriage. Her dress was made of numerous folds of dark blue cloth. The billowing fabric made her totter a bit before her feet landed on the street. She regained her sophisticated posture and entered the hat shop next to the clothier's store.

A small medicine shop was squeezed in between a grocer and a corn dealer. If he had the coin, Egan could have bought theriac for Kerrin. It was sure to be good medicine if the wealthy bought it, but the shop was too far from home. At least Egan thought he was far from home. He felt far from home.

People bustled through the street in complete disorder, creating paths in the crowd for the random distinguished citizen or wealthy merchant whose expensive clothing naturally set them apart like a rainbow from the clouds.

Church bells rang, causing a frenzied atmosphere as folks finished their daily exchanges and hurried for home.

"There's no more bread for the day," said an irritated woman as she exited a bakery across the street.

"Thomas Croofe can never meet the demand," a man answered. "Another baker will replace him if he ain't careful."

"Not to my standards," Egan heard nearby, but he could not identify the speaker.

"He was a skinner on Budge Row!" exclaimed another, causing a cackle of feminine laughter.

"I'm astounded he weren't beheaded at the Tower!" a woman responded, adding to the mirth.

"Call tomorrow," a slurred voice echoed down the street followed by the slam of a heavy door.

The crowd started to decline as the light waned into early evening. Egan glanced over at Pitt, who was curled up sound asleep on the cobblestones. He looked thin and lifeless.

"Need a bit of luck, child?"

Egan looked up at a solid woman with a quick smile and tenacious blue eyes. Wispy strands of hay colored hair escaped from a dilapidated straw hat that was bent down at the sides by a scarf tied under her chin. "Are you two behaving yerselves?" She asked.

"Yes, and we've had a good day of business," Egan answered.

"I says to meself, now there's two fine boys of business. Good fer you. Is yer friend all right?"

"He's all right."

"Well, when you be needing a bite, visit me corner over there. I'll give you a good price on a boiled potato."

"I like potatoes."

"Me too, but I guess that be the Irish in me. Not much a good potato can't fix."

"Me Da was Irish."

"Well, what do you know. We be family."

"Do you know the Whitcombe's in Fermanagh?"

"I can't say that I do, dear."

"Oh, well that's me Da's clan."

"I wish I knowed them. We'd be fast friends to be sure. I better be off now, dearie. Slán abhaile!"

"Slán."

The woman proceeded with her large pot down the street and smiled back at Egan before disappearing around the corner.

Pitt was right, Egan thought, this was quite a city.

CHAPTER XI

"Charles, are you finished buffing the ragout spoons?"

"Yes, sir."

"Bring them here."

Charles Greville collected four large silver spoons and walked them across the workshop to Lamerie.

Lamerie lifted his eyeglass and inspected the first spoon.

"The bowl of the spoon is dull."

"It be difficult to buff the curve."

"What did I ask you to do?" Lamerie's voice was stern.

"Buff the spoons."

"Until...."

"Until they shine."

"Does this shine?"

"Parts do, sir."

"The correct answer is no, Charles. They do not shine. Do you think George Treby will be satisfied with partly buffed spoons? Begin again," Lamerie ordered.

"Would you look at the others?"

"Do the others shine?"

Charles glanced at the spoons in his hand. "No, sir."

"Then get to work."

Lamerie checked his temper as Charles stomped back to the buffing table, dropped the spoons in a clanging pile on the table, and grabbed a pad of compressed wool.

Lamerie glanced sideways at Bennett Bradshaw, who was working diligently as if he had not heard the exchange.

"Bennett," Lamerie's voice was calm.

"Yes, sir."

"Is the relief mold ready for the border on the Thomas Western dish?"

"Yes, sir."

"Is the silver heated?"

Lamerie observed Bennett lift a crucible from the hot coals with long metal tongs.

"Yes, sir. It's the perfect temperature – cherry red molten metal."

"Good. You may pour the mold," Lamerie said.

Charles let out an exasperated huff.

"Bennett, pour the mold please."

"Yes, sir. Thank ye, sir."

Lamerie watched as Bennett checked the holes on the mold and made sure the passages were clean. Bennett then tested the grips, following every step of Lamerie's training. The mold was held firmly in the upright position.

Bennett pulled his gloves up tightly between his fingers, picked up the crucible with the tongs, and carefully moved it over the mold. He tipped the crucible over the hole furthest away from him and poured a small stream of the liquid metal into the mold. When he saw that the hole was full, Bennett moved on to the next hole. The silver ran out before the last hole was filled to the top of the mold.

"Sir, I may have poured too much silver in each hole. This side mold may not be filled." Bennett admitted.

"We shall see on the morrow. Clean up for the evening."

"Yes, sir."

Bennet hung the tongs on the hook by the hearth and swept silver scrapings from Lamerie's work table into an empty wooden bowl.

Charles set the compressed wool aside and began to remove his leather apron.

"Young man, your work is not yet finished," Lamerie bellowed.

"But it's the end of the day."

"The day will end when those spoons shine."

Charles tossed a spoon across the room. "This ain't right. You let him pour a mold while I do chump work."

"Perhaps you should stop acting like a chump. You will finish the buffing tonight, or you won't enter this workshop again." Lamerie glared at the young man.

After a minute of strained silence, Charles crossed the workspace, picked up the spoon, and returned to the buffing table.

"Good night, sir," Bennett said.

"Good night, Bennett."

When Bennett left the workshop, Lamerie sat down and resumed his work engraving delicate trellis patterned panels within a circular border on a round silver plate.

"Yer staying with me?" Charles asked.

"Yes."

"Why? So I don't run off with the silver?"

"Are you planning to? There are terrible consequences for thieves." Lamerie seemed amused.

"Like there be consequences for marking and selling silver crafted by yer Huguenot friends like it was yer own?"

"Charles, how would you like to live on the street?" Lamerie asked.

"Not at all, sir. These spoons will shine, sir."

CHAPTER XII

"Now keep yer mouth shut," Pitt instructed Egan as they approached the back door of Master Armory's house. "Twig."

"After today, I wonder if you can."

"I can."

"You almost got us in trouble with that footman. You step a toe out of line or question sumfink and you is whipped and probably me too. Twig?"

Egan nodded.

"I mean me words. Don't say nuffink. Don't smirk. Don't even look at him. Keep yer eyes on yer feet."

"I won't say nuffink, Pitt."

Egan snapped his head down and followed Pitt into Master Armory's house. Egan studied the movement of his feet as he walked. His right foot stepped out straight and rolled to the back as his left foot stepped out a bit crooked and pushed back for his right foot to take over again. Egan wondered if he always walked crookedly. He had never known it before if he had. The thought came to an abrupt halt when he smacked into Pitt's back.

"Umpf," Egan grunted.

Pitt turned toward Egan, grabbed him by the shoulders, moved him to the side, tapped his head downward again, and turned to face Master Armory. The master was lounging in a wingback chair in the parlor. He set down his book, snuffed at his pipe, and held out his hand.

"Here are our earnings today, sir," Pitt offered Master Armory the handful of coins. "Two shillings and a sixpence. We were hired for a new account, a Mister Hollings." Pitt handed Master Armory the card.

"A great house and you did not fetch me? What have I told you?"

"Sir, Mister Hollings instructed the work to be done at once," Pitt explained.

Master Armory considered the claim. "Very well, I could have charged twice that fee, but I suppose you did yer best. I will introduce myself to Mister Hollings and establish regular services. Both of you may join me on the next visit."

"Thank ye, sir," Pitt responded, nudging Egan.

Egan turned his head askew to look questioningly at Pitt. Was he supposed to do something? He knew he was not supposed to say anything.

"How did he do?" Master Armory asked.

"Well enough, sir. He swept five holes by hisself without me help."

"Good. Looks like you might have been worth the coin I paid." A few drops of spit flew from Master Armory's mouth towards Egan.

Egan flinched. "How much did you pay fer me?" he asked.

Pitt grabbed the back of Egan's neck in a firm grip. Egan closed his mouth and lowered his eyes.

"Get out of me sight," Master Armory hissed.

"Yes, sir." Pitt pulled Egan out of the room and back down the hallway towards the kitchen.

The aroma of baked quail in the kitchen teased them, and Egan's stomach growled.

"Good lord, even yer stomach is noisy." Pitt wiped his good hand across his brow and laughed.

"Pitt?"

"Yeah?"

"I'm sorry I said sumfink."

"Yeah, I know."

Egan followed Pitt down the back staircase. Although the air was damp and unpleasantly cold in the cellar, the soft candlelight seemed to welcome the weary broomers. Egan placed his bucket and brush back on the ring of dirt in the corner where he had it been that morning. Other buckets and tools were forming a line along the stairs.

Will and Rory sat on the floor looking at some colorful cards. Iggy was curled up in his sacks, avoiding the group and pretending to be asleep.

"Did you see Tick up there?" Will asked Pitt.

"Naw, not yet here."

"I found a set of cards," Rory announced.

"Found them where?" Pitt asked.

"In a wanker's pocket. Me hands are sticky." Rory shrugged.

"Come play," Will invited.

Egan went over to his pathetically thin sack in the corner and sat down. He plumped up the day's ashes for a pillow and placed it behind him. It was an improvement.

Egan looked up as Andrew came down the stairs. Adam sulked behind, keeping to the shadows.

"Hey, Pitt. Hey, Egan," Andrew greeted. "How was yer first full day sweeping?"

"I made it to the top!" Egan said.

"He did all right," Pitt agreed. "Wot's up with Adam?"

"He walked into the corner of a railing. He thinks I pushed him, but I didn't."

Adam stuck out his bottom lip and stomped his way to his bed of ash. "Did so, you arse," he muttered under his breath.

"Takes one to know one, you snivelin snotty nose!"

"I just blowed it!" Adam sniffed.

Andrew ignored him. "Wot are you playing?"

"Noddy. Join in," Pitt offered.

"I want to play," Adam whined.

"Yer too little," Rory said. "This game is only for us older broomers."

"Yer an arse," Adam repeated, this time to Rory, before throwing himself onto his sacks of ash with his back to the group.

Egan retreated to his corner. If Adam was too little to play, so was he. Iggy was already entrenched in his ashes.

"Any of you brooms seen Miss Eleanor lately?" Will said as he laid down a card.

"Mister Ruckston's daughter?" Pitt asked.

"Yup."

"The girl with the enormous ears?" Andrew spouted.

"They are not. At least not anymore. I was in Mister Ruckston's store this morning cleaning his chimneys. Miss Eleanor came downstairs to help customers. Well, she was wearing her hair up on her head instead of in braids. And her ears don't show no more."

"But her ears are still enormous under her hair."

"Yeah, but Andrew, you can't tell. She looks normal," Will grinned.

"You fancy her then?" Pitt asked.

"Naw, I don't go for mush. I just think she's nice."

"Mush? You look positively sniggered!" Andrew said.

"Maybe a bit," Will admitted.

The boys chuckled, and their focus returned to the cards. The room grew still. Then quietly from the corner of the room, Adam sang out in a high-pitched voice, "Oh Ellleeaanorrr, big-eared Ellleeaanorrr."

"Adam, stop before I cuff you," Will threatened.

Adam immediately became silent.

"Hmmm," Andrew hummed pensively.

"Wot?" Will challenged.

"I just hummed," Andrew answered.

"But you've got sumfink to say, me thinks."

"Not really, naw, nuffink worth saying."

"Well, Mister Ruckston 'as a right good setup. If Eleanor took a fancy to me, maybe he would pay me debt to Master Armory. I'd learn clerking and Eleanor and me could..."

"Could wot? Take vows? Yer thinking of marrying big-eared Eleanor?" Pitt teased.

"Yes."

"Will, we aren't fit for marriage. Mister Ruckston wouldn't let you pay a visit to Eleanor, much less court her."

"That's yer problem, Pitt. You can't see beyond the walls of this cellar, but we're almost out of here whether we have five guineas or not. Master Armory don't keep broomers much past fourteen, and I'm almost too big for flues anyway. We need a plan. What if he sells us to the Americas?" Will argued.

"I have me own plans."

"Well, I knew life before sweeping and sure as spit I'll see life afterward."

"Life with big-eared Elleeaanooorrr...," Adam taunted. Will stood up, took two steps, and cuffed him in the back of the head.

Adam gave an exaggerated yelp and then wavered, "I 'pose I deserved that."

Iggy smirked. It wasn't a laugh, but a smile cracked his face, and he grunted a bit in amusement.

"Hey, Iggy just smiled," Pitt said.

Iggy's smile faded. "It's not like I don't know how. You lot just aren't that amusing."

"That be true," Pitt agreed.

The card game resumed just seconds before a yelp followed by a painful crying echoed from upstairs.

"It's Tick. I forgot 'bout him," Will said.

Will pushed up from the floor as Master Armory threw Tick down the stairs and slammed the door, bolting it shut. Tick hit the wall then tumbled down the steps. He fell onto the floor at the bottom, curled himself into a ball, and wept.

Will was at Tick's side in a moment.

"Tick, you hurt?"

"I was short a haypenny. Only a haypenny," he wailed.

Will waved the other boys away as he placed a comforting hand on Tick's back.

"Did you spend the coins I gave you?"

Tick nodded.

"All of them?"

"I was hungry."

"I knows temptation. It ain't easy. We will sweep together on the morrow to make sure you get enough coin. I shouldn't have left you on yer own."

"Master Armory told you to."

"Yeah, but we can sweep together and report to Master Armory alone. I'll watch over you and he will never know of it."

"Promise, Will."

"I promise."

"Don't coddle him! He ain't nuffink to put yer neck out fer," Rory said.

"We looks out fer each other, Rory," Pitt said.

"Eejits," Rory muttered as he collected the stolen cards and placed the stack in his pocket.

"Time for sleep you sots," Pitt ordered.

"Tomorrow will be better, you'll see," Will assured Tick.

"Only if yer with me," Tick whimpered.

Egan looked over towards Pitt.

"How old are you, Pitt?" Egan asked.

"Around thirteen, I think."

"Will Master Armory sell you?"

"Naw, he needs me until you eejits remember yer place."

"That'll never happen," Andrew chuckled.

Egan gave Pitt a faint smile, but all he could think about was Pitt leaving him.

CHAPTER XIII

Exhaustion held Egan captive in dreams.

Da grinned as he taught Egan to tie a carrick bend with two pieces of weatherworn rope. The image distorted as the rope wrapped around Egan's neck with a choking grip.

Kerrin cheerfully hummed "Bessy Bell and Mary Gray" while bending discarded straw into dolls. The dolls began to move on their own and in a fury of anger scratched Kerrin's face and hands, causing thousands of red bumps to erupt over her skin.

Mum said a nighttime prayer, kissed his forehead, and tucked a quilt under his chin. The quilt became a blanket of ice, smothering him. Egan tried to escape out from under it only to awaken in the dark cellar where his confused mind panicked in the unfamiliar space.

Each moment of happiness twisted into terror. Each time he woke, Egan wept silently until he drifted back to sleep.

"Up you." Pitt nudged Egan's side with his foot.

"Ain't it Sunday?" Egan asked, struggling to lift his fatigued body. "Are you expecting Master Armory to take us to church?"

"Don't he go?"

"He goes, but that don't mean we do. We're needed on the streets, not in a church."

"You should still say prayers," Adam chimed in. "Me Mum always said prayers for us, and I say them for her and sometimes for Andrew when he is nice to me."

"I'm always nice to you," Andrew said as he wrapped an arm around Adam's neck and hugged him.

"Me Mum taught me to pray," Egan said.

"God doesn't listen to the likes of us," Rory said.

"He does too," Adam countered.

"God listens to everyone," Pitt challenged Rory. "But we ain't going to church, so get moving."

The bolt slid across the door at the top of the stairs.

Egan's limbs ached from climbing the day before, and each joint protested with pain as he followed the other broomers up and into the kitchen.

Lamps placed around the room enhanced the light from the fire and cast shadows about the room. Miss Clara scooped a bowl of gruel for each of the boys.

"You are awful quiet this morning boys, but I suspect there'll be good cheer when spring comes."

Egan accepted the last bowl from Miss Clara and hungrily slurped the bland, gray substance. Warmth spread through his body, easing the hunger pains.

"It's not long before the sun rises earlier and warm weather comes." Miss Clara said. She dunked a rag in a bowl of water and rubbed a bar of soap against the fabric to create soapsuds.

"Come here you," she said to Tick.

Tick stepped forward, closed his eyes, and scrunched his face as Miss Clara attacked the thick black streaks caused by his tears the night before.

"Faces should be washed now and again, and not just by tears."

Miss Clara rubbed Tick's face red. He looked young and vulnerable without the layers of soot.

Miss Clara lifted his chin, "Yer tears be gone, Tick. A good washin' keeps them away for a while."

Tick smiled at Miss Clara. "I hope it be so, Miss Clara."

Miss Clara rinsed the rag and moved towards Egan. "Yer still right clean," she announced, scrubbing Egan's face in a downward spiral motion and pinching his cheek in approval. Mum used to pinch his cheek. He had never liked it, but now he missed it.

"I found this for you love. You'll be needing one."

Egan unfolded the coarse cloth Miss Clara had handed him. The makeshift climbing cap was like the one Pitt used. The stitching was jagged, unlike Mum's small even stitches, but the holes were strategically placed to protect his eyes, nose, and mouth.

"Was that Reeves' cap?" Tick asked.

"It was, and it's awful glad to have a new owner." Miss Clara patted Egan's head.

"Thank ye," Egan said, looking up at her.

Miss Clara smiled at Egan and proceeded up the line to grab at a reluctant Iggy and scrub his face clean. Iggy could hardly keep hold of his bowl or stand straight on his feet as the washing jostled his thin body about.

"Who's next?" Miss Clara held up the soiled rag and looked down the line.

"It be time for me to get sweeping," Rory announced.

"Me too," Will echoed.

"I washed last week," Andrew proclaimed with a hand held up defensively in front of him.

Miss Clara frowned at Andrew then pointed the rag towards Pitt.

"Thanks, but I do me own washing," Pitt said.

"So you do. Better than most. Where's Adam hiding?"

Pitt stepped aside so Miss Clara could get to Adam who was standing in the corner. "You, young man, never wash."

"I never need washin!"

"No one is naturally clean, especially not you." Miss Clara attacked Adam's face, neck, and ears with fervor before moving him by the neck towards the basin for more water.

"Yer such a sight. I couldn't get you clean with a well of water and all the soap at McGivney's store." Miss Clara scoured the black stains on Adam's skin. When he protested, a corner of the dirty cloth dropped into his mouth. Adam gagged.

"Stay still!" Miss Clara ordered.

The boys laughed, and even Egan found a slight grin. The mirth ended when Master Armory staggered into the room, disheveled from a late night at the pub.

"Pitt, you and the runt are with me this morning," Master Armory slurred.

"Yes, sir,"

Master Armory stumbled out of the kitchen.

Pitt placed his empty bowl on the table. "Let's go, Egan."

"I'm not a runt."

"Sure you are."

"Am not."

"Are too," Adam chimed in. His rosy cheeks shined through streaks of soot. Miss Clara was only partly successful in cleaning him up.

"Am not."

"Are too. First it was me, then Iggy, and then Tick. There's only one runt at a time, and now it's you."

"Yer always gonna be a runt." Andrew slung his arm around Adam's neck and pulled him towards their pile of tools.

"I was a runt once too," Pitt whispered with a lopsided smirk.

Egan grunted, retrieved his sweeping tools and bag of ash, and followed Pitt out the door.

Egan and Pitt plodded after a staggering Master Armory, careful to avoid his erratic steps. The winter morning was freezing, but Master Armory seemed oblivious to the cold. He muttered to himself and stopped walking. He was confused, maybe lost. Egan glanced at Pitt, who waited five steps behind Master Armory. Egan imitated Pitt's stance and his respectful downward gaze.

Master Armory began walking again after a minute. They followed him up the street back in the direction they had just come. They were almost back to Master Armory's house when he veered off into the opposite direction.

Master Armory led the boys past the marketplace towards a narrow street of row houses. The tall, spindly buildings stretched eerily above Egan, seemingly twisting, and protruding into the taciturn gray sky.

Pitt looked at the rooftops and twitched apprehensively. Egan followed his gaze. The pointy rooftops were steep with lines of chimneys rising from the angled sides.

Pitt leaned closer to Egan as they trailed Master Armory. "Notchy nines," Pitt whispered.

Egan responded with a blank look.

Master Armory shuffled up to a house three doors from the main street and pounded on the door.

"I brought me boys," he yelled up at its second-story window. "Open up. It's morning, and I brought me boys."

The door opened, revealing a young kitchen maid. "Go away you! We didn't call for a sweep."

Master Armory appeared stunned. "George?"

"Do I look like I be George? Off with you now!" She exclaimed and closed the door as harshly as the quiet morning would allow.

Master Armory stumbled backward away from the door.

"Daniel!" a voice hoarsely whispered from down the narrow street. "Over here old chap!"

"Ah," Master Armory turned and stumbled across the street. "The dark hid me way."

"Whiskey has done you in my friend. Come in and rest yerself."

The man helped Master Armory into the house and closed the door leaving the boys outside.

Egan collapsed next to the door with a grunt, thankful for a time to rest.

"Don't get cozy. He'll be out here for us soon."

"Wot's a notchy nines?"

"Nine-inch holes. There's a hearth tax on each chimney 'cause there is taxes on everything. So, builders got smart and connected one hole to lots of fireplaces so as to pay only one tax. Only the hole be hard to sweep 'cause it's a nine-inch square and joins up with other nine-inch squares."

"Like the holes yesterday?"

"Naw, yesterday there was climbing room mostly straight up. Fourteen inches easy. These be tiny and crooked; a maze of pitch-black holes running through the house. You get turned upside down or fall and yer stuck easy."

Egan shivered.

"Missus Bixby told me that most broomers that got dead were in notchy nines or shoddy brick holes that crumbled, and Missus Bixby would know," Pitt said.

"Wot do we do, Pitt?"

"We climb to the roof and brush as far as we can get. We don't ever veer sideways none or the soot will trap us."

"And wot if I gets trapped?"

"First, keep yer wits about you. If you gets turned around or buried in soot and can't tell which direction is up, just spit. Spit always rolls down. Then climb up 'til yer on a roof somewhere," Pitt instructed.

"Wot if I can't spit?"

"Then piss. It rolls down too."

"Only babies piss their pants."

Pitt sat down beside Egan. "Remember it's just five guineas to freedom."

"Five guineas be a lot." Egan yawned and leaned up against the railing.

CHAPTER XIV

"**R**esting, are we?"

"We're at yer service," Pitt jumped to his feet to face the woman standing in the open door.

"You don't look it. Brush the grime off yerselves before comin' inside," the woman directed.

Egan followed Pitt out onto the cobblestone street, carefully avoiding the refuse that littered the street. The boys vigorously stomped the dust off their clothes until the woman nodded in satisfaction.

She led them into the front hall and closed the door behind them.

"Yer to act smart. No funny business."

"Yes madam," Egan said. Pitt nodded.

"Yer master is in the study. Follow me."

The broomers followed the woman down the hall and into a side room that smelled of pipe tobacco and books. Egan walked straight towards the large map that decorated the far wall of the room and stared up at it.

Master Armory was seated in a tapestry chair, still recovering from his intoxicated stupor. He looked intently at Egan.

Before Master Armory could speak, Pitt said, "This hole be a notchy nines, just me expertise." Pitt stepped out of his shoes and peeled down his britches.

"Yer eager," Master Armory observed.

"I'd like to be a real apprentice and then a master sweep one day, sir. I needs all the practice I can get. Egan is a right good broomer though, sir. You'll see at the next house just how good, sir."

Pitt set his tools down by the fireplace. He pulled his sweeping mask over his face and stooped into the hearth.

As Pitt's feet disappeared into the chimney, Master Armory grabbed at Egan's neck and pulled him across the hallway to the dining room.

"You take this hole, runt."

"Yes, sir."

Egan stripped down to his small clothes and pulled his sweeping cap over his face. He stooped into the hearth and hesitated. The hole was narrow. He was not sure he could fit. There were no ledges to pull himself up. The air was thick with dark with cold smoke. He could not see any light shining down from the top.

"Climb up and scrape it down, runt."

"Wot?"

"Climb up and scrape it down," Master Armory repeated.

A struggle between anger and helplessness raged in Egan's bones. He was afraid. Immobilized, Egan attempted to stall. He ducked out of the hearth.

"I can't…"

Master Armory struck Egan's face with such force that sent Egan's head flying into the corner of the fireplace brick. Blood trickled down Egan's neck.

Master Armory lifted Egan off the floor by his collar and growled in his ear, "I am not asking, runt. I am telling you. CLIMB UP AND SCRAPE IT DOWN!"

The gash throbbed and Egan's sight blurred, but he ducked back into the chimney to avoid another blow. He looked up. Pain sparked white flecks before his eyes; Egan could see nothing else. He stared intently into the black hole, trying to see something, anything. Suddenly his left leg jolted involuntarily in pain. He looked down as Master Armory's hand poked at his ankle with a sharp needle. He jerked away.

"Climb runt!" Master Armory pricked Egan again with the needle.

Egan shrieked. He placed a foot on the side of the hearth and pulled himself into the small hole to avoid another prick from the needle. The hole was too narrow to climb with his feet, and there were no metal rungs to aid him. He felt with his hands and found one uneven brick to grip. Egan pulled himself up with his hands and anchored himself with his elbows, knees, and back.

Out of Master Armory's reach, Egan stopped to collect his courage. He took a deep breath and slowly let it out. Then he inhaled a suffocating breath of smoke and began choking. Master Armory had filled the hearth with straw and was lighting a fire under him. The warm smoke enveloped his sweeping mask as he gasped for air. Egan's limbs flew into action, trying to escape the flames below.

Egan started to scream, but he didn't have the breath. He had to get to the roof. He scooted up on his elbows, thighs, and knees, desperate to reach the top.

The hole slanted sideways, and Egan crawled less awkwardly for a short distance, watching for soot to fall and suffocate him. As the hole bent vertically again, Egan lifted himself upwards. He scooted up and then slid his right knee up too far, wedging himself in the suffocating space. He strained to push himself up, but fear immediately sapped his strength.

The notchy nines had trapped him. Egan wriggled and twisted, but his body was irretrievably stuck. Horror whispered promises into his ear.

He pressed his hands and forehead against the filthy bricks and surrendered to his fear. Pain erupted from his chest in shrieking sobs. Urine streamed in a heated torrent down his bare leg and over his toes. Egan was overcome with shame.

Smoke started streaming up through the small cracks between his body and the bricks.

"Fire!" Egan screamed, gasping for air. He was overcome with fresh terror as he struggled to move.

"Egan! Egan! I'm here! Climb up to me voice." Pitt shouted down the chimney to Egan.

"Pitt?" Egan cried.

"It's just a pirate cave, Egan, the sky is at the top. Search for the sky!"

Egan whimpered.

"Egan! Yer only end is through this hole. Climb, damn you! Climb! I will not lose another broomer! Climb!" Pitt shrieked.

"Pitt! I can't! I'm stuck!" Egan cried.

"You must. Climb!" Pitt screamed.

"Pitt," Egan wailed.

"Hold on. I'm coming!"

All the light around Egan vanished as he heard Pitt climb into the chimney and inch downwards.

"Egan, reach up for me leg. Tell me when I'm close to you."

"I can't see you."

"I'm not far above you."

Pitt felt something brush against his foot.

"Was that you?" Pitt lowered himself a wee bit further.

"I feel yer foot, Pitt. Me leg is stuck against me chest."

Pitt's leg dangled down towards Egan.

"Grab me leg, and I'll lift you free."

Egan grasped Pitt's leg. Pitt strained to lift his leg upwards.

Egan shrieked as the bricks tore the flesh from his right knee. He released Pitt's leg and anchored his weight on shaking elbows and feet. Egan began to creep upward.

"Now climb!" Pitt ordered.

Egan squinted back the tears and bellowed in anguished resolve. He pushed himself up on limbs that seared with pain. Particles of grime fell from above as Pitt climbed out of the hole.

"Yer all but out. Climb to me."

Egan's eyes filled with tears as Pitt's damaged and calloused hands looped under his armpits and pulled him onto the roof.

CHAPTER XV

"Egan! All right you?"

Egan's eyes flickered open.

"Pitt?" Egan pulled the sooty mask from his head and sat up. He breathed in the cold winter air. His body shivered.

"Egan, put yer head in the hole and shout 'all up' so Master Armory can hear you," Pitt ordered. "Do it!" Pitt pushed Egan towards the hole.

"All up," Egan said down the hole. His voice sounded shaky and weak.

"Louder!"

"All up!"

"Now get in and scrape yer way down."

Egan stared vacantly at Pitt. "You want me to get back in there?" Egan's knees and elbows burned with pain where the brick had pulled his skin away. Blood and urine trickled down his body. He began to shake as fresh tears rolled down his cheeks.

"Master Armory is not forgiving."

"Pitt! I can't Pitt! I can't!"

"Get back in that hole and scrape it down."

"No! Pitt, no!"

"Get back in the hole!" Pitt shouted as he backhanded Egan across the face.

Egan flew back to the roof and scooted away from Pitt. Stunned, he glared at Pitt.

"I'll not ask again." Pitt pointed towards the chimney.

Keeping a wary eye on Pitt, Egan tugged the sweeping mask back over his face, picked up his brush, and climbed over the crown of the chimney.

He lowered himself down, squeezing between the bricks. Egan anchored himself with his elbows and feet, only using his knees when necessary. He came to the spot where he had been stuck. A sob escaped his throat, and he continued to climb down.

When the chimney began to slant sideways, Egan realized that he had not been cleaning the bricks, and Master Armory might be listening for brush strokes. Egan put his brush to work, pounding on imaginary clumps of soot to convince Master Armory that he was working.

Master Armory was waiting for him at the bottom. He pulled Egan out of the hearth, tore the sweeping mask off his head, and rudely inspected his face.

"Looks like Pitt took care of you for me," Master Armory sneered, his thumb digging into the bruise forming on Egan's cheek.

Egan winced.

"He might make a decent apprentice after all."

Master Armory grasped Egan's neck and directed him to the next room. Without hesitation, Egan pulled the mask back on, stooped into the hearth, and began to climb.

Egan brushed the brick as he climbed. The work distracted his mind from the strange angles and perilously small dimensions of the chimney. Egan was careful, always checking his ability to move. The notchy nines would not trap him again.

Egan emerged onto the roof and shouted, "all up" down the hole for Master Armory's benefit. He examined his torn flesh and then wrapped his arms around himself and cried as the cold air bit at his exposed skin. He had a few moments alone before Pitt emerged from a chimney across the roof. Egan quickly turned his back on Pitt and climbed down into the hole.

The parlor room was empty when Egan cautiously emerged at the bottom. He peered out into the hallway and then retrieved his tools from the dining room. Egan swept the parlor hearth, shoveled the waste ash into his sack, and scrubbed his footprints from the floor with Missus Bixby's rags.

Egan repeated the task in the dining room. As he was sweeping out the hearth, a boy about his age entered the room eating a piece of bread. Egan stood.

The boy shrieked and ran from the room.

The reaction startled Egan. He looked around to see what frightened the boy and then realized that the boy was scared of him.

Egan finished sweeping the hearth, dressed himself, and waited in the hall. He kept the sweeping mask on to hide his tears.

About midday, Master Armory left Pitt and Egan at the Little Conduit in Westcheap. Sweeps and broomers milled around, ready to bid for the next customer.

"Master Armory has a midday meal with his Missus," Pitt said.

Egan stared silently at the cobblestones. He had yet to remove his sweeping mask.

"He may come back, but we can leave if we find work. We find our own scratch on the street. A broomer who can't find a turnip innit worth much."

Egan did not respond.

"You don't know, Egan, wot Master Armory would have done if I hadn't done it."

Pitt picked up one of their rags and a bucket and left Egan sitting on the ground.

Egan needed the silence. He needed time alone.

Pitt returned a few minutes later with some water.

"Let me see yer knees," Pitt said. He reached for the hem of Egan's pant leg. Egan immediately cowered and began to cry.

"I'm not going to hit you. Yer scrapes need cleaning, just like Missus Bixby said."

Pitt struggled with his deformed hand to roll up Egan's pant leg and inspect the scraped skin. Pitt carefully applied the cold rag to the wounds, cleaning the soot from the blood.

"This will hurt," Pitt warned as he scrubbed some soot from flesh that was already scabbing over. The scab tore free, and blood poured from the wound.

Egan flinched.

Pitt rinsed the rag in the water and used his good hand to squeeze it out over Egan's knee. The water washed away the grit.

"Missus Bixby says you got to keep yer scrapes clean or yer to die of infection. Will you do the rest?"

Egan nodded as he rolled up the other pant leg and proceeded to clean the gashes in his other knee. When finished, he pulled his pant legs down against the cold air. He removed his wool sweater and pulled up his sleeves. Blood had seeped through his shirt. He dabbed at the cuts along his arms and washed the blood from his hands.

"Master Armory would have hurt you bad if I hadn't done it," Pitt said.

"I know."

"You done real good, Egan."

"No, I didn't, I pissed meself," Egan choked.

"Naw, you were just pissing out the fire under you. Every broomer has pissed a fire out least once."

A laugh escaped from Egan's chest.

"Sometimes I drink lots just so I'm ready if there's a fire to piss out," Pitt added. "You gave that fire a good strong piss."

Egan pulled off his mask and weakly smiled at Pitt.

"It innit easy, Egan, but you done good."

CHAPTER XVI

"**M**ister de Lamerie, which mark should I use?" Bennett asked.

"Use the old mark," Lamerie responded.

"Will you be taking these spoons and salvers to the Goldsmith's Hall for hallmarking then?"

"Yes. The wardens have been sniffing around, and my new mark may have been recognized last week at George Treby's party," Lamerie said.

"Will you register it then?"

"I would if it weren't for the bloody taxes. You can't sell a piece without a proper hallmark. You can't hallmark a piece without paying the duty. Keeps a man from making a living. At least the sterling standard for silver plate was restored. Still, we'd all be out on the streets without a sale or two on the side."

"What will you do if you get caught?" Bennett asked.

"Pay the fine. Spend a week in Newgate Prison." Lamerie brushed some silver shavings away from the design he was engraving.

"I heard talk from another apprentice that the king's advisors want to punish counterfeiting hallmarks as a felony, punishable by death," Bennett said.

"I doubt that will happen. It's too stiff a penalty for duty dodging," Lamerie assured his apprentice.

Lamerie carefully carved the fronds of a fern into the mold, creating a delicate pattern.

"Is this the right mark, sir?" Bennett interrupted.

Lamerie glanced at the iron stamp that Bennett held towards him. The mark was a crown and star over "LA," the first two letters of his surname, right above a fleur-de-lis. Lamerie had registered this mark when he became a freeman in 1713.

"Yes, that is right."

"I've been thinking about my mark," Bennett said.

"It's never too early to make plans for the future. Let's have it. What will your mark be?" Lamerie asked.

"Like yours, except scripted initials "BB" with a crown and rose."

"Very English, wise choice. I sometimes wonder if I should use a fleur-de-lis in my mark. It's too French, and very few Huguenots are registered with the Company of Goldsmiths."

"You are, sir."

"And my mark is not respected as it ought to be," Lamerie stated.

Bennett stamped a spoon and placed it in a wooden crate with other items to take to the assay office at the Goldsmith's Hall.

"Sir?"

"Yes."

"Sir, I have concerns about Charles."

"What about?" Lamerie asked.

"When he attends customers in the front shop, well he has a charming manner and is good for business, but being around the jewelry and such, unattended, I just…"

"If that boy steals from me, I'll pack him off to Newgate to rot."

"Yes, sir."

"In fact, I kind of hope he does," Lamerie said with a wink. "He tries my patience."

Bennett laughed and nodded. "Mine too, sir."

"Make sure those spoons and salvers are stamped and packed tonight," Lamerie ordered. "I intend to leave for the Hall early and avoid the crowd. I have matters to discuss with Master Beaufort."

"Yes, sir."

CHAPTER XVII

The first rain in April was a welcome deluge upon London's filth. The air was fresh. The earth was new.

The broomers stripped down and ran naked through the falling water. The heavy drops smeared the grime on their bodies. Egan reveled in the feel of clean skin as brown water ran through the gutters and washed the waste of London into the River Thames to the south and River Lea to the west.

The storms increased in strength, bringing unusually strong winds, thunder, and lighting. Master Armory sent the brooms out alone each morning before he headed to the pub and drank through the storms. When the rain hammered down upon the cobblestones and Master Armory was away, Miss Clara let the broomers sneak back into the damp cellar until the sky grew calm. Stormy afternoons were broomers' holidays.

Egan wanted to run naked in the rain again, but Adam warned him about the risks of bathing more than once a year.

Instead, the broomers resorted to other entertainment. The older boys played cards. Adam objected to being excluded from the game, so he created a game called "ash sack skipping." The broomers jumped erratically from sack to sack without touching the floor until two broomers ended up on the same sack. From there, the game transformed into a rowdy competition to see who could wrestle the longest without touching the floor.

Adam cheated, of course. He was small, but aggressive, and ran down the larger broomers just to start a fight. "Ash sack skipping" became a giant wrestling match with the trophies being black eyes and bloody noses. The game appealed to Adam's restless nature, but the others tired easily.

Wasted from exertion, the older broomers resorted to noddy. Rory had brought another stack of cards, between the two sets there was a full deck. No one asked if Rory had stolen the cards, the broomers just accepted the fact that Rory was a thief. Sometimes his sticky fingers were helpful to their cause.

Adam bounced around the vacant sacks by himself, prodding the others to join him. Tick joined him for a while. Iggy fell asleep.

Egan stared up at the ceiling and thought about the way Mum had hugged him that last night before selling him. She loved him. Egan knew she did. He needed to find her and Kerrin and give them his savings. He had fourteen pence and four farthings in his socks.

"How long have you been here, Pitt?" Will asked one afternoon.

Pitt lifted an eyebrow at Will. Egan raised himself up on his elbows to listen.

"You, Eli, and Rory were here when Master Armory took me, Iggy, and Reeves from the parish," Will said.

"Pitt was here before me," Rory added.

"Then Andrew and Adam, then Eli died, and then Tick came. You have been here through all that," Will continued.

"I have been here the longest, but me story is me own."

The broomers respected Pitt's response.

"Me father is in prison," Rory offered.

"We know," Andrew and Adam said in unison.

"I got nipped stealing and the constable turned me over to Master Armory for a coin," Rory continued.

"We know," Andrew and Adam repeated.

"Wot about you then?"

"Our family was sent to the workhouse after father was trampled by a horse. He couldn't work."

"But he is still strong," Adam added defiantly as he bounced across the sacks.

Andrew shook his head slightly. "Adam and me paid our parent's workhouse fee."

"The horse never meant to hurt him," Adam assured from across the room.

"I went back to the workhouse once to look for them after Pitt let me sweep on me own. They weren't there no more," Andrew said.

"They will come get us soon," Adam said, bouncing on his sack.

Andrew shook his head and looked at the others playing cards. "Will, wot was the orphanage like?" he asked.

"Better than here," Will responded, "Although I thought it was the worst. Iggy, Reeves, and I chose to leave when Master Armory came 'round looking for apprentices."

"This is better than down by the River Thames," Tick interjected. "There's no food down there, and nabbers were always around looking for kids to sell to the Americas."

"Some kids got nabbed from the parish yard," Will confirmed. "Tied up and taken before anyone could stop them."

"Most of us hoped for a roof to sleep under, but no one wanted to be on one of them ships to the Americas. I had good luck," Tick concluded.

"Good luck?" Egan questioned.

"I didn't belong anywhere before here," Tick answered.

"We don't belong here," Pitt reminded in a stern voice. "Everyone is saving for five guineas, right?"

The mumbled replies were overpowered by the sound of rolling thunder.

CHAPTER XVIII

It was not long before the spring rains became a curse. The broomers' earnings were low, and their guts ached from hunger.

The first few mornings, the broomers hauled their extra ash to Bishopsgate to sell to farmers who bought it to fertilize their fields during the spring planting. Egan sold all the ash he had collected, keeping only the thin sack he inherited from Reeves. Coin was better than a full gut, and a full gut was considerably better than sleeping in comfort.

Despite the extra coppers, work was scarce. The boys left earlier in the morning and walked the streets, but most houses had their chimneys cleaned the month before. The broomers resorted to lying. They knocked on doors and advised residents that their chimney smoke looked dangerously close to starting a fire. The approach worked well in the early morning when the flues were not too hot to climb and the servants were gullible. But too many Londoners were wise to that trick, and the broomers were chased away.

"Curses me stomach," Egan muttered as he and Pitt turned away from a closing door.

"Thinking of food only leaves you hungrier than you were before."

"How much have we made today?"

"A sixpence."

Egan groaned. "There's an Irish woman near Stocks Market. She sells boiled potatoes."

"Coins are better than a full gut," Pitt reminded.

"I'll take it from me savings, just a farthing or two," Egan pleaded. "We could split a potato then find the next job."

Pitt relented. "Lead the way," he said.

Egan was getting quite good at navigating the area around Master Armory's house, especially the route from the Little Conduit to Stocks Market. Street vendors set up a few yards past the market. Egan scanned the lot looking for a battered straw hat. When he spotted her, he approached and waited until she turned around. Her blue eyes twinkled through the strands of straw-colored hair.

"Well, I'll be. It's me fellow Irishman! Didn't think I'd see you again. Come for a boiled potato?"

"Yes, madam," Egan answered.

"I don't be grand enough for madam. I be just Missus Winchester," she introduced herself. "Wot might yer name be?"

"Egan, Egan Whitcombe."

"Fitting for a little fire sprite."

"How much for a potato?"

"A haypenny."

"I'll take one." Egan unwound the burlap from around his foot and dug two farthings from his sock. He handed them over and rewrapped his foot.

"Is that yer friend there?" Missus Winchester pointed towards Pitt.

"Tis." Egan beckoned Pitt, but he wouldn't come over. He waited patiently for Egan on the corner of the street.

"I'll give you two potatoes for another farthing. Half price," Missus Winchester tempted.

"How big are the potatoes?" Egan asked.

Missus Winchester smiled and scooped two piping hot potatoes from her pot with a large wooden spoon.

Egan dug another farthing out of his sock and handed it to her.

Egan wrapped his hands with the edges of his sleeves and took the two large potatoes from Missus Winchester.

"Share one with yer friend," she winked.

"I will. Thank ye!" Egan exclaimed. His belly groaned in anticipation.

"Go on now. Off with you!"

"Thank ye!" Egan repeated as he ran towards Pitt.

The boys devoured the potatoes. Pitt hugged Egan's neck clumsily with his distorted arm, and they took off down Bearbinder Lane. Egan had never been to this section of the city and was content to let Pitt lead.

Pitt watched chimneys and yelled 'Sweep!' every few buildings. The street was quiet compared to Stocks Market until the broomers neared a courtyard where dozens of boys ran about playing a game Egan did not recognize.

"Is this a school?" Egan asked.

"It's the Merchant Taylor's School. Them is wealthy blokes."

A few boys noticed Pitt and Egan and ran towards the edge of the lawn. They started jeering at the soot-stained broomers.

"Look, it's Lucifer and his pet!"

"Demons! Aufs! Goblin children!"

"They carry the plague!" one boy yelled. "Run far away!"

"Ignore them," Pitt said. "They don't know how to wipe their own noses."

Egan eyed the boys with envy. Each one had shoes on their feet, and he was a haypenny and a farthing further from freedom than he had been that morning. Guilt overwhelmed him. Pitt was right. Savings was better than a full gut because freedom was better than sweeping.

"Sweep!" Pitt yelled after they passed the school.

"Sweep!" Egan joined in.

Egan's eyes widened as the broomers turned onto Candlewick Street. The upscale shops boasted candles, lanterns, silk draperies, and cloth. The clientele arrived and departed in carriages with full livery staff and well-groomed horses. The shopping along the street was a social affair.

"You there, sweeps!" a man called to Pitt and Egan.

"Aye, sir, at yer service sir," Pitt responded.

"A tanner to you chaps if you'll clean the street in front of my shop," the man offered. "Most unfortunate amount of dung today." The man pointed to the area in front of his tallow candle shop. Patrons avoided the section. Sidestepping took them to a competing business.

"Yes, sir!" Pitt responded.

"Watch out for horses," Pitt cautioned Egan, "they gets spooked easy and bite."

"Horses bite?"

"You bet, and it hurts more than you would think."

Pitt pulled Egan through the crowd of people, carts, and carriages to get to the dung. They shoveled into their pails using their sweeping tools. The pails filled too quickly. Egan carried the pail around the corner and emptied it onto the adjacent street. He ran back to Pitt for the other pail. The boys cleaned the area, collected the shilling, and proceeded up the street. They offered their services to the merchants they spotted and collected half a crown between them.

"This is better than sweeping holes," Egan said.

"This is wot I do in the summer sometimes," Pitt stated.

"In the summer? Why?"

"When Master Armory goes to the country, we gets to roam free a bit. Summer in London is the best."

"We don't sweep in summer?"

"We do if we want to. Let's go towards Budge Row. We still need two coppers."

CHAPTER XIX

hen the dark clouds rolled away and the sky turned a
brilliant blue, every face in London turned upwards
towards the sunshine. Every window opened to the street to
let the fresh air in. Winter's cold, grey drizzle had yielded to spring,
which would eventually surrender to summer.

The first morning in May was cool with a crisp vapor that hovered
above the cobblestones. The air stirred with the promise of a long day
of perfect weather. In the darkness, the broomers started down the
alley towards the main street armed with buckets, bags, poles, and
brushes.

"We sweep together today," Pitt announced.

"I saw windows open yesterday," Will said.

"Aye, the sun is teasing us," Pitt said.

"Wot?" Egan asked.

"The sun is teasing us, making us think summer is here."

"Summer will be here soon."

"Not soon enough, but this be the best time of year for a broomer."

"Why's that?"

"Open doors and windows. Fresh air. Spring cleaning. Lots of
coin. We're practically guests in every house."

"We sweep together cause every house wants a sweep whether
they need it or not. We make more money if we work streets
together."

"I'm not spending the day with you louts," Rory said and walked
away.

"And a good riddance to you," Adam said.

"Come on, we'll start at the Little Conduit, get our first job, and
then work the street."

The broomers were flagged by a servant on the Old Change before
getting to their first destination. They spent the day sweeping through
the Bread Street Ward; starting negotiations were sixpence per flue
with a lesser price if compensation included some food. The larger
houses paid the high price, but the poorer homes shared their bread
and conversation for a discount.

By the third day of May, the broomers had swept near every house in the Bread Street, Cheap, and Cordwainer Street Wards.

Egan's socks jingled as he walked.

"Better strap down those coins. No need to invite robbers or let Master Armory know you have savings," Pitt told him.

Egan moved all his coins from his socks to his drawstring purse at the next house. He would separate his sweeping coins from his savings before getting back that night. The small pile of coins thrilled him. Most of it was Master Armory's, but still, he had never held so much money at one time. The businesses and residents on Budge Row had been either generous or ignorant. Either way, Egan's spirits were high.

Pitt had assigned him the chimneys on the second and third floors with a reminder to listen in the flues for Andrew or Adam coming up beneath him.

As he laid down his tarp and tools, a clean little boy entered the bedroom. Egan stood and waited for the boy to say something. The boy studied Egan for a few moments.

"Were you bad? Did you disobey?" he asked.

"Wot?"

"My father says he'll sell me to a chimney sweep if I'm bad. Were you bad?"

Egan looked at the other boy.

"No. Me Mum needed the money."

The boy held out a glass to Egan. "Here. This is for you."

"Wot is it?"

"Milk. Drink it."

"I've heard of milk." Egan accepted the glass and tasted the creamy substance. Finding it agreeable, he drank the entire glass. "Thank ye, I rather liked that," he said as he handed the glass back to the boy.

"Do you like climbing chimneys?"

"No."

"Yer not a demon, are you?"

"No, I'm a boy."

"Me too."

Egan heard Andrew call "all up" nearby and was reminded that he needed to get to work.

"I'm heading up," he said to the boy.

Egan ducked into the chimney and brushed the sides as he climbed the cold flue. He called "all up" at the top and brushed his way back down to the bedroom. The clean little boy had gone.

Towards the end of the day, the broomers bought two loaves of bread from a street vendor and divided it up among themselves.

"I'm going to see Rex and the others before the day's done. Anyone joining me?" Pitt asked as he chewed.

"No, I'm going with Andrew," Adam said.

"Well, I'm going with Pitt," Andrew said.

"I'll join you, Pitt," Adam said.

"Who's Rex?" Egan asked.

"He's the king of the broomers, at least he used to be. He was crushed by a toppling chimney a few years back. He and other old broomers live near the water pump down Cornhill."

"I'm beat. I'm heading back to the cellar," Will said.

Iggy and Tick joined Will.

"How far is it?" Egan asked.

"Down the Cornhill. Not far."

"I'll go," Egan said, following Pitt.

"Rex is a cripple, don't stare at him," Pitt warned.

"He looks real bad," Adam added.

"Could be any one of us," Andrew said.

The street widened past a poulterer's shed into a busy thoroughfare lined with merchants and their customers.

Pitt led Egan, Andrew, and Adam towards a crippled boy folded on the ground near St. Michael's. The boy's lean legs crossed over each other at old angles beneath an unnaturally curved spine.

"Hallo, Rex!"

"Pitt! Yer a sight for sore eyes! I was just thinking 'bout me broomer friends."

"Rex, you remember Andrew and Adam."

"Of course, fellows. Good to see you!"

"This is me new recruit, Egan."

"Hallo, Rex," Egan greeted as he sat down on the corner with the others.

"Where are the others?" Pitt asked.

"Wes was picked up by the constable last fall. I haven't seen him since. Soot warts got Noel last winter. He cut them off hisself, but they festered, and he died."

"You seen Harley about?" Andrew asked.

"Nabbers got Harley last week. They is selling him to the Americas. The nabbers didn't want me. They can only sell ones that can walk."

"Aren't you glad they didn't take you?" Egan asked.

"Naw, least I'd have a place to sleep. Not much work 'round for a cripple after I got too big to fit in a flue."

"Well, we've a bit of luck this week," said Pitt.

"Spring sweeping time?"

"Yup." Pitt retrieved a shilling and gave it to Rex.

"And this too," Egan said, handing Rex the heal of one of the loaves of bread.

"Thank ye. Sure wish I was still sweeping."

"Me too, Rex. Remember when we filched that bread when the baker didn't pay us?"

Rex sniggered. "He was too fat to run after us. You yelled saying he should have his arse whipped."

"Pitt stole sumfink?" Adam did not hide his disbelief.

"Only 'cause he refused to pay us. His ovens were hot too. We shoulda pushed him in them ovens," Rex said.

The broomers laughed as Rex bit into the bread with a grateful sigh.

"This is sure nice of you. Have you seen Corbett's broomers lately?" Rex asked.

"Not since Brien died. Casey is good though," Pitt said.

"He hasn't been 'round to see me," Rex said.

"I'll tell him where you are if I see him."

"Thank ye, Pitt. Tell him I miss him but that he'd better be saving."

"I will. Say Rex, who helps you to the workhouse to sleep?"

"The workhouse won't take me no more, but St. Michael's Parish is good to me. Father Wilton gave me this blanket."

"That's good, Rex. How have you..."

"Pitt! Run!" Rex shrieked and pointed towards the street. "The constable's coming with nabbers! Run!"

The constable and three men had surrounded the boys and were closing in.

The broomers rushed to their feet, grabbed their tools and sacks, and ran.

Adam darted between two of the men and ran towards Cheapside.

A hand reached for Egan. Egan grabbed the hand and bit it as hard as he could and then dashed after Adam.

Two men descended upon Pitt.

"Pitt!" Egan screamed, turning around and running back towards Andrew and Pitt.

"Run home!" Pitt yelled.

"Leave them be! They're working boys," Rex yelled.

Egan felt Adam grab his arm and pull him away.

"Follow me!" Adam yelled, running behind St. Mary Woolchurch and onto Bucklersbury. Adam weaved between buildings and streets, taking the nabbers on a wild goose chase. Only, the nabbers were not following them.

"Stop running you eejit!" Pitt yelled from a street away.

"They ain't following no more," Andrew gasped.

Egan pulled Adam to a stop.

"We showed them, those nabbers!" Adam's cheeks were red with exhilaration.

"Where are we?" Egan asked.

"I don't know. Who cares? Did you see their faces!"

"You done good," Pitt said, walking up behind Adam.

"Where are we?" Egan asked again.

"Near St. Paul's. Let me catch me breath."

"They think they got us! They don't got us!" Adam yelled, beating the air with his fists.

"They woulda let us go. Master Armory owns us. They can't sell us," Andrew said.

"They can if they're fast enough. If that ever happens again, you run and get Master Armory. Twig?" Pitt said.

"It won't happen again. They won't get us," Adam said.

Egan looked at Pitt and nodded.

"Good, we go this way," Pitt pointed down the alley.

Egan followed Pitt down an alley to Friday Street, and London became familiar once again as they walked towards Master Armory's house.

"Pitt?"

"Yeah?"

"Wot do we do when we're too big for the flues?" Egan asked.

"If we don't got five guineas, we get sold to someone else unless yer cripple and get put out on the streets."

"Like Rex?"

"Yeah, but we are saving so we can choose wot we want."

"I'm hungry again," Adam said.

"Weren't you listening to Pitt? We need savings so we don't end up on the streets like Rex," Andrew said.

"I need food too! There's a hole in me stomach."

"Quit whining before I give you another hole in yer head."

"I like the holes in me head. Me nose, me mouth, me ears."

"Adam?" Pitt said.

"Aye?"

"Shut yer mouth. It's the big hole in front of yer face."

"Aye, Pitt."

"He says that to me too!" Egan told Adam.

"Egan…"

"Aye, Pitt."

Egan and Adam sulked, looking down at their feet as they walked behind the older boys. Both were quiet until Adam walked straight into a lamppost and fell backward onto the ground.

"It weren't me. I didn't do nuffink!" Egan said.

Blood gushed from Adam's forehead.

"I'm fine! I'm all right! Me head hurts is all."

Pitt and Andrew helped Adam to his feet and helped him stay upright as they walked back to Master Armory's house.

Part Three
Southwark, 1721

"As happy a man as any in the world, for the whole world seems to smile upon me!"

-Samuel Pepys, 1632-1703

CHAPTER XX

The spring clean did not last long in London; soon manure, human refuse, and trash littered the spring's freshly washed streets. The summer heat allied with the humidity and filth to invade London with a fetid stench. Sweat dripped off unwashed bodies. Disease festered in every corner. There was not a street in London where one could escape the foul reek of the city. Windows and doors were shut again until the mild weather and rain that would come in August.

Those that could afford to travel vacated London during the summer months to avoid the unpleasant odor and sickness.

In early July, the Armory household prepared for a holiday.

"Master Armory secured a cottage in the country. We plan to leave when the carriages are packed and will be back when the weather turns," Miss Clara informed the broomers.

"Are any of us going?" Pitt asked.

"Master Armory has not yet said. Be ready just in case."

When the broomers came back to the house that evening, the door was locked. Miss Clara had left a sack by the back door containing the remaining scraps from the kitchen and two loaves of fresh bread.

"Hurrah!" Will yelled, which was followed by joyous shouts from Pitt, Andrew, and Rory. Iggy remained complacent.

"Where do we sleep?" Adam asked.

"Wherever we wants to," Pitt explained.

"I have no place I wants to be," Tick said. His face was ashen.

"We follow Pitt," Egan told Tick.

Tick nodded. "I don't want to live on the streets again."

"Come with me if you want," Pitt began, "or go yer own way if you want and come back when the sun cools. Either way, everyone comes back with a crown for Master Armory. You'll get yer hide torn if you don't come back on yer own or if you come empty-handed."

Pitt's voice was edged with severity. "We're on our own for the summer, but we still belong to Master Armory."

Rory nodded at Pitt and walked away.

"Where's he going?" Tick asked.

"Doesn't matter," Will responded.

"Are we sticking together?" Pitt asked the others.

They nodded.

"I go where you go," Will confirmed.

"And me," Egan added. Egan wanted to go home, but he needed Pitt to show him the way. Until then, he would follow Pitt.

"With me, everyone earns their own scratch," Pitt stated.

They nodded.

"Well, come on then," Pitt said and started walking away.

The broomers followed. Two blocks into their summer, Adam announced that he left his pail and sweeping tools at Master Armory's house. Annoyed, the broomers waited for Adam to run back and retrieve his things.

When they were on their way again, Pitt led them through unfamiliar parts of London, weaving through horses and pedestrians alike. Tick and Egan looked about with curiosity as the neighborhoods transformed with each step. Fashionable row houses lined wide streets that bustled dangerously with hurried carriages. A short alley away poor tenements rose from the ground in a ramshackle pattern of despondency. Egan cringed at the blight, bitterly aware of the coins hidden beneath his makeshift burlap shoes. These people were one copper away from the workhouse.

The buildings improved as the broomers approached the next street and found themselves in a quaint fishing quarter. Egan's heart quickened. They were approaching the River Thames. He could smell the water. He could hear the current lapping against the docks. Egan gasped when the buildings cleared and the river appeared. Pitt was taking him home.

The broomers ran towards the hill above the River Thames and looked down. The river stretched out below them, glistening in the setting sun. Egan looked towards the London Bridge, proudly straddling the mighty river.

Egan looked at Pitt. "Can we cross to Southwark? Out of London?"

"Let's do," Pitt answered.

The broomers walked along the River Thames to the foot of the London Bridge. Travelers waned with the sun, and the broomers could pass without difficulty by the shops and houses crowding the surface of the bridge. An occasional carriage sent them fleeing safely to the side of the narrow path. Otherwise, the bridge was theirs to conquer.

The distance across was shorter than Egan remembered. Occasionally, there was a narrow crevice between the merchant shops on the bridge. Egan peered through the increasing darkness towards Jacob's Island, searching for familiar sights. The vessels upon the River Thames were mere shadows.

The boys exited the bridge through the Southwark gate. The night guards did not trouble themselves with vagrant children.

Across from the bridge house on Tooley Street stood an old church, crumbling in disrepair and neglect. The tall tower jutting from the side of the building appeared haunted in the moonlight.

"This is St. Olave's," Pitt announced in a hushed voice. "I passed by here last winter with Master Armory."

Pitt quietly led them around the decrepit building to the graveyard. A few wooden coffins had been buried too near the stone foundation and were rising through the soil. Rotten corners of wood jutted up at eerie angles.

In the back corner far removed from the crumbling building stood two large grey alder trees; one leaned precariously towards the River Thames. Pitt led the broomers to the trees and began to settle in.

"Won't the spirits be getting us?" Tick asked.

"Naw, a graveyard is a grand place to rest," Pitt responded.

"Just ask the departed," Will joked, propping himself up next to a headstone.

"Look, this here be the best. It's like Robinson Crusoe's island without the cannibals. Remember last summer in Hyde Park where we fought for space and our tools were stolen?" Pitt inquired.

"This beats Hyde Park," Will agreed.

"All the climbing boys are in Hyde Park, and business is scarce. We have this place to ourselves and can stay as long as we don't get caught," Pitt reasoned.

"Caught by the spirits?" Tick asked again.

"Caught by the rector or the gardener or someone else who is still breathing," Andrew replied with a smirk.

"It looks like no one comes here," Will observed, "Least of all a gardener." Tall grass and creeping vines covered the tombstones. Will bent a broken branch from one of the alder trees further down against the ground, hiding the broomers from the street.

"Don't fear the dead Tick. Spirits be just stories," Andrew said.

"No, they're not, Tick," Adam said. "Andrew, don't you remember Old Lady Eldred who walked the streets wailing about being in hell just two weeks after she died?"

"No one remembers that Adam because it never happened," Andrew responded.

"It did too. Father told me so."

"Well let's hope she innit buried here," Andrew conceded.

"We'll be safe here. It's hallowed ground." Iggy said.

"Wot's that mean?" Tick asked.

"It's been blessed by a minister. Evil spirits have been banished."

"How would you know?" Adam challenged.

"Because there's a cross on the wall there," Iggy pointed, "that's wot the cross means. Evil is banished. That's wot the priest told us in the orphanage."

Pitt brought out a loaf of Miss Clara's bread and divided it seven ways. As a special treat, some turkey and cheese wrapped in cloth were towards the bottom of the sack. Pitt divided the bites of turkey among them and passed around the wedge of cheese. In order of seniority, each boy took a bite. Egan ate the last small chunk; the distinctive taste clung to his tongue.

The broomers rarely ate an evening meal, and they savored each bite of the feast.

"Thank ye, Miss Clara!" Will yelled up through the alder branches and into the sky.

"Thank ye, Miss Clara!" the broomers echoed.

"I love thee, Miss Clara!" Adam shouted.

The broomers giggled.

"Well, I do love her. I'd love any girl who cooked me turkey."

"Make sure you tell her that during yer next washing," Andrew teased.

Each broomer made himself a niche in the overgrown grass and settled down for the night.

"Good thing Master Armory didn't take us to the country," Tick observed as they lay on the ground looking up into the branches of the trees.

"You'd be lucky to go to the country," Pitt said. "There's no need for broomers in the country."

"Don't country folks have chimneys?" Egan asked.

"Yeah, but they don't use broomers to clean them," Pitt responded.

"Wot do they use?" Egan's mind swam with the things he could do if Master Armory didn't need him.

"Birds." Pitt's smile betrayed the coming story.

"Yer tricking us," Will dismissed Pitt with a swish of his hand.

"It's true," Pitt vowed.

"You may as well weave yer tale," Andrew surrendered. "We're listening."

"I spent me sixth summer in the country," Pitt began. "Master Armory brought me with him to make some coin for him. When we got there, the Missus at Hansley Corner told me the country folk had no use for climbing boys and that I might as well leave. I didn't understand, so she took me down to the lake to fetch a bird. I caught a right nice duck and carried it back to her cottage. Then the Missus took the duck from me, grabbed it 'bout the neck, and climbed up on her roof. With its wings batting around in turmoil, the Missus pushed the wretched thing head first into the chimney."

Egan and Iggy gasped appallingly in unison.

"The duck flapped its wings as best it could, trying to fly, but it couldn't get out of the hole. Soon, the room started filling with smoke because the duck was blocking the chimney."

"Wot did you do?" asked Adam.

"The Missus built up the fire, but instead of making the duck fly out, she slowly cooked the feathers off him. The flames stretched higher as the duck baked. Soon enough, without feathers, the duck was so roasted that it fell down through the blocked ash and right into the Missus' soup cauldron."

"Naw," Egan balked.

"Yes, sirs, that duck was as bare as if she had plucked him herself. Course, he still had all his innards. The Missus gutted the duck before serving it. Still, she near cleaned her chimney and cooked dinner all at the same time."

"That's silly," Will began.

"Silly maybe, but true."

"So, wot are you saying? You think we should sell ducks instead of sweeping?" Andrew asked.

"Naw, just saying you'd be lucky to live in the country."

"Did you really see that?" Egan asked.

"I ate some of him too."

"Really?" Iggy asked.

"Aye, tasted like soot," Pitt concluded.

"I know wot soot tastes like," Tick said.

"All broomers know wot soot tastes like," Adam said.

The broomers turned quiet and began to fall asleep. With full bellies and open sky, the day's events seemed unreal to Egan.

"Pitt?" Egan whispered.

"Aye?" Pitt answered with sleep in his voice.

"I want to go home, Pitt."

"I know."

"It's here close, innit?"

"Aye."

"Will you show me the way?"

"Will you come back?"

"I will."

"Then I'll take you there."

"When will you take me, Pitt?"

A tranquil yawn was Pitt's only answer. Exhausted and content, Egan fell asleep under the leaning alder to the melodic current of the River Thames.

CHAPTER XXI

Egan opened his eyes in the darkness. The grass was wet and cool. First light drew near. He yawned and stretched out his limbs.

"Is it time to get up?" Tick whispered.

"I think so," Egan responded.

"Why is everyone still asleep?"

"Don't know."

"Should I wake them?"

"No, you should not," Pitt grumbled and rolled onto his side.

Egan closed his eyes again. His weary body welcomed the rest.

"Egan, you going back to sleep?" Tick asked.

"Aye."

"I guess I'll just be awake by meself then."

CHAPTER XXII

Birds chirped in the limbs of the grey alder trees. The shrill sound roused the broomers as the sun lifted into the sky. On a normal day, Egan would have swept near eight holes before sunrise. Waking with the sun in St. Olave's graveyard felt like a holiday.

In the daylight, St. Olave's acknowledged its age. It had survived the great fire of 1666 but had been poorly maintained since. The church appeared abandoned except for a few signs of the parish curate's care.

The broomers devoured the last loaf of Miss Clara's bread, collected their belongings, and crept out of the cemetery.

"Meet back here every night after dark," Pitt instructed. "Be careful that yer not seen entering the graveyard."

The broomers nodded and set out, anxious to explore. Will, Tick, and Iggy went west. Andrew and Adam went south. Egan followed Pitt east.

Egan's anxiety grew as they walked down Tooley Street. This place was vaguely familiar. He recognized the hum of business as tradesmen began the day's work. Wharfingers, outfitters, biscuit-bakers, store-shippers, ship-chandlers, slop sellers, block-makers, rope-makers, engineers, and other merchants crowded together along the street. Egan tightly gripped his pail. Home was near.

Pitt stopped in the middle of the awakening street.

"This is it. I don't know where yer home is, but this is where Master Armory bought you."

Egan looked down Tooley Street. He would find his way if he went east along the river. What would Mum say to him?

Egan trembled. He turned back to Pitt, "I don't want to go alone."

"I'll go with you."

Pitt placed his withered arm across Egan's shoulders and pressed him forward.

The broomers walked along the River Thames, threading in and out of the wharf traffic. They approached the landing where the

Earnest Vesper docked. On impulse, Egan stopped and looked for Da's ship. It wasn't there.

From the dock, Egan could find his way blindfolded. He walked faster down the side street and then broke into a run. He knew this place.

Egan ran past the street where Mister Carrington kept shop. He ran past the neighborhood cistern. He ran to his door. He pushed the handle, but the door was latched from the inside. He knocked wildly, excited to see Mum's face. Excited to be held in her arms. Excited to laugh with Kerrin. Excited for this moment that had come at last.

The door was drawn open in a hesitant answer to Egan's forceful banging. Egan sprang forward to grasp Mum in his arms but drew back sharply when he saw the face of an unknown woman. It was a kind face, but the spindly woman at the door was not Mum.

Egan backed up.

"Who are you?" Egan cried.

Egan frantically searched the street, looking for an explanation.

"Wot is it lad?" the woman asked.

"Me Mum. Who are you?"

"Are you lost child?"

"Me Mum. This is me house."

"Yer mum's moved on, lad. Me family leased this flat last spring."

Egan looked wildly up and down the street. "No. This is me home! Where is me Mum!" he shouted at the woman and tried to push the door open. "Mum! Kerrin!" he shouted into the house.

"She's not here!" the woman yelled back. "She's moved on!"

"Where? Where is she? Where did she go?"

"I do not know, child. I'm sorry," she said and slammed the door closed.

Egan banged his fists against the door. "MUM!" he shouted.

"She's not here!" Pitt pulled Egan away from the door. "She's not here anymore."

"Where is she?" Egan yelled at Pitt.

"I don't know, but I'll help you find her. Who did yer mum know 'round here?"

"She is gone. Kerrin is gone."

"Let's find them. Who did yer mum know 'round here?"

Egan looked up at Pitt.

"Do you know anyone 'round here?" Pitt rephrased the question.

"Mister Carrington."

"Good. Where might we find this Mister Carrington?"

"He runs the shop, just over there," Egan pointed.

Pitt nodded and directed Egan down the street towards Mister Carrington's store.

Egan entered through the front. The shopkeeper finished counting coins and peered down through his spectacles at Egan and Pitt.

"And how may I help you, young sweeps?" Mister Carrington inquired.

"Mister Carrington, it's me, Egan Whitcombe."

"Tis you! I hardly recognized you through that soot. So yer a climbing boy now."

"I am, sir. Mister Carrington, have you seen me Mum? She left me."

"Not since spring I'm afraid."

"Where did she go?"

"I don't know. I didn't know she left until the new tenant visited the shop. It was after yer sister made it through the sickness," Mister Carrington said.

"She said she would come for me."

"I'm sorry lad. Maybe she went to the east end where there is work."

"Thank ye, Mister Carrington," Egan nodded and turned to leave the shop.

"Egan, me chimneys could use a cleaning. Would you like some work?"

The words took Egan back a year. Mister Carrington had so often said, Egan, I have packages to deliver or floors to be swept. Would you like some work?' There was kindness in those words.

"Yes, sir."

"We're the best sweeps in town sir," Pitt added.

"I have no doubt," Mister Carrington replied.

The shop had three fireplaces, one in the main store and two in the living quarters. Pitt swept the two in the back while Egan cleaned the one in the front, talking with Mister Carrington as he swept the hearth. Egan took care to sweep better than he ever had, scraping the bricks new.

"Very fine work, very fine work indeed. I'll be ready when winter blows to town."

Mister Carrington paid the broomers two shillings each. It was an exorbitant amount for such little work, but the boys did not protest.

"Where are you staying?" Mister Carrington asked. "So I can tell yer mum if I see her."

"St. Olave's cemetery," Egan blurted out.

Pitt elbowed him in the ribs. "We stay with Master Daniel Armory near Distaff Lane in the Bread Street Ward in London. Come September we will be by the Little Conduit in Westcheap every afternoon."

"If I see her, I will let her know."

"Thank ye, sir." Egan smiled at the old shopkeeper.

The broomers gathered their tools and exited into the street.

"Where do you think they are?" Egan asked.

"Don't know. Just keep looking wherever you go."

The broomers walked down to the docks and spent the afternoon watching the activities at the wharf.

Watch and learn me trade, Da had said as he pointed out the various merchants to Egan. Da knew every ship that sailed down the River Thames and could name the vessels coming in that day by the merchants waiting on the dock. Coal, timber, hay, sugar, tea, tobacco, wine, grain, and fur, it all came to London through the water.

You must live every day as if I am coming home tomorrow, Da had said. But Da wouldn't be home tomorrow or the day after that. Da was gone. Mum and Kerrin were gone.

"We'll find them," Pitt broke the silence. "Yer mum and sister. Just like Robinson Crusoe and Friday."

"Friday?"

"Friday was Crusoe's friend. Crusoe helped Friday save his father from cannibals or mercenaries or sumfink."

"But I don't know where they are."

"I'll help you find them and then we'll sail to the Americas and grow tobacco."

Egan smiled up at Pitt. "Five guineas to freedom."

"Five guineas to freedom," Pitt echoed.

CHAPTER XXIII

As the sun began to set, Egan and Pitt walked back towards St. Olave's, hoping it would be deserted enough to settle in early. Master Armory was not waiting to collect their earnings, but the broomers still debated whether to spend their coins. They decided to stop for a bowl of porridge on Tooley Street, splurging a haypenny each for a full stomach.

The substance was thick and had been sitting in a pot all day, but the boys devoured it all the same. The smell of the simmering mutton stew was a delicious torment beyond their means.

As they approached St. Olave's, Pitt was noticeably upset at the sight. Will was cutting brush away from the tombstones with a chaffing knife while Iggy raked the excess vegetation into a pile.

"Wot are you doing? Suppose someone sees you!"

"Someone already did. The curate, he knows we're here," Will said. "He has a room at the back of the church and saw us last night. He was sitting on a tombstone waiting for us when we came back."

Pitt nodded, accepting the news. "So wot are you doing?"

"The curate said we could stay if we helped out, and he gave us lamb stew." Iggy's face was consumed by a wide grin.

The gruel murmured with an unsettling gurgle in Egan's stomach.

"Where's Tick?" Egan asked.

"Sleeping off drunkenness," Iggy replied.

"Wot?" Pitt was confused.

"The curate is old," Iggy added, "really old."

"Wot's that to do with anything?" Pitt asked.

"The parishioners are building a new church in Horselydown. There's no coin for upkeep here, and the curate is too old to do it hisself. I agreed that we would help him if it's right with you," Will said.

"It's more than right, Will. You done good."

Will beamed with a wide smile.

"But why is Tick drunk?" Pitt asked.

"Oh, we earned a mug of ale hauling crates at St. Savior's Dock. Tick drank most of it."

1 2 2 | A. M. WATSON

"It was funny," Iggy snorted.

"We'd better let him sleep then. Well, how can we help?" Pitt asked.

The broomers spent the next hour clearing out the front corner of the graveyard. They collected the clippings in their burlap sacks and dumped the overgrown grass into the river.

When Andrew and Adam joined the broomers, darkness was spreading across the graves and work abandoned until morning. Resting beneath the alders, the broomers shared the events of the day while Tick struggled to wake up.

"I'm never drinking ale again," Tick vowed.

"You drunk too much, Tick, and missed the story," Iggy said.

"Wot story?" Egan asked.

"We met this old sailor at the Rose and Thorn that told us about a giant sea creature he'd seen," Will said.

"None of those tales can be believed," Andrew said.

"But he seen it hisself," Will stated.

"Wot he say, Will?" Egan interrupted.

Will mischievously raised his left eyebrow. "He said that past the Irish Shore, there's a vicious sea monster the size of a small island. It lures unsuspecting ships in to dock at her tail fin. When the sailors disembark to explore wot they believe is dry land, she raises her head from the deep water and devours every last man. Chomps them in half with her long fangs. Leastways, that's wot the sailor said."

"And how would he know?" Andrew challenged.

"Well, he was a sailor on a slave vessel heading to the Americas. They spotted a small island where land hadn't been charted. 'Land ho!' the sailor in the crow's nest yelled, 'land ho off the port bow.' The captain took the helm to see the wee island resting less than a league ahead. He veered the ship to the left and weighed anchor along the island's shore."

Andrew rolled his eyes as Will continued.

"After days at sea the crew was anxious to step on dry land, but the island was strange. The grass was all furry, and there wasn't any sand. There were fin-like trees along the shore. *It's too small to inhabit*, the captain said, *but we will enjoy our ale and meat by fireside tonight*. The men all cheered. *Gather wood and meat*, the captain ordered. *We set sail in the morning*."

"The crew couldn't find any wood on the land. So, they tore apart the ship's railing, arranged the rails like kindling, and called for the captain to lite a fire. The scorching heat woke the sea monster and she dove deep into the ocean. Wot the sailors thought was land, disappeared under their feet. Some drowned straight away because they couldn't swim. The others swam for the ship, but the monster returned and satisfied her appetite for flesh."

The younger boys were mesmerized by the story. Andrew sighed critically and looked to Pitt.

"How would the sailor know about this?" Pitt questioned. "How did he survive?"

"He was aboard the ship relieving his bowels when the others were devoured," Will explained.

"If he was using the pot, how does he know wot happened?" Pitt continued.

"I don't know. Maybe there was a porthole that he looked through while finishing his business."

"Why didn't he poop on the island?" Egan asked.

"Heck if I know. Maybe he is shy."

"Wot happened next?" Adam asked.

"Well, the sailor named hisself captain and returned to England where he sold the ship and all the slaves. He swore that he would never take to the sea again. He said the monster haunts his dreams and would find him if he even stepped a toe into the River Thames."

Tick belched.

The broomers laughed.

"You should have seen Tick," Will bellowed, "he asked the barkeep for another ale and then fell off his stool, drooling like a babe."

"It's not funny," Tick moaned, holding his head in his hands.

The broomers laughed louder, and suddenly Iggy joined in. His screechy, high-pitched snort startled the broomers into a stunned silence.

"Are you hurt, Iggy?" Egan managed to ask.

Iggy clutched his sides and rolled onto the ground, shaking his head sideways.

"I think that is his laugh," Pitt observed, making Iggy snort loudly.

The boys slowly erupted in laughter again, which made Iggy snort and laugh harder. The squeals succeeded each other until he was out of breath and coughing.

"Don't make me laugh," Iggy begged, "it hurts."

"Iggy!" Egan managed to gasp, "You sound like a pig dying!"

"Sumfink was dying," Pitt confirmed, rejuvenating the broomer's laughter.

"I can make all kinds of noises," Iggy said. He then snorted like a pig and followed it with his squealing laughter. Iggy cawed like a crow, hooted like an owl, and chirped like a lark.

"That's pretty good," Andrew complimented.

"Listen to me rooster," Iggy crowed a couple of times and then farted loudly.

Iggy squealed, and the boys completely fell apart, rolling on the ground laughing.

"Keep that thing away from me!" Pitt laughed, pushing away from Iggy's backside.

"Wot animal was that?" Egan gasped and the laughter increased.

"That was all me!" Iggy screeched.

"That's nuffink!" Andrew said, letting a louder fart loose. "Top that!"

"I can top it!" Adam yelled. A determined look crossed his face, and he released a tiny, high-pitched fart that reduced the group to hysterical laughter again.

Then Egan let one rip.

"Ewww!" Iggy squealed. "That sounded oily!"

Each boy contributed to the contest as often as he could, trying to outdo the last.

"I can't breathe!" Pitt panted. "Air, I need air."

CHAPTER XXIV

E gan woke during the wee hours of the morning. He smiled to himself, rolled over, and went back to sleep.

Rising with the sun was a luxury, Egan decided a few hours later as he stretched in the sunshine.

The curate, who ambled across the cemetery favoring his right leg, called out to the broomers. Pitt eyed Will uneasily.

"Good morning, young sweeps," he greeted.

"Good morning sir," Pitt answered for them.

"I am John Whalley, the curate of St. Olave's."

"I'm Pitt, sir, and that is Will, Iggy, Tick, Egan, Andrew, and Adam. We mean no trouble here. We'll move along if you like."

"And so young Will told me yesterday," Curator Whalley responded. "So many children run these streets. I usually collect them and find a suitable place for them."

"Sir, we have a position with Master Daniel Armory in London. He is expecting us to return next month. Please, sir, we can't be sent away, or he will have me hide."

Curator Whalley considered the boys for a moment. "I've discussed your presence with Preacher Erington, and he agrees that you may stay for a while if you clean up and earn your keep."

"Thank ye, sir, we will," Pitt answered for the group.

"Tis Sunday and services begin in a few hours. Get yourselves down to the river to wash up," Curator Whalley handed Pitt a small brown square.

"Sir?"

"Tis soap. Use it to scrub your skin clean."

"I don't need washin'," Adam started to protest, but Andrew hushed him with a nudge to the ribs.

"Hurry now, I expect you at the service."

The broomers ran around to the back of the church and down towards the River Thames. They stripped their clothing and waded into the water.

"Do I have to?" Adam whined from the bank.

"Get in. You need it more than anyone," Andrew insisted.

Adam reluctantly got into the water.

The boys passed the soap and scrubbed themselves until smears of black swirled about their bodies. None of them passed Pitt's inspection. Pitt climbed to the bank and sorted through their clothes. He pulled small clothes from the pile and tossed them into the river.

"Use the clothes to scrub yer skin with the soap. And wash yer heads."

The boys helped each other scrub backs, necks, and spots that were missed.

Egan helped Iggy scrub the back of his neck and noticed long purple scars down his back.

"Are those stripes from Master Armory?" Egan asked.

"No," Iggy responded, "from Rory."

"Rory?"

"It don't matter," Iggy deflected, ducking back into the water.

Egan was perplexed. Pitt had struck him once, but it weren't hard enough to leave a scar. As the boys dressed, Egan approached Iggy again.

"Why did Rory whip you?"

"I pay Rory two coppers a day. One day I didn't have enough. Either Rory whipped me for being short or Master Armory did, and I chose Rory."

"But I don't pay Pitt," Egan said.

"You pay when Rory watches after you."

"That ain't right."

Iggy shrugged and walked back towards the church.

Before long, the broomers were clean and redressed in their soot-stained rags. Adam complained that his small clothes were wet and sticking to all the parts he shouldn't talk about, but Andrew shushed him as they entered the back of the church. Curator Whalley directed them to the bench at the back of the sanctuary, and they did their best to imitate the parishioners by kneeling, standing, sitting, and praying at the proper moments.

At the end of the service, Preacher Erington introduced the broomers, stating that the climbing boys would be attending services throughout the summer and learning their catechism. Only Will and Iggy seemed to know what that meant.

The parishioners welcomed the boys and brought them articles of clothing, well-worn but tidy and clean compared to the rags they wore. They were each given a pair of stockings, but there was only one pair of shoes that fit Iggy and Andrew. The boys agreed to swap the shoes every other day. Egan concealed his coins in the new stockings beneath his burlap shoes, setting aside his wool socks during the summer heat.

One Sunday a family brought the boys tea, milk, and little cakes the likes of which the boys had never eaten. They eagerly accepted the gifts and sat with the family near two hours, talking and answering their questions. If the parishioners started a school, would the boys attend? They wanted to start a school where the poor could learn. The older boys politely responded that they wanted to learn to read, while Egan told them he didn't want to go to school because he wanted to be a sailor. The comment earned Egan a harsh stare from Pitt.

During the hot summer days, the broomers fared well, never being without work or a meal. The parishioners hired the broomers to sweep their chimneys, most of which were cool and unused in the summer heat. Will scraped the holes in St. Olave's and patched one of the chimneys that was wearing thin near the top. The boys cleaned up the cemetery and set about helping Curator Whalley with the vicarage chores.

During the week, Preacher Erington taught the boys the letters and how to spell their names. Adam told the old preacher that his name was Clarence because Adam was sure that the name Clarence had more letters in it than Adam and he wanted to learn as many letters as possible. Preacher Erington taught him to write the names Adam and Clarence while explaining the sin of dishonesty.

A mid-July Sunday was especially eventful. Preacher Erington christened nine babies during the service. The parishioners were delighted by the offspring, smiling at the soft cries and gurgles of the young. Egan watched the fathers. A butcher, soldier, schoolmaster, bricklayer, weaver, and brush maker were among them; there were no sailors like Da. Egan wondered if Da brought him to church when he was born.

Preacher Erington requested that the young sweeps remain after the service for the marriage of Mister James Goodford and Miss

Elizabeth Clear. The broomers remained seated on the back bench with the Curator Whalley.

"Wot are we staying for?" Tick asked Pitt in a low voice.

"Chimney sweeps are good luck on yer wedding day. King George said so." Pitt answered.

The wedding was like one of Mum's stories, the ones Kerrin liked about lords and ladies. They pledged to honor and serve each other until death. Egan found it a rather formal affair, nothing as exciting as a joust.

Preacher Erington declared that the two were married and they turned to walk down the aisle. Egan sighed, he was glad it was over.

Adam stood up and blurted out, "Muh lady, the heavens sing of yer beauty." Then he blew the bride a kiss.

Egan did not know that you were supposed to do that in the ceremony, so he quickly stood up and blew a kiss to the bride too.

The bride was stunned. After a moment, she giggled and approached Adam and Egan. She kissed them both on their cheeks and gave each a tuppence.

"Thank ye, young sweeps," she said and rejoined her groom.

"You two are not to attend any more weddings," Curator Whalley scolded.

"That's not wot you do?" Egan asked.

"No, it is not."

Egan slunk back onto the bench.

Adam, however, looked quite proud of himself.

CHAPTER XXV

The summer days wove into a comfortable pattern. The broomers woke with the sunrise, dined on the bread the curate left for them each morning, and spread out to earn coin.

Iggy found regular work at a bakery, stoking the coals and placing the bread and biscuits into and out of the hot ovens. Pitt, Egan, Andrew, and Adam met the ship chandler on Tooley Street and hired themselves out for whatever work was available. The boys delivered goods to and from ships, shoveled silt away from the docks, filled wooden ship seams with pitch, varnished decks with linseed oil, and cleaned out latrines.

The chimney sweeping business waned in summer, but Will and Tick were not deterred. They walked through the streets advertising their services with a song:

"Sweeping chimneys keeps them neat,
Sweeping's best in summer's heat,
Come winter night when all is cold,
No trouble you'll have with smoking coal.

Scrape yer chimney and scrape it good,
Scrape it to burn coal or wood,
If you sweep in summertime,
In winter's chill, it will burn just fine.

Chimney fires burn so bright,
Casting off a dreadful light,
Get yer chimney cleaned all round,
Before a fire burns yer house down."

Will and Tick kept busy sweeping flues and sometimes were given a copper for their song.

Every Saturday afternoon without fail, the boys would wash in the river for Sunday services. Adam outgrew his revulsion of water when he discovered splashing. Like 'ash sack skipping,' bathing sometimes turned into a wrestling match, after which another scrubbing was necessary to remove the mud.

The summer days seemed to last forever and yet the cooler nights betrayed the coming autumn. A melancholy settled over the boys; each one knew their freedom was coming to an end.

"Do you have a story tonight, Will?" Egan asked during a pause in the conversation.

Will stood in false bravado, waving his arm up and into a deep bow. "Me fellow broomers…"

"Here we go again," Andrew breathed in exasperation.

Will, ignoring Andrew, continued. "I'm going to share the secret of how Queen Catherine of Valois smiled long after death stole her last breath. It's a story I've been saving for a night such as this."

"Wot are you hashing now?" Pitt arrived at the tree and plopped down beside Andrew.

"This story is true," Iggy defended. "Right stupid, but true. I knowed it."

Andrew's eyes shot up to his raised brow in irritation, but he held his words. He glared at Will. "Well, continue."

"I don't need yer permission. In fact, I don't want you listening."

"Just be out with it."

Will returned Andrew's glare, then wiped his face of irritation and once again became the ostentatious storyteller. "When Queen Catherine of Valois died, she was buried in the royal tomb at the palace. Her grandson Henry VII was ashamed of his grandmother, but I'm not sure why. Maybe it was because she was French. That aside, he wanted her removed from the royal grounds and ordered that her tomb be taken to Westminster Abbey. By an unfortunate accident, the lid of her coffin slipped off and cracked in two. The Queen's corpse was out in the open for all to see."

Around the fire, eyes widened in intrigue.

"Over two hundred years later. Samuel Pepys, an officer of the Royal Navy, fell into a melancholy stupor. For weeks, he wallowed in despair. No one knew wot ailed him. On his birthday, Pepys went to Westminster Abbey to be prayed over by the clergy. But when a clergyman could not be found, Pepys walked around about the graves pondering the fact that he too would soon be dead. Then his eyes saw Queen Catherine, lying in her open coffin. Pepys could feel her pain and loneliness. So, he sunk his arms into her coffin and embraced her cold, dead form. Then he lifted her up to his lips and kissed her deeply."

"Ewwwww!" The boys erupted into echoing revulsion and laughter.

"One fit bird," Pitt sighed.

"A corpse? She'd be shrunken and moldy…it's foul!" Andrew said.

"Shakespeare hisself said *fair is foul, and foul is fair*," Pitt retorted, and the laughter about the fire rekindled.

"How do you know Shakespeare?" Andrew challenged.

"Shush! Let Will finish," Pitt said.

"Well, after the kiss, some of the clergy said that Queen Catherine's decaying mouth turned slightly upwards in the corners, so that for all eternity those that gaze upon Queen Catherine of Valois, lying uncovered in her stone coffin, will see the thrill and rapture that the Royal Navy left behind on her lips."

"That's not true," Adam shouted.

"Is too!" Iggy said.

"You wanted a story!" Will said. "Besides, you can go to the Abbey and see her yerself."

"Truly?"

"I've seen her," Pitt offered, lending credibility to Will's story, "but I don't know that she was smiling."

"Well, she is, and not long after the kiss, Pepys was elected to Parliament. It was the Queen's kiss that done it, I think. Changed Pepys fortunes in an instant. Maybe one day I'll kiss her meself."

"Me fortune will turn without kissing, but I don't want to be in Parliament," Egan said.

"I do. I want to rule everything," Adam said.

"I just want me own house with me own sheep and cows to eat," Tick said.

"Wot do you want, Pitt?" Will asked.

"I have me wants like any broomer. We all want the same things."

The boys fell quiet. Autumn was approaching far too swiftly.

Adam broke the quiet reflection, "We should perform the charm of good fortune."

"How's that go?" Egan asked.

"Well, you hold a candle between both palms and walk three times around the person you want to charm. The person says wot he wants most, and upon the dawn of the next Sunday, his life will slowly fill with good fortune."

"It doesn't work," Andrew muttered.

"It does too. Father told me it does," Adam responded defensively.

Andrew shrugged.

"Why does yer fortune change on Sunday?"

"It's the Lord's Day," Iggy stated incredulously. "You wouldn't be expecting yer luck to change on a Wednesday, would you?"

"But the Lord made Wednesday just like he made Sunday," Egan stated.

"Yer one of them heathens," Adam said, pointing at Egan.

"Sunday is a holy day," Iggy stated.

"I'm not a heathen," Egan mumbled, "I'm learning the catechism same as you."

"Sunday is a holy day," Iggy repeated.

"Wot is a heathen anyway?" Adam asked randomly; no one was listening to him either.

"So, we perform the charm on Saturday, that way we have less time to wait for our fortunes to change," Pitt decided for the group. "Adam, wot do we need for the charm?"

"A lighted candle. We can take turns getting charmed."

"We have to do it this week because Master Armory will get back from the country soon," Pitt stated. "Who has a candle?"

The broomers looked at each other in silence.

Pitt rephrased, "Who can get a candle?"

"I can ask Curator Whalley if we can borrow one," Will offered.

"Good. Iggy, can you bring a hot coal from the baker's shop to light the candle?"

Iggy nodded and struck his fist to his heart in a mock salute. "I nobly accept the duty."

"If we all walk around each person," Tick piped up, "The charm should take stronger."

"I'm not sure it works that way," Adam said.

"I thought the Irish never doubted the power of a charm," Will accused.

"We're Scottish," Andrew retorted.

"Doesn't make much difference – Scottish or Irish."

"It does make a difference," Andrew asserted.

"I'm Irish," Egan said. "Wot's wrong about being Irish?"

"Quiet down. It was just a bit of fun. We're all peasant serfs here, no matter wot blood runs through our veins," Pitt stated.

"Well," Tick declared, straightening his posture, "Our luck is about to change."

CHAPTER XXVI

A s the clouds darkened Saturday evening, the boys gathered beneath the grey alder trees in St. Olave's cemetery. Each one was freshly scrubbed from their weekly bath in the river and content from the dinner of mutton stew they had just eaten with Curator Whalley. The aging man had offered them a partially burned candle with strict instructions not to set the cemetery on fire.

A few hot coals smoldered under a pile of dirt in Iggy's sweeping pail.

"One sits in the middle and says out loud wot they want while the others walk around him three times," Adam instructed.

Andrew rolled his eyes.

"Who holds the candle?" Will asked.

"The person walking around should, but since we are all walking around maybe the person sitting should hold it," Adam answered.

"I'll go first," Tick announced and sat down in the middle.

Iggy dug out a hot coal with his shovel and held the wick of the candle to it until the candle lit. He handed the candle to Tick, and the boys circled around him.

"Now we walk around him three times," Adam instructed.

Tick squinted his eyes shut and recited his wishes. "I want somewhere to sleep every night and a full belly every day, and I want me own horse, and I want to stay here and learn to read with Preacher Erington, and then I'll be rich," Tick finished, satisfied with himself.

"Iggy, yer next," Pitt directed.

Iggy took the candle from Tick and sat in the center of the circle. The boys started circling him.

"I want me luck to change. I want to join the clergy, and I don't want to see Rory ever again."

Iggy abruptly stood. "Who is next?"

"Rory innit that bad," Will said.

"He is too. I hope he gets nabbed and sold to the Americas this summer. Who's next?" Iggy demanded.

No one moved. Iggy handed the candle to Egan.

"Yer next, Egan."

Iggy rejoined the circle and pushed the boys to start walking around Egan. Egan sat down.

"I want five guineas to pay me debt to Master Armory, and I want to sail the seas like Da. I want to find Mum and Kerrin and take them to America and buy them a house they never have to leave. And I want to grow tobacco," Egan finished.

"Tobacco? You smoke?" Tick asked.

"I don't smoke," Adam answered.

"I weren't asking you."

Egan stood and handed the candle to Will.

Will sat. "I want to pay me debt and then marry Miss Eleanor Ruckston and then set up shop as a ship chandler the rest of me days."

"Ellleeaanorrr," Adam started, who was promptly cuffed by Andrew.

"Take the candle, ya eejit," Will stood and handed the candle to Adam.

Adam began speaking before he could sit down. "I want to buy me own ship and sail the seas with Egan and then buy me own church and then buy me own horses and then buy me own house, but I don't want to get married, and then I want to kiss Queen Catherine and be really lucky and then be king," Adam finished.

"Is that all?" Andrew asked flippantly.

"No, I want to smoke too but not too much because I heard that tobacco turned Old Lady Eldred's teeth brown. And I want me parents back. And that is all."

"Yer next," Adam handed Andrew the candle.

Andrew sat. "I want to pay me debt and go to the country where I'll grow food and keep cows and chickens. I'll build me a cottage, and it'll be grand. And I'll take Adam with me because he innit going to be the king."

"You can't wish for someone else. You canceled me wish! Now I need to go again," Adam complained, reaching for the candle.

"Shut it," Andrew said.

Andrew stood and handed the candle to Pitt. The boys waited. Pitt sat quietly, and they began circling him.

The broomers finished the third circle and stopped. Finally, Pitt spoke. "I want to leave London."

Pitt extinguished the candle, and the boys settled into their green beds.

The next morning the broomers attended the Sunday service, returned the candle to Curator Whalley, and said their goodbyes. They thanked Preacher Erington and Curator Whalley for the food, clothing, and work they were provided. All the boys, even Egan, promised to return if St. Olave's opened a school.

Reluctantly, the boys walked back over the bridge into London.

Part Four
London, 1721

"Such a measure (to reform the use of children in chimney sweep trade) we are convinced from the evidence, could not be carried into execution without great injury to property."

-Lord Sydney Smith

CHAPTER XXVII

It was another week before Master Armory and his Missus returned from the country. John, the Armory's manservant, returned early to ready the house. He introduced himself to each broomer and let them in the house at night to sleep in the cellar.

The broomers wandered the streets singing Will and Tick's song, creating new verses, and looking for work. Each one had collected a crown's worth of coins for Master Armory, but they needed savings for the winter when work and food were scarce.

Egan had saved one whole guinea and three shillings over the summer. It was an extraordinary sum compared to the shilling and a sixpence he had saved sweeping. Pitt had helped him count his coins at St. Olave's. He needed three guineas and eighteen shillings.

Rory did not return until the morning of Master Armory's arrival. Egan suspected that he had watched the house and waited to return until the last minute. He plunked down the steps and went straight to his sacks, ignoring the other broomers.

"First sign of Rory's old ways and I'll take care of him," Pitt had promised Iggy on the way back from St. Olave's.

Iggy reverted to his solemn isolation, repelling attention and efforts to engage him in discussion.

The first morning of regular sweeping came the day after Master Armory's return.

"Good morning, boys," Miss Clara called down the stairs. "Best be getting going as I can hear Master Armory stirring."

The broomers stretched, still sleepy in the early morning hours.

Sacks and tools in hand, the boys lined up at the bottom of the stairs, Pitt first followed by Rory, then Will, Iggy, Andrew, Adam, Tick, and Egan. It was as if the summer had never happened.

The broomers ascended and placed their tools in the short hallway. Master Armory was waiting for them in the kitchen.

Pitt handed Master Armory a handful of coins, "Here's me summer earnings, sir," he said, signaling the other broomers to follow. Wary of the sum in his socks, Egan emptied his pockets and handed Master Armory the coins.

"Let me get a look at you," Master Armory sneered, looking at the broomers.

"Where'd you get them clothes? Stole them? Spent me coin on them?"

"From a parish, sir," Pitt answered.

The other broomers kept their heads down.

"Me boys don't need charity. Don't I take care of you to yer satisfaction?"

"You do, sir," Pitt replied meekly.

"The lot of you grew over the summer, probably eating more than yer share. I have little boys for little flues, best you heed it, or you'll be out on the street."

"Yes, sir," the broomers murmured.

"No porridge for you this morning. Out to the streets with you. At least three shillings by nightfall."

The broomers quickly gathered their tools and ran out the back door and down the alley.

"At least it's a free morning," Andrew said as they stopped at the end of the alley.

"Three shillings, Andrew. Did you hear him?" Will asked.

"Of course I did."

"Master Armory thinks we kept summer coin from him," Pitt said. "Earn wot you can today, and that's wot you give him. Three shillings or not. Whipping or not. Twig?"

"Twig," they agreed.

Adam's belly growled.

"Curses me stomach," Adam muttered.

"Get used to it," Rory remarked.

"Shut it, Rory," Pitt said.

The broomers formed their usual semicircle and then took off in the various directions they were facing. Egan followed Pitt.

The two broomers settled into a comfortable pace. Work was plentiful in the richer neighborhoods as the households prepared for winter. Most of the chimneys were cool in the early autumn weather and easy to climb.

Moments before sunrise, Egan reached the top of the first chimney, stuck his head out and yelled, "All up!" into the silent morning. He hoisted himself up, hanging by his armpits on the chimney ridge, and admired the view. The world was different looking down on things that usually looked down on him. The helpless feeling faded as the rooftops spread out before him. He was an equal with the treetops. He shared their breathing space, their gentle wind, their observation point.

Egan glanced around London, looking first for the River Thames, and then for St. Olave's bell tower. He yearned for the grey alder trees in the cemetery as he yearned for home. A home that no longer existed, he reminded himself.

"All up!" A climbing boy yelled several buildings over.

Egan looked to see if he could find the broomer, but the boy had already vanished. Egan ended his short break and anchored himself back into the chimney. Using the end of his broom, Egan hit the bricks to break up the thick layers of soot that had collected the past winter. The black substance began to break apart into small pieces and fall to the hearth below.

The broomers were hired to address an emergency at one fine residence. Egan glanced at Pitt nervously. Emergencies usually meant burning brick and flues too hot to climb.

The chimney in question was warm, but not hot. The emergency consisted of a sharp burnt smell that clung to one's nostril hairs.

"You've burnt yerself a critter," Pitt explained to the frazzled cook.

Egan scooted up the chimney and found a nest of squirrels that had established the wrong summer residence. He dropped the charred critters, sticks, and leaves down the hole and proceeded to scrape down the bricks.

As the afternoon waned, Pitt and Egan had scraped twenty-three holes, removed six bird nests, and nine charred squirrels. It was a good day, but they were each short seven pence.

Egan fretted over the amount and wanted to compensate their earnings with his savings. Pitt appeared unconcerned.

"Master Armory will whip us either way. He needs to remind us he's the master."

"I knowed he's the master."

"Then take the whipping, Egan, and keep yer mouth shut."

Egan nodded and followed Pitt towards Distaff Lane.

Around the corner from Master Armory's residence, Iggy was handing a tuppence to Rory.

"It's good you remembered yer place," Rory sneered.

Pitt's wrath ignited. He threw his tools to the ground and charged Rory. He grasped Rory's shirt and pushed him against a brick building.

"No broomer hurts another broomer, never! Don't you know that?" Pitt yelled at Rory. "We takes it from Master Armory, but not each other. How dare you steal coin from Iggy!"

"He owes me!" Rory protested.

"How?" Pitt demanded.

"I'm an apprentice. He works for me!"

"He does not, and if you hurt him or steal from him again I'll give you to the nabbers meself and sell you to the Americas. Twig? Twig?" Pitt shouted in Rory's face.

"Twig," Rory relented, but anger and humiliation sparked in his eyes.

Pitt released Rory's shirt. "Give Iggy back his coin."

Rory pulled the tuppence from his pocket and returned it to Iggy.

"Get out of me way," Rory said as he pushed by Iggy.

"Thank ye, Pitt," Iggy sniffled and picked up his tools.

"I made you a promise. And I mean to keep it."

The broomers delivered their earnings to Master Armory, each boy being short of the daily requirement.

Master Armory's whip slashed through their respectable clothing to rip open their skin. When Master Armory made his point, the blood-stained broomers were dismissed to find refuge in the cellar.

CHAPTER XXVIII

Master Armory pointed to Tick, Egan, Adam, and Iggy. "Pitt and all you littlest ones are coming with me today. Everyone else earns at least two shillings."

"Yes, sir," the broomers responded.

The morning was cool. Egan thought he could smell the shift to autumn; the city was somehow fresher than the day before. It was not possible that the city was cleaner; he could see that the smoke had already begun to leave its dark coating of dust on the windows that lined the street.

While these chimneys boasted of smoldering fires, two streets away people could barely spare coin to burn coal when the winter winds howled through their cracked walls. It was just as well; chimney fires often burned down ramshackle dwellings. Still, freezing indoors in the winter was a luxury that the homeless envied.

Master Armory led his broomers to a magnificent estate house, the likes of which Egan had never seen. Behind the tall rod iron fence, the resplendent facade boasted of large windows and a front door wide enough for the passage of a carriage. Crimson and golden leaves decorated the mature oak trees that defined each corner of the house.

The broomers followed Master Armory to the fence, where he rang a bell affixed to the gate. A well-dressed man appeared from a standard door in the back of the house. Egan decided that if he lived in such a house, he would always use the impressive door in the front. It was too grand a door not to be used all the time.

"Mister Daniel Armory, master chimney sweep at yer service," Master Armory introduced himself to the gentleman.

"You are expected," the man replied, opening the gate for the group to enter. The grounds were immaculate. Every bush was faultlessly pruned, and the cobblestone pavement was freshly washed.

Up close, the house dwarfed any structure Egan had seen. It was larger than most of London's churches. And yet the imposing outside could hardly rival the lavishness of the interior. Egan gawked at the flowered tapestries, wide windows, marble statues, and portraits that furnished the house.

A team of servants met Master Armory and the broomers in the formal dining room where a table stretched long enough for fifty people. Egan's mouth watered thinking about the exquisite and bountiful food that was served in the room.

A gentleman in a black suit gave instructions to the servants.

"Dobbs, you shall escort two boys to the second floor." A servant stepped forward.

"You two," Master Armory pointed at Iggy and Tick.

"Yes, sir," they responded and followed Dobbs out of the room.

"Michael, you shall take two to the third floor." A servant stepped forward.

"You two," Master Armory pointed at Egan and Adam.

"Yes, sir," they replied and followed Michael out of the room.

Michael stoically walked to a back staircase and ascended several flights of stairs.

"Did you get a look at this place?" Adam asked Egan.

"If you touch anything, the guards will carry you off to the Tower where my lord shall cut off your head," Michael stated.

Adam and Egan froze in the middle of a step.

"Wot?" Adam gasped. "Truly?"

"Touch something and find out," Michael tempted.

Adam twitched. Egan grabbed one of Adam's hands and dragged him up the stairs after Michael.

The broomers started in opposite bedrooms. It was clear that Michael didn't know about the flues because the boys soon ran into each other as the holes combined.

"Egan!" Adam greeted, "I'll scrape up if you scrape down."

Egan looked across the bricks. A long narrow flue descended into the darkness below. Adam scrambled up the hole, not giving Egan time to object.

A few feet into the third hole, Egan's feet found a soot clogger. He scooted lower and pushed at the sides of the chimney with his bare feet until soot broke apart and fell into the hole.

"Hey! Who's up there?" Pitt shouted.

"It's Egan. Sorry Pitt! There's a clogger up here."

"I'll scrape it. Climb out and go to the next fireplace," Pitt ordered.

Egan climbed the hole until it converged with three other flues and lowered himself back into the fireplace where he had started. Michael was waiting, disinterested and bored. Egan swept the cold ashes into his empty sack and set the hearth instruments back in order.

"Ready for the next one," Egan told the servant as he gathered his tools and discarded clothing.

Michael led Egan across the hall. "Go on," he pointed to the fireplace.

Egan lifted the fire screen and set it to the side. He pulled his brush from the bucket and climbed up into the hole. Egan knew that Armory expected him to do a full sweep, so he decided to climb up to the roof and then scrape down until he met another broomer.

This chimney was relatively clean. Egan swept in a quick, half-hearted fashion so he could get to the grimy areas. His slapdash scraping stirred up needless clouds of dust and left wee clumps of soot undisturbed in the crooks and crannies of the brick. Neither Pitt nor Master Armory would approve, but neither one would see this hole.

Egan chuckled at the thought of Master Armory climbing a chimney. If Master Armory were a broomer, sticking pins in his legs and lighting a fire under him would never get him up the chimney. He simply would not fit.

Egan reached the roof and yelled "all up" and quickly scraped his way back down. As he approached the hearth, Egan gripped the expanding sides and deposited his feet into the left hole. He started to scrape down when he heard a stifled cry echoing up the hole.

Egan tucked his brush into his pants and shimmied down the bricks.

"Who's down there?"

"Egan?" Iggy choked. His voice was muffled. "Egan, I'm stuck."

The narrow flue ended in a wide hearth below.

Iggy cried out in pain.

"Iggy? Where are you?"

"Egan," Iggy cried.

Egan examined the bricks until he found the narrow tunnel extending sideways just below him. He descended and looked into the hole.

"Iggy? You in here?"

Egan slid his hands into the hole and felt for Iggy.

"I can't breathe," Iggy rasped. His voice was close.

Egan ducked and pushed his head and shoulders into the hole, but couldn't find Iggy.

"Wiggle yer feet," Egan ordered, desperate to find his friend.

Egan thought he heard a slight shuffle. Egan pressed further into the hole. Egan found Iggy's feet and grasped hold of his ankles.

"I'm pulling you back," Egan said.

Iggy mumbled something incoherent.

Egan pulled Iggy back, burying the boy in a pile of soot. Egan scooted himself back and pulled on Iggy again. Egan felt his feet enter the vertical chimney as he scooted back, pulling Iggy with him.

Iggy had stopped moving. Egan bent his legs upwards, not finding a good angle to lower his legs downward, and scooted back again. At the edge of the sideways flue, Egan twisted himself into a standing position and reached back into the flue. He grasped Iggy's legs, pulled him from the sideways hole, and dropped him into the hearth below.

Iggy began choking.

"Pitt!" Egan screamed as he lowered himself and pulled Iggy from the hearth. "Pitt!" Egan scraped the soot from Iggy's eyes, nose, and mouth. Iggy inhaled deeply, desperate to fill his lungs with air.

Master Armory bounded into the room. "Wot is this?"

"Iggy was stuck," Egan explained.

"Where did all this soot come from?"

Piles of soot from Iggy's body had fallen onto the clean floor.

"From a side flue," Egan explained.

"Get in there and clean it out," Master Armory ordered.

"Yes, sir," Egan's voice wavered. Master Armory raised his fist and took a step closer to him.

"Yes, sir," Egan repeated. He pulled his brush from his pants, ducked into the fireplace, and looked for the opening. Locating it, he climbed up and pushed himself into the sideways hole, arms out and face forward. Egan slithered forward until the soot started lining the edges. Iggy must have kept going, not knowing how much soot was ahead. Egan swept some of the soot into a pile and scooted back out of the hole, brushing the pile with him.

At the flue entrance, Egan swept the pile into the hearth below. The ash hit the bottom and billowed out into the room. Master Armory started cursing, and the hearth was quickly covered with burlap. The darkness made it more difficult to work. Easing further into the hole, Egan found where Iggy became stuck. The flue bent upwards at a ninety-degree angle, making it impossible for Iggy to bend upwards without turning over. If he had turned over, he would have been suffocated from the soot that fell from above. Egan pulled together a modest pile of soot and backed out of the hole. Five trips later, the corner was cleaned out.

"All clean!" Egan yelled into the hearth. A corner of the burlap was pulled away.

"Climb back upstairs," Pitt's low voice commanded from the hearth.

Egan climbed and entered a room he didn't recognize. One of the broomers had already swept the hearth free of ash. Egan remembered he was supposed to be sweeping on the third floor. He entered the converging flues and climbed upward. Michael was waiting in the doorway when he dropped into the chimney.

"Finally," Michael groaned.

Egan swept the hearth, wiped his feet clean, picked up his belongings, and followed Michael down the hall to the next room.

The grandeur of the house faded as Egan swept chimney after chimney. Soon Egan felt trapped in the grand rooms with high painted ceilings.

When the hall of rooms was finished, Adam and Egan walked down the stairs with Michael and arrived in the kitchen where they had entered the house.

Master Armory collected the fee and handed the gentleman his card. "Me little boys cleaned yer little flues better than any other sweep. You won't have trouble come winter, and if you call on me in the spring, I'll offer you a special fee."

"My thanks," the gentleman responded without emotion, took the card, and led the group outside to the back gate. The man locked the gate behind them and returned to the back door.

"A shilling each before nightfall," Master Armory instructed, depositing the newly earned fee into his pocket.

"Yes, sir," the broomers replied in accord.

Master Armory walked away.

"Don't we get the rest of the day off? I thought we did," Adam complained once he was out of earshot.

Iggy attacked Egan with a fierce hug around his shoulders.

"Wot happened?" Tick asked.

"Iggy got stuck, and Egan pulled him out." There was a glint of pride in Pitt's voice.

Egan smiled timidly. "I was just there."

"I want to buy Egan a meat pie," Iggy beamed.

"That's a grand idea!" Adam exclaimed, "I love meat pie!"

"And some ale!" Tick added.

"Is yer name Egan?" Pitt asked Adam. "And don't you remember, Tick? No more ale for you, ever." Pitt grinned.

"Savings is better than a full gut," Egan said.

"Aye, but I got out of that hole 'cause of you," Iggy said.

"Yer me friend, Iggy," Egan said.

"Yer me friend too," Iggy responded.

"No ale, but let's get a meat pie. It's on me," Pitt said.

Pitt pulled Egan into a side hug. "You done good," he said.

CHAPTER XXIX

A month later, it was Egan's first day to sweep alone. He was given a long wooden pole and instructed to stick to the streets he knew. Egan watched Pitt walk away, and he was tempted to trail him, staying a few yards back. Instead, Egan decided to courageously accept the assignment of sweeping on his own and wait for business at the Little Conduit.

Fog covered the streets, clinging to Egan's skin like a mantle of early snow seeping into his body. He drew in a quick breath; the chill coated his lungs as the fog absorbed the warmth that escaped from his mouth in a cloud of steam.

Winter was near. He could feel it. He could hear it. It was the first morning since early March that the cobblestones took heed of solitary travelers by echoing back their steps in a sharp, crisp manner. He could hear the winter silence coming; it was the sound of falling snow, the sound of refuse freezing in the streets, the sound of ice. Winter brought a rare lonely quietness. Egan shivered. He missed Pitt.

A man soon arrived at the Little Conduit, bundled for the cold and seeking a sweep.

"Tuppence a chimney, more if there's a clog, fire, or angled brick," Egan boldly stated his price.

"The chimney is stopped up," the man admitted.

"Is it hot?" Egan asked, feeling confident as he bartered with his first customer on his own.

"Not too hot, I lit a fire and smothered it when the chimney smoked."

"I'll clean it for a sixpence," Egan stated assertively. It was much too high a price.

"Done," said the man.

Egan gasped and then nodded.

The man led Egan in the direction of Moorgate. Egan feared that the work was on the other side of the wall. The man looked wealthy, too wealthy to live outside the wall, but they were coming close to the edge of London. The man led Egan past a large brick building with white pillars and big windows.

"Wot is this place?" Egan asked, ever curious.

"This is Armourers' Hall. It holds the largest collection of armor and weapons in the world, so I'm told."

"For fighting pirates?"

"Pirates and other enemies of England."

"Could I see in there?"

"Are you a member of The Worshipful Company of Armourers and Brasiers?"

"No."

"Then probably not. However, you could join the livery when you get older."

"I don't think so. I'm going to sea like me Da."

"Good choice, my lad. I myself work for the Honourable East India Company."

Egan stopped in his tracks. "Do you sail the seas?"

"I don't sail the ship, but yes. I've been to the East Indies three times, trading silks mostly."

"I wish I could go with you."

"Someday you might."

The man led Egan to a house and opened the door. Entering the house, Egan became aware of the smoke sifting into the hall. He went directly into the room without being invited and set his tools down by the smoking fireplace. The room was a formal parlor, not often used.

Egan stripped down to his small clothes, pulled his sweeping mask over his head, and stooped into the hearth. Egan ignored the tears welling in his eyes as they reacted to the smoke. His eyes were persistently red and swollen; there was naught to be done about it.

Up the hole, there was no sign of light. Egan retrieved his pole and climbed up into the chimney. The bricks were still cold. After a distance, Egan poked his pole up into the chimney as Pitt had taught him.

Be as far away from cloggers as you can get until you see the sun, Pitt had told him.

If Egan were too close to the built-up soot, it could fall and stick around his mask, and he would be unable to breathe.

Egan's pole reached up into the darkness. It didn't strike against anything except the walls. Egan scooted himself up a few more feet and tried again. The pole smacked the hardened soot, sending a cloud of dust downward. Egan struck harder and then harder. The pitch started to break away, falling towards Egan and then into the hearth. Egan struck it until an opening broke free to the sky.

Egan dropped his pole into the hearth, braced his back on the brick, planted his right foot on the opposite wall, and began to climb again. About halfway to the clogger, Egan began to scrape. Winter snow melting into the chimney had created a soot wall that was so thick it had formed a second chimney inside the hole. It was impossible to climb through, so Egan scraped from the bottom up.

He chipped away at the soot with the end of his brush. After what seemed like hours, he finally reached the top. He did not give a yell, only paused to look at the view. Through the fog, he could see lanterns that hung from the city's wall being extinguished to save lamp oil during the day. Egan looked towards the River Thames, but it was too far away to see.

Egan ducked down and brushed the sides down as he descended. At the bottom, he shoveled the soot into a burlap sack and gathered the tools.

"Yer fireplace won't smoke now, sir. Do you have other fireplaces for me to see to?" Egan asked, hoping to spend more time asking his questions about the sea.

"No, that will be all," the man handed Egan a shilling. "You were up there a good amount of time, warranting a larger fee."

"Thank ye, sir!"

Egan pulled on his clothes and placed the shilling in his pocket.

When Egan was ready, he stepped toward the front door. "Good health to you, sir."

"And to you, young sweep. Also…"

Egan turned back towards the gentlemen.

"If you should want to be a ship's boy when you get a bit older, the East India House is on Leadenhall Street. We are always looking for good workers, and I think you should apply."

"Thank ye, sir. Leadenhall Street. I will, sir," Egan grinned and headed out into the street. He turned to look once more at the man as he closed the door.

Egan skipped happily through the next hours. The man thought Egan would be a good ship's boy. The man must have recognized the Irish in him.

In the late afternoon, Egan walked towards Stocks Market. He argued with himself about his purpose in heading that way. He was looking for work, he told himself. Really, he meant to pay a visit to Missus Winchester and buy a boiled potato. His spirits were high, and his will was weak without Pitt around. It was just a farthing or two he decided.

"Hallo, there me little fire sprite!" Missus Winchester's blue eyes sparkled in the afternoon sun. "I haven't seen you since spring. Come for a boiled potato?"

"Hallo, Missus Winchester! Wot's yer price today?"

"A haypenny for you."

Egan handed her a coin from his pocket.

"Here you are," Missus Winchester said, handing the hot potato to Egan. "A hot meal is necessary for us hard workers."

"Where does yer mister work?"

"Who knows. The laggard was a drinker. He left years ago and probably died somewhere drowning in his own spit."

"Me Da died at sea," Egan told her, biting into the potato.

"Dying at sea is too good for me husband. He left after beating me son half to death. Me son was only five and never the same in the head after that. No man who beats his own son is worth the ground he stands on, I says to him that day. I will take the boy away, I will, if you harms him again, I say. Then he hit me too, and I just knew it."

"Knew wot?"

"That I couldn't fix him."

"Me Da spanked me lots."

"Spanking for discipline is a lot different from beating."

"Then good riddance to him," Egan concluded, finishing the last bite of potato.

The woman chuckled, "A very good riddance to him. Where's yer friend today, love?"

"I'm old enough to sweep on me own."

"And how old might that be?"

"Seven, maybe eight by now. I don't know, but I'm bigger. Only I can't get too big because then I won't fit in chimneys."

"That wouldn't be so bad."

"I need to fit until I can pay me a debt, and then I'm going to sea with the East India Company."

"Yer debt?"

"I owe Master Armory five guineas."

"That's a large sum."

"Tis. I need to find work. Thank ye for the potato!"

Missus Winchester winked, "Yer welcome, sprite. Come back and see me!"

Egan gathered his tools and wove his way through the street vendors. He liked Missus Winchester. Her life had been horrifying, but she still smiled, and her eyes sparkled.

Egan traced his steps back towards the Little Conduit.

"Sweep! Sweep!" he called out.

He was rewarded with several chimneys at a large residence, enough so that his first shilling of the day could be tucked securely into his sock. He proudly delivered two shillings worth of coins to Master Armory that evening.

"It was his first day sweeping on his own," Pitt told Master Armory.

"You are worth the price I paid for you runt," Master Armory sneered and dismissed the boys.

Pitt whispered, "You done good, Egan."

They were the first broomers back to the cellar.

"Pitt, I met a sailor today that works for the East India Company. The house is on Leadenhall Street. He told me to apply to be a ship's boy," Egan rattled off excitedly. "Let's go, Pitt. We could be hired as ship's boys and sail the seas. Master Armory would never know where we went. We could leave and never come back. He would search the winter through and never find us."

"They wouldn't take me with me hand."

"But they would. There is a whole world out there, Pitt. Me Da told me stories of the places he had been, and the sailor I met has been to the East Indies three times. Three times, Pitt!"

"Egan, we owe a debt to Master Armory. Five guineas, you know that. A man always pays his debts."

"Like Robinson Crusoe." Egan's countenance fell.

"And Friday. As soon as we pay our debts, I'll help you find yer family and then we'll join the East India Company and sail the seas just like Crusoe and Friday. But we can't run, Egan."

"Wot if yer free before me?"

"Then I'll find yer family for you. I take an oath that I won't sail the seas without you."

"Then I take an oath that I won't sail the seas without you," Egan returned.

The boys shook hands, binding them to their promises.

"We'll never be free if we run," Pitt said.

"I know. Five guineas to freedom," Egan mumbled.

CHAPTER XXX

The winter arrived in full force, and work became scarce. Chimney sweeps with climbing boys were popping up all over London, undercutting Master Armory's prices.

Egan walked to the outskirts of London only to come back empty-handed. If he could endure it, Egan submitted himself to Master Armory's wrath and accepted the lashings. Other days, he withdrew coins from his treasured savings.

On Christmas Eve, Egan found himself wandering through a curvy, narrow street, calling out his services. He trudged through the hours, waiting for London's merriment to pass. He wanted to return to the cellar to spend Christmas with the other broomers. Will and Iggy said that they would tell the Christmas story that the pastor told them in the orphanage. Miss Clara was making them dinner. Egan would miss it all if he could not earn a shilling by nightfall. It would not be Christmas if he spent the day alone.

Egan circled neighborhoods and streets thinking about Christmas before realizing that he was lost. Egan crossed a prominent street, thinking it would take him to the London Wall. Instead, he ended up weaving through more buildings and houses.

The afternoon grew dark. Egan had never been alone at night in London, much less this part of the city. He could find his way back to Master Armory's house if he found the London Wall, or the River Thames, or even Throgmorton Street, but he recognized nothing.

The candle lighters had long since lit the street lanterns; between the lampposts, the night glowed with falling snow. The unfamiliar houses were brightly lit as families gathered together to keep Christmas. Joyful conversations rang out from the pubs. Egan looked for someone to ask for directions, but no one traveled the frozen streets.

He could go into a pub or knock on someone's door, but Egan did not want to. He pressed towards the river, but after an hour, he knew he was again heading in the wrong direction.

A few steps down the street, an old man wrapped in tattered blankets had chosen a doorway to sleep in. As Egan approached him, he could smell the stink of alcohol and refuse.

"Which way is it to the River Thames?" Egan asked the man.

The man wobbled as he adjusted his eyes on Egan. "He left by the river. He left by the river and never come back."

Egan stepped away.

"There be dragons in the river. The dragons got him, and he never come back."

The old man reached for Egan but collapsed in a drunken stupor when Egan ducked beyond his reach. Egan ran across the street and through an alley. The man shouted after Egan, "He never come back. The river. He never come back."

Egan ran until he heard the soft words of a song drifting from a church. He stepped up to the chapel's doors and listened to the words the people sang.

"While shepherds watched their flocks by night all seated on the ground, the angel of the Lord came down, and glory shone around.

'Fear not,' said he, for mighty dread had seized their troubled mind, glad tidings of great joy I bring to you and all mankind."

Egan opened the door and slipped into the back of the sanctuary as the singing continued. He placed his tools on the floor and crept closer to listen.

"To you in David's town this day is born of David's line, the Savior who is Christ the Lord and this shall be the sign.

The heavenly Babe you there shall find to human view displayed, all meanly wrapped in swathing bands and in a manger laid."

Mesmerized by the harmonious beauty of the song, Egan jerked with surprise as a large hand grasped his shoulder. The hand belonged to a man of towering stature dressed in a long black robe with white lace about the collar.

"Welcome to St. Helen's. Are you escaping the cold, lad?"

"Yes. No. I mean, I don't know," Egan stammered. "I've never been here before. I was on me way towards the River Thames and heard the singing. I..."

"My, you are quite lost."

"Yes, sir. I'll be on me way."

Egan tried to turn back towards the door, but the hand's firm grasp was unrelenting.

"Come," the man said. He directed Egan up the aisle to the front of the church. "Please make room for this young lad," he quietly asked a gentleman on the front row, who promptly moved his family over. The robed man sat Egan down on the long bench as the song finished:

"All glory be to God on high and to the earth be peace,
Goodwill, henceforth, from heaven to men begin and never cease.
Begin and never cease."

"Caught his eye, did you?" the gentleman asked Egan.

"Who is he?"

"That is Pastor Benjamin Robinson. He's well respected and studied in the scriptures."

Pastor Robinson ascended to the pulpit, opened the book in front of him, and read:

"Matthew 1:21, And she shall bring forth a Son, and then shalt call His name Jesus: for He shall save His people from their sins."

Pastor Robinson looked out at the congregation and continued in a deep, strong voice that echoed down from the wooden rafters, "The celebration of the birth of Christ hath been esteemed a duty by most who profess Christianity. Christ came to take our natures upon him, to die a shameful, painful, and accursed death for our sakes; he cleansed us by his blood from the guilt of sin, and now, my brethren, he is a mediator between us and his offended Father."

Egan looked up at the arched ceiling, studying the church. It was different from St. Olave's but just as beautiful. He had never sat at the front of a church before. Egan looked up to the pulpit.

"Shall we yearly celebrate the birth of our temporal king, but not the birth of our Lord Jesus, the King of Kings? Let the birth of our Redeemer, which redeemed us from sin, from wrath, from death, from hell, be always remembered; may this Savior's love never be forgotten.

"And as, my brethren, tis the time for keeping Christmas, be ye mindful of the poor, like this child who is subjugated to a life of merciless toil."

The pastor stretched his upturned palm towards Egan, who slunk down in his seat. He should not be sitting in the front of the church. Paupers should stand in the back.

"This lad was wandering lost, unable to find his home among the ashes, and instead sought refuge in the Lord's church. If the Lord has smiled upon you and blessed you with an abundance of the things of this life, return that blessing upon the poor of this world.

"My dear brethren, let us celebrate and keep this Christmas, with joy in our hearts. Now to God the Father, God the Son, and God the Holy Spirit, amen."

"Amen," the parishioners echoed.

"Amen," Egan said.

Pastor Robinson descended from the pulpit and walked to the back of the church to wish people glad tidings as they left. Egan stayed in his seat. The pastor had so deliberately placed him there, and he wondered if he should get up. The gentleman he sat beside did not move either. Egan stared wide-eyed up at him.

"Happy Christmas to you, young lad." The man placed a sixpence in Egan's palm.

"Thank ye, sir! Peace be with you," Egan recited the Sunday greeting from St. Olave's, hoping it was correct to say in this church.

"And also with you," the man responded.

The man patted Egan's head, seeming not to notice the grime that smeared onto his clean hand. Just as the man walked down the aisle to the back door, a young girl walked up to Egan and offered him a red and white clay marble.

"Happy Christmas!" she giggled and skipped away.

"Happy Christmas!" Egan yelled after her.

A thin, elderly woman grasped Egan's hands and lifted them. Egan unfolded his fingers to reveal the coin and the marble. Egan studied the woman. She was tidy, but her clothes were shabby and worn.

"Are you hungry? You can have it." Egan lifted his palm, offering the coin to her.

The woman shook her head. She placed a farthing on the top of the shilling and folded Egan's fingers back over his palm. She patted his hand with a smile that shone out from her cloudy brown eyes.

Several more followed the old woman's lead. Egan soon lost count of the coins he held in his palms. As the church emptied out, the pastor beckoned Egan to the back of the church.

Egan met the pastor and held out his hands. "Look! Wot am I to do for it?"

"Tis a gift that is freely given. Take it as a blessing from God."

"But why would they give me coin for no work?"

"Because the love of God dwells in them. You see, God loves us although we have nothing to offer him. Have you a pocket to tuck it away for safekeeping? One without holes?"

Egan nodded and secured the money into the pocket he used for the sweeping coins. He kept the marble out and rolled it about his palm with his fingers.

"I've never had a marble of me own. A girl give it to me."

"It's a Christmas gift."

"I've never had a Christmas gift, except from me Mum."

"Now, young sweep. Where might you be headed?"

"Distaff Lane but I'd know me way if I could find the London Wall or the River Thames or even Thames Street."

"Well let's snuff out the candles and then I'll walk with you until you find your way."

Pastor Robinson handed Egan a candlesnuffer, and they walked along the arches of the church extinguishing the light.

"Yer church is grand," Egan said.

"It is. Been here near 300 years now."

"You've been here for 300 years?"

Pastor Robinson chuckled. "No, though some days I feel that old. The church was built near 300 years ago, but many ministers preceded me. I pray many more follow me. This church was designed to serve the Lord, what power could destroy its walls?"

The last candle snuffed, Pastor Robinson donned a long woolen coat and scarf, collected a lantern, and shut the great wooden door behind them.

"I often walk the streets of London at night, tis peaceful, if a bit cold, this time of year," Pastor Robinson said.

"Don't you fear robbers?"

"Why? Are you a robber?"

"Naw…well, once when I wanted a sweet from me sister Kerrin, I pretended to be Jack Hall the Highwayman, and I stole it from her and ate it. It made me Mum upset. Said she didn't want to see me swing from Tyburn Tree like Jack Hall. Stealing is wrong."

"Thankfully, God forgives."

Egan looked up at the man and smiled.

"How long have you been a chimney sweep's boy?"

"Mum sold me to Master Armory last winter. Today was me first day to get lost. If I didn't have all this coin, I'd be whipped. He may make me sleep outside anyway." Egan shuffled his burlap wrapped feet through the snow.

"You weren't far off course. As we turn the corner, we'll be on Bishopsgate Street, which leads to the London Bridge or to Threadneedle Street, which may be a better route for you."

When they rounded the corner, Egan still did not recognize the area. He was glad that the pastor continued to walk forward.

"Does your master attend to your education?"

"No, we're the kind of sweeps that work all days. There are some broomers that go to church, but Master Armory says our type is different. We are needed more than those others, so we don't have time for learning."

"I see. Do you want to be one of the other types of broomers?"

"Somedays, but I really want to go to sea like me Da. He was going to get me a position as a ship's boy, but he died before I was big enough. He wasn't a pirate if you think that."

"I did not think a smart lad such as yourself could be the son of a pirate. Reflected in you is a father that was a fine man," Pastor Robinson said.

Egan beamed. "Do you have children?"

"Several. They were at the church tonight. My wife Anne walked them home after the service ended. I believe the youngest gave you that marble."

"That was yer daughter?"

"Aye."

"I really like it. Will you tell her I really like it?"

"I will."

Pastor Robinson turned Egan to the left, and suddenly the buildings looked familiar.

"That's Throgmorton there, innit?"

"Tis. If you follow that street to Cheapside, you'll be close to home."

"Thank ye, sir. Happy Christmas!" Egan shouted as he ran through the snow.

"Happy Christmas," Pastor Robinson returned the greeting.

Egan ran until he tired and then walked as fast as he could back to Master Armory's house. When he arrived, the back door was locked.

Egan set his tools down, pulled the coins from his pocket, and knocked on the door. Someone should be awake on Christmas Eve. Egan knocked louder and then pounded his fist against the door.

The bolt slid aside, and the door creaked open. Master Armory stood in the opening.

"You think you can come back this late and still have a place to sleep?"

Egan held the coins up to Master Armory.

"I got lost. Here are me earnings, sir."

Master Armory took the money from Egan and counted the coins.

"Get down to the cellar," he ordered.

Egan gathered his pail and tools and rushed to the cellar, expecting Master Armory's belt or whip to lash his backside. The punishment never came. Egan hurried down the dark stairs, set his things down, and scrambled to his ashes.

Master Armory closed and locked the cellar door. Egan listened as his heavy footsteps crossed the kitchen and disappeared up the stairs.

"All right, Egan?" Pitt whispered.

"Yeah, but I got lost."

"Why didn't Master Armory whip you?" Tick asked.

"I gave him lots of coins."

"Shut it," Rory hissed. "I'm trying to sleep."

"I'm glad yer back," Iggy whispered in the dark. "Miss Clara gave us turkey with a biscuit. I saved some for you. It's on yer sack near the wall."

"Thank ye, Iggy!"

He felt around and found the food and hungrily devoured the morsels.

"Happy Christmas, Egan," Iggy whispered.

"Happy Christmas, Iggy."

The Christmas greeting echoed around the dark, cold cellar.

CHAPTER XXXI

The temperature fell and ice collected along the banks of the River Thames, slowing the water until the river became hazardous to sail. The price of coal increased as wealthy citizens stockpiled fuel. The river merchants made a handsome profit on the coal they brought down from Newcastle.

As with the deluge of rain the prior spring, the broomers were confined to the cellar on the days of brutal cold. Pitt, Rory, and Will went with Master Armory to respond to an emergency one afternoon, but otherwise, the broomers entertained themselves.

The game of "ash sack skipping" was revived, providing a way for the broomers to stay warm, and Miss Clara brought the boys bread and tea in the afternoon. Master Armory bellowed angrily upstairs, frustrated with the loss of earnings.

"If Master Armory is so upset, why innit he making us sweep?" Tick asked.

"Because folks don't smother their fires when it's this cold. Makes it too dangerous for us," Will responded.

"Last year we were outside freezing and still never earned a farthing," Andrew added.

"Is that wot happened to Reeves?" Egan asked.

"Not really," Pitt said. "Master Armory is careless only when he's drunk. If he loses us, he loses business. He never meant to lose Reeves."

"But he whipped him," Iggy interjected. "Master Armory whipped him because he wasn't bringing back enough coin, and the next day he didn't come back. Tell him, Pitt."

"We found Reeves near Thames Street. Someone had roughed him up and stripped him bare. They took everything but that sack of ash yer sitting on," Pitt said.

"He bled out and froze to death! He was scared to come home, and he froze out there all alone," Iggy cried.

"Master Armory made us carry him to the peasant pit," Andrew said.

"Wot's that?" Egan asked.

"The ditch at All Hallows Staining where they put the poor dead people," Pitt said.

"The gatekeeper charged us the three pence to take his body. Pitt paid for it with his savings," Andrew said.

The cellar grew colder.

"Reeves was a faithful broomer. The best of us," Pitt said.

"I'm glad it happened. Now we get to stay inside when it's too cold," Rory said.

"You arse!" Andrew yelled.

"Everyone's thinking it. I just said it."

Andrew pushed Rory towards the wall. Rory's hands came up in surrender.

"Cut it out," Pitt warned.

"He was the best of us," Iggy said.

Rory retrieved his cards, and the older boys gathered around.

"Anyone remember that frost fair a few years back?" Pitt asked.

"Frost fair, wot was that?" Will asked.

"The River Thames got so cold that it froze over for miles. Ships got stuck for months in the ice."

"Naw, really?" Andrew was ever skeptical.

"This is not a story. It really happened."

"I want to hear the story," Adam piped up.

"Pitt just said it wasn't a story," Andrew countered.

"Wot happened, Pitt?" Egan asked.

"Can I see yer marble again, Egan?"

"Shush, Adam!" Egan said, handing Adam his marble. "I want to hear Pitt's story."

"A few years back, folks say that Jack Frost hisself visited London. He froze every drop of water, including the River Thames."

"He froze the entire river? That ain't possible," Andrew said.

"Shush, Andrew," Will whispered.

Pitt continued. "The water froze into icy crystals that spread out from the pillars under the London Bridge. Soon the entire river was frozen, and ships of all types were trapped in the ice for months. The sailors climbed out of the ships on rope ladders and went home for the winter."

Egan tried to remember if Da's ship was ever stuck. He wished Da had stayed home last winter.

"But Londoners make the best of everything. Instead of yielding to Jack Frost's mischievous trick, merchants moved onto the river and set up shop. It was like a summer fair, with merchants and gypsies and tinkers. There were tailors, chandlers, printers, carpenters, grocers, and even a pub. You could get boiled potatoes, meat pies, tea, and almost anything else at the fair. There were races, football games, and archery contests. There was always sumfink fun happening at the fair. When thieves started sniffing around, people moved onto the ice to live so they could guard their shops."

"Wasn't that too cold?" Tick was engrossed in the story.

"Naw, there were braziers of coal burning. A tailor and seamstress sewed suits and dresses right out on the ice. Measured people in their underclothes to do it too. It was that warm. And an ox was roasted on a spit right in the middle of the river.

"The river was frozen cold, but there be a layer of fog over the ice. People said that ghosts walk on the river, howling with the wind. Some said it was Jack Frost hisself. Others said they were spirits of mental patients from Bedlam Asylum still wailing in their madness. It made no matter to me, but when the living moved out onto the ice, the dead didn't like it."

"Pitt, you'll give Adam nightmares," Andrew protested.

"Will not. I'm tough, and you knowed it," Adam said. "Wot happened next?"

"Well, the ghosts danced about in the dark at the edge of the firelight for the first few weeks. They howled warnings, but the merchants refused to leave. An old sailor told me that globes of curious blue light circled the frost fair at night. His first mate went to see wot the lights were, but they flickered out and reappeared further out onto the ice. His first mate followed the lights and never returned. The next night, the lights reappeared and claimed three more souls. The third night, no one followed the lights.

"The ghosts became angry that they had not collected any souls that night and vowed to claim the entire fair. The next night, a faint tapping sound joined the blue orbs. Tap, tap, tap, tap, tap. The tapping was followed by a quiet cracking sound. The sounds grew louder and soon the ghosts were shifting ice. They lifted the frozen surface into the air and crashed it down into the riverbed below.

"Constables ordered everyone to vacate the River Thames for fear that the ghosts would move upon the land. The shopkeepers, barkeep, gypsies, sailors, and thieves gathered their belongings and fled to sure ground as the ice melted away underneath them. During the frost fair, the ghosts realized that when water freezes they are free to walk on the land. Next time the River Thames freezes over, the ghosts will walk through London and take the souls of all who get in their way."

All eyes were wide open, red, and blotchy from sweeping and frightened as the wind howled outside.

"Maybe the River Thames froze over this very night," Pitt concluded.

Andrew grabbed Adam around the chest from behind. "Yer mine!" he whispered in a raspy voice.

Adam screamed a high-pitch girly scream, and the broomers erupted into laughter.

"You arse!" Adam yelled, wrestling Andrew to the floor. Tick, Will, and Rory jumped into the fray, shouting and laughing hysterically.

"Did that really happen?" Egan asked Pitt.

"Don't know. I wasn't stupid enough to sleep out on the ice, but that's wot the sailor told me."

"Shush!" Miss Clara ordered. From her bent position, she looked into the cellar and tried to make sense of the sight. "Shush you boys! Wotever is going on down there?"

The broomers stopped wrestling and looked up at Miss Clara from the pile on the floor.

"They started a fight with me!" Adam complained.

"I'm sure that's a whopping lie. Now hush before Master Armory sends you out into the cold!" Miss Clara scolded.

Grumbling in protest, the broomers untangled their limbs and resumed their places.

"If you behave, I'll bring you sumfink to eat a bit later," Miss Clara tempted. She gave them another look of warning and stepped back through the cellar door.

Adam growled and incited another wrestling match, but when Andrew pushed him off, he retreated to his sacks to pout.

"Give back me marble, Adam." Egan held out his hand.

"I don't have it!"

"You do too!"

Adam shrugged and started looking around his sacks.

"There were fires everywhere when Reeves froze," Iggy said.

"If any of you gets that cold and can't get back here, sneak into a pub and hide in the corner or under a table until morning. If you can, drink some ale. It warms the insides," Pitt instructed.

"Except for Tick. No ale for Tick," Will laughed.

"I like ale," Tick responded.

"We know," Will and Iggy said at the same time.

The boys erupted into laughter again, but Pitt hushed them before Miss Clara returned.

"Is anyone playing?" Rory asked, holding up his cards.

"I am!" Adam yelled.

"No, you're not," Andrew said.

"Am too. I just found Egan's marble."

"Wot difference does that make? Yer not playing."

Adam returned to his pout while the older boys started a game of cards.

Egan, Iggy, and Tick drew pictures in the dirt floor with their fingers - a frozen river, tents on the ice, and ghosts that hovered at the edges.

"You think they're here, the river ghosts? Because we talked about them? Will they take us?" Egan asked.

"They will if you follow the blue lights," Rory said from across the room.

"It's just a story, Egan. Besides, me Da always said that we should fear the living, not the dead," Pitt said.

"Reeves' spirit is still here," Tick said. "I feel someone watching over me sometimes, and I think it's him."

"Reeves follows me too," Iggy admitted.

"Wot does he want?" Egan asked, thinking about the sack of ashes beneath him.

"He wants to live," Iggy said. "Even if he has to be a broomer, he wants to live."

"And he wants five guineas," Tick said.

"That too," Iggy agreed.

"We need a better picture," Egan decided, wiping the lines from the dirt.

"We need sunshine."

"And grey alder trees," Tick added.

"And a church and cemetery," Iggy said.

"And the river!" Adam jumped from his sacks and joined the younger boys. He used the marble to trace waving lines in the cellar floor.

"And Preacher Erington," Egan added as the boys set about recreating their summer at St. Olave's.

The drawing came with stories, some true, some not, and some with bits of each. The broomers' memories were skewed by the comparison to the present, as are all memories that become distorted with time. The cellar was warmed by good cheer that afternoon, the last of ephemeral Christmas.

CHAPTER XXXII

Charles Greville stumbled out of the Lamb & Flag and into the crowded streets of London. Bennett followed, trying to steady the inebriated apprentice.

"Gin! Never a better drink! I think I'll get some more," Charles slurred as he turned around to go back into the pub.

"Come, we've work tomorrow. Mister de Lamerie will give you chump work if you show up pissed again," Bennett turned Charles back around and pushed him towards St. Giles Street.

"You've no real talent as a silversmith, my friend," Charles slapped Bennett on the back. "What will you do when the Hall rejects you?"

"So what if I'll never be a master. I'll work in a shop. It's a good trade."

"Gin. You should make gin."

"Yer drunk."

"Bloody bastard, don't tell me I'm drunk. I know when I've had enough," Charles shouted.

"Let's get back. You can sleep it off."

"Get away from me." Charles pushed away from Bennett and stumbled back towards the reveling crowds.

"Don't drink yer last shilling!" Bennett called after Charles.

"Bullocks you bloody rogue! Go on and lick Lamerie's boots if you want to," Charles responded.

Charles ambled towards his own destruction free of judgment. A crowd of noisy men surrounded a makeshift cockpit constructed behind the butcher's shop. Money exchanged hands all around the ring as bets were placed on two roosters, one with a red ribbon tied on its foot.

Charles dug into his pockets and retrieved a crown and two shillings. "Huzzah!" he exclaimed. "I ain't down to my last shilling. What does he know?"

Charles studied the two roosters. Both looked plucky, but the one with the red ribbon sported scraggily feathers. It had been in another fight that evening.

"Two shillings on the gamecock with the black tail feathers," Charles slapped the coins on a desk in front of a stout fellow who was writing out bets.

"Here's yer bet," the man said as he handed Charles a strip of paper.

Charles slipped the bet into his pocket and pushed his way between sweaty, inebriated bodies until he stood at the edge of the ring.

"Last call for bets!" the stout fellow called.

"Fight! Fight! Fight!" the crowd began to chant.

"All bets are in. Gentlemen, release yer birds!" a man in the pit shouted.

The gamecocks were released by their owners and charged at each other. Metal had been attached to their natural spurs, causing blood to gush violently from claw wounds. The black-feathered bird slashed the other bird's wing, causing it to drag on the ground, then pursued the wounded bird across the pit.

"Huzzah!" Charles yelled as the black-feathered cock ripped a lethal slash in the other gamecock's wee neck.

Men cheered or started fights in anticipation of paying their debt.

Charles reached for his winning ticket, but his pocket was empty. He checked his other pockets, which were also empty.

"Who took me bet?" Charles shouted.

"I did," the man at the desk shouted back.

"No, not you. Someone took it from my pocket!" His eyes darted across the room and spotted a soot-faced boy smiling at him from across the room.

"You there! Thief!" Charles yelled. But before he could shove through the drunken crowd, the boy had disappeared.

CHAPTER XXXIII

"Egan, I need you," Pitt whispered, shaking Egan awake.

"Wot?" Egan murmured.

"Master Armory has a job and yer coming. Come on. Get up, Friday! I need yer help."

Egan stumbled to his feet, groggy with exhaustion. Miss Clara was not in the kitchen, and the hearth was cold.

Master Armory was waiting at the back door with a lantern.

"You took yer sweet time," he spat and stumbled outside.

Master Armory staggered down the alley and up towards Cheapside. He smelled of decayed spirits and was in a foul mood.

Pitt and Egan followed closely behind, careful not to speak or otherwise provoke Master Armory into a drunken rage. Master Armory was never cheerful after a night of drinking, but working in the early hours of the morning darkened his temper even more.

Master Armory led the broomers to a brewery. Jack Calvert, the proprietor, stood waiting by the door.

"It's about time. I was about to call on the sweep down the street."

"I said I would be back, and here I be," Master Armory grumbled.

Inside, black billows of smoke sieved into the room through the large brick fireplace at the back of the room.

"The iron pipe in the flue is clear, but something is blocking it up above," Mister Calvert was saying. "Sure you put those bricks back the right way last time?"

Master Armory grunted at Mister Calvert.

Pitt and Egan approached the large fireplace and set down their tools.

The fire had been extinguished in the hearth, although the bricks were still blistering hot to the touch.

Pitt pulled his sweeping mask over his face, ducked into the billowing smoke, and looked up the hole. He quickly stepped out of the hearth.

"The chimney is aflame. I'll have to break through the block from up on the roof and push the burning part down into the hearth," Pitt informed Master Armory.

"Climb," Master Armory commanded.

"Sir, it's too hot."

"Climb."

"Master Armory, I won't make it. It's too hot."

Master Armory traced his soiled finger down the scar on Pitt's face. "Climb," he slurred.

"Yes, sir." Pitt trembled and backed away from Master Armory.

The corners of Master Armory's mouth turned upwards as he narrowed his eyes. His mouth formed the word "Climb" as he stumbled backward towards the bar.

"Egan, give me yer shirt."

"Wot?"

"I can't climb without more protection. Give me yer shirt."

Egan stripped off his shirt and gave Pitt his climbing mask and rags.

"Wrap this 'round you too."

Egan held up the empty burlap sack and helped Pitt secure it around himself with a rag.

Pitt stooped to remove his shoes.

"Put on me shoes," Pitt commanded in a low voice, pushing the shoes towards Egan.

"Wot 'bout yer feet, Pitt?" Egan whispered. "Missus Bixby said..."

"Put on me shoes, Egan," Pitt repeated softly.

Egan nodded.

Egan unwrapped the burlap from his feet. His coins clanked at the bottom of his wool socks. He gasped. Pitt gave him a warning glare. Fortunately, Master Armory appeared not to have noticed the sound of the hidden coins. He quietly poured the coins in his socks into Pitt's shoes.

Pitt put on Egan's wool socks and wrapped his feet in the strips of burlap.

Egan slid on Pitt's shoes. Egan's feet were too small. He untied the laces and pulled the straps tighter. He did not know how to retie the laces as Pitt did, so he knotted the straps and stuffed the extra length into the side of the shoes.

The shoes were heavy on his feet.

Pitt pulled the two sweeping masks over his face. He stretched the pairs of gloves over his hands. Pitt picked up his pole. His arms and legs were shaking. Pitt gave Egan a wary shrug and then hoisted himself into the hearth. Egan watched as Pitt's feet disappeared up into the hole.

The air was thick with smoke. Pitt jabbed his pole upwards, but it hit nothing. The air was too thick to see through, but even if it was clear Pitt was too afraid to look up. Somewhere above him, a fire raged.

Pitt climbed another foot and thrust his pole upwards. Still nothing. The chimney grew hotter. He reached an iron pipe, which was installed to keep the decrepit bricks from caving in. The pole was still too short.

Careful to avoid touching the iron sides, Pitt anchored his knee against the brick below the pipe and pushed himself up. The heat baked his flesh. He knew he needed to get out soon. He stabbed the pole upwards.

Flaming debris fell upon his body, lighting his sweeping mask and clothing on fire.

Pitt screamed and lost his grip on the burning hot bricks. One of his legs dropped down to the hearth while the other bent at the knee and wedged against his chest, stopping his fall. He dropped the pole and pulled the burning masks from his head.

His skin immediately blistered from the heat. Pitt shrieked and tried to push himself to the side, pull himself up, and push his leg down. None of his efforts gave him the leverage to free himself from the chimney. Engulfed in flames, Pitt exhausted his strength in a shriek of terror.

"Pitt! Pitt!" Egan screamed into the hearth.

"I cannot move," Pitt whimpered.

"I'm coming for you," Egan yelled.

There was no answer.

Egan plunged into the hearth and began to climb. The hot air burned his eyes. Not far up the chimney, one of Pitt's legs hung down.

"Pitt!"

The hot bricks burned through Egan's undershirt. He patted out flames that caught the fibers of his clothing. His cheeks blistered with the heat. He used his toughened elbows and Pitt's shoes to anchor his climb. He reached Pitt's leg and attempted to pull him down. Wedged into the narrow flue by his knee, Pitt's head lolled down towards the hearth. His eyes bulged, and his tongue drooped from his mouth. Pitt's clothes smoldered in flames.

"PITT!" Egan screamed at the sight and scrambled down the hole. "Pitt! He's stuck!" The smell of burnt flesh permeated the brewery.

Master Armory grunted and shoved Egan out of the way. He bent into the hearth and raised the lantern up the chimney. Master Armory withdrew from the fireplace in disgust.

"Climb and pull him down," Master Armory ordered.

"I can't. He's stuck," Egan protested, shuddering sobs escaping from his chest.

Master Armory lifted his hand. Egan forced himself to crawl back to the fireplace. He climbed up to Pitt, the heat boiling new blisters on his already charred skin.

Egan grasped onto Pitt's dangling leg and freed himself from his footholds. With all his weight on Pitt's leg, Egan attempted to twist and tug Pitt free. Pitt did not respond.

Egan's efforts only pulled Pitt's back lower, wedging his body tighter into the chimney. His hold slipped, and he fell into the hearth, knocking his head against the side of the brick. Dazed and miserable, Egan crawled out of the hearth and lay upon the slatted floor.

"Mister Calvert," Master Armory addressed the proprietor, "Call on the mason."

"The mason?"

"Yer fire killed me sweep. The only way to get him out is to remove the bricks." Master Armory's voice raised.

"I expect you want me to pay for this work!" Mister Calvert returned.

"And the price of me best boy!" Master Armory argued.

"You will pay for this damage, not me!" Mister Calvert yelled at Master Armory.

Pitt's body barricaded the dwindling fire in the chimney and pushed the smoke upwards to the sky. The room began to clear.

Entertained by the commotion, patrons drifted into the brewery and ordered a round of ale.

Egan stared up at the ceiling. Tears ran down his blistered face. Every part of him was in pain, but nothing compared to the weight on his chest. He could not accept what happened or what was happening around him.

"Ten guineas! I could buy a horse for that sum!" Mister Calvert shouted at Master Armory.

As the men argued, the brewer's clock began a slow, agonizing announcement of the hour. Egan counted as he thought.

Clang. Pitt was not dead. He was just stuck.

Clang. The mason would get Pitt out.

Clang. The mason would be there soon.

Clang. Pitt was hurt, but Missus Bixby would fix him.

Clang. Five in the morning. People do not die in the morning. Death sneaks up on you at night.

Egan looked towards the fireplace, and his eyes landed on his feet. He was wearing Pitt's shoes. Pitt never took off his shoes, not even to sleep.

Egan pulled himself over to the fireplace, grabbed the lantern, and looked up the hole. At the sight of Pitt's face, charred and swollen, dripping blood, Egan cried in horror.

"Pitt!" Egan screamed. "Pitt! No! Pitt! No! No!"

Master Armory pulled Egan from the hearth and grabbed the lantern from his hand. He carried Egan forcefully through the pub and pitched him out into the street. The burned skin on Egan's arm rubbed off onto the cobblestones.

"Go fetch the others," Master Armory shouted at Egan.

"Pitt…," Egan wailed, curling himself into a ball on the street.

Master Armory approached Egan and kicked him in the gut, bouncing the frail body. "Go!" he yelled.

Egan slowly pulled himself to his feet, clutching the pain in his stomach. Through tears that clouded his vision, Egan hobbled through the darkness. Torment wailed within his soul.

CHAPTER XXXIV

The broomers were in the kitchen with Miss Clara when Egan stumbled through the door.

"Egan? Egan! Wot happened?" Will asked.

"Pitt. Master Armory says to come, all of you."

Egan turned and staggered back towards the brewery with the broomers following.

"Wot happened?" Will asked again.

"Fire. Pitt is stuck," Egan tried to explain, but his thoughts were muddled. Every few steps he choked on his tears.

Arriving at the pub, Egan stood outside the door and stared. Rory reached around and led the boys through the door. A mason was on a ladder demolishing the front of the chimney near the ceiling. He slammed an iron bar into the mortar and pushed a brick into the flue. The brick crashed through the chimney, but it didn't fall to the hearth. Terror descended on the broomers as they realized what was happening.

The mason chipped away at the next brick, freeing it and handing it down to Master Armory. The mason opened up a narrow space.

"Lantern," he requested.

Master Armory handed him the lantern from the fireplace mantel.

The mason held the light close to the hole and looked inside. He reached into the hole and removed the first brick. He handed the brick and the lantern to Master Armory and proceeded to chip away at the mortar.

After freeing several more bricks, the mason measured the opening with his arms and descended the ladder. "That should do."

Master Armory nodded and climbed the ladder.

"Boys!" he yelled. The broomers approached the fireplace.

Master Armory glared at Egan and looked for Will. "Will, climb and push him up when I say."

"It's real hot, Will," Egan whispered a warning to Will.

Will nodded and ducked into the hearth. Egan watched his feet disappear just as Pitt's had an hour earlier. Egan listened to the sounds of Will's movements.

"Ready," Will called out to Master Armory.

Master Armory leaned into the hole above.

"Push," Master Armory ordered.

Master Armory clutched Pitt under the armpits and struggled to lift him up through the hole in the bricks. Egan watched in misery as Master Armory dropped Pitt's lifeless torso onto the bricks outside the hole. Pitt's scorched arms dangled.

"Catch him," Master Armory ordered, pulling Pitt's legs from the hole and lowering him down towards the broomers' outstretched hands. Egan backed into a corner as the boys placed Pitt on the floor.

"That's not Pitt," Tick said, shaking his head.

Master Armory descended the ladder and bent down to inspect the body. Pitt was unrecognizable. His short hair was gone. His skin had been burned away with his clothes. His face was distorted in terror.

Master Armory angrily kicked Pitt in the side a couple of times. The body heaved indifferently. Life's breath had long since abandoned the scant bones.

"Get that thing out of here!" Mister Calvert insisted.

"Take him to All Hallows Staining," Master Armory ordered.

The broomers remained still, looking at Pitt's crumpled form in shock.

"The peasant's pit! Now! Take him!" Armory lifted his fist and yelled.

Adam's heart snapped, and he erupted with a cry, "But it's Pitt!"

Master Armory backhanded Adam, throwing him to the floor. "He's no use to me now. I'd lament the death of a dog I hated more."

Will helped Adam to his feet, and the broomers bent to lift Pitt's body.

Rory and Will, being the largest boys, stooped to put their arms around Pitt's middle while Egan, Tick, and Adam grasped the lifeless shoulders and head. Andrew and Iggy grasped the knees, and the boys lifted the blistered body. Pitt's blood rubbed onto their blackened clothes as his body lay suspended, burned, and broken in their arms. A reddish black mark of blood and soot remained upon the floor.

The broomers exited the brewery into the cold winter morning. Those out on the quiet morning streets parted for the boys to pass. The climbing boys were noticed only for the entertainment value of the corpse they carried. People stared and then pulled their eyes away from the mutilated body. A woman opening the seamstress shop let out a shriek of revulsion before fainting in the doorway. Several onlookers rushed to revive her. No one offered to help the little boys struggling to carry their fallen friend.

Outside the church gate, the boys found a young clergyman praying over a recent grave. Solemnly, he beckoned the boys forward.

"Have you money for a private burial?"

"No, Reverend," Will answered.

"Bring him here," the clergyman instructed, pulling a cloth up to cover his nose and mouth.

The broomers followed him to a section in the far back of the graveyard where a large pile of earth had been removed from the ground. The smell of death grew stronger with each step. The poor hole was near six or seven feet wide and deep, very deep. The bottom was already stacked three deep with bodies.

"Throw the body in," the clergyman instructed.

Egan's eyes filled with tears as he looked up at the man, silently pleading for a moment of compassion.

Above the face covering, the clergyman's eyes softened. "Put him down on the ground."

The boys followed this second command, arranging Pitt carefully on the damp grass. The clergyman drew a wee book from his robe and began to read from its pages.

"Unto thee, O Lord, do I lift up my soul. Remember, O Lord, thy tender mercies and thy lovingkindness; for they have been ever of old. Remember not the sins of my youth, nor my transgressions: according to thy mercy remember thou me for thy goodness' sake, O Lord.

"This is the word of our Lord, Psalm 25." The clergyman closed the book, bowed his head, and prayed, "Lord, may your mercy be bestowed upon this child. May you bless him with the grace he knoweth not in this life. Take him into your arms and heal his wounds so that he may know your everlasting love. Amen."

"Amen," the boys echoed softly.

"I shall see to the body. Would you like to say any words before you depart?"

Iggy shook his head and backed away; his expression told the story of the grief he fought to control.

Andrew choked back tears, "Farewell, Pitt."

"Farewell, Pitt," the others echoed.

"I love thee, me brother," Will said.

"An tiarna déan trócaire a anam," Rory muttered.

Egan began to back away but then collapsed on the corpse in gasping cries of pain. "Wot 'bout the sea? You've never seen it, Pitt, you've never seen it," Egan wailed.

The clergyman wrapped Egan in his arms and lifted him from the ground. The clergyman started to walk them away from the peasant's pit, but Egan's blackened hands clawed at the departing robe. The clergyman drew Egan to his side and hugged him fiercely, allowing the pain to dispel into piercing cries of sorrow.

"He didn't want to climb. He was scared," Egan choked.

"Death has a thousand doors my lad, one for each of us."

"But why, Pitt?" Egan sobbed.

"It was his time. When your door comes, you'll walk through and leave someone crying over you. It's just the way of this world."

"Only Pitt would have cried for me," Egan murmured. He released the clergyman's robes and stumbled between the gravestones to the street.

"Sweep with me today," Will beckoned to Egan.

Egan shook his head and walked away. He wandered through the approaching daylight until he was back on Distaff Lane. He snuck into the house and went down into the cellar to curl up on his ashes. He surrendered to the respite of a troubled sleep.

CHAPTER XXXV

E gan woke to the dim light of the cellar.

He could not stay here anymore. He could not stay here without Pitt.

Egan sat up and stared at Pitt's shoes. Pitt had given Egan more than his shoes. Pitt had given Egan all of his hope. Egan removed the thin cloth pad in each shoe and collected the coins that Pitt had carefully arranged in the soles. Some coins were stacked four deep.

Egan looked at Pitt's coins. He recognized the guinea, shillings, and pence coins, but two other types were new to him.

Egan wished Pitt were there to count the money. He knew he needed five guineas, but could not figure out how much the coins were worth. Anyone who saw his coins would rob him or cheat him. He needed Pitt.

Egan carefully arranged the coins in the shoes and placed them back on his feet. He could think of only one person that could help him. Egan climbed the stairs and slipped through the kitchen, which bustled with the cooking of Master Armory's evening meal. Two people he did not recognize worked alongside Miss Clara, frantically setting about the food.

Egan quietly exited through the back door and found his way through the alley. He sought out the narrow street where Pitt led him on his first day in London. The buildings and people no longer overwhelmed him. The wealthy were as invisible to Egan as he was to them.

Egan found the alleyway door that he sought and knocked softly.

A bulky man answered and peered down at him.

"Is Missus Bixby in?"

"No, young sweep, but come in. I can help you," the man answered.

"Are you Missus Bixby's mister?"

"I guess I am," Mister Bixby chuckled. "Come sit up here." Mister Bixby patted the embalming table.

There were no bodies lying about as before. Egan thought that he should have brought Pitt here and used his savings for a proper burial. The shoes were heavy on his feet.

Egan stepped up on the stool and slid himself onto the table with a grunt of pain.

Mister Bixby helped Egan out of his shirt and then cut the remaining charred clothing away from his skin.

"Not even the dead should look like this," Mister Bixby muttered, inspecting Egan's wounds. The undertaker started to clean Egan's charred skin with a rag and saltwater. Egan winced as the rag cleaned the gash on his head.

"Sir, I need some help," Egan began.

"I see that you do."

"Not doctoring help, but other help," Egan said, hoping he could trust this man.

"Let's take care of this first."

Mister Bixby applied a foul-smelling ointment that seared into the blistered flesh with a potent burning sensation.

"It will help you heal," Mister Bixby said in response to Egan's reaction.

The undertaker pulled a clean rag from the shelf and wiped Egan's face, cleaning the grime from the blisters. He went to the back room and brought out a shirt.

"This should fit. He was a wee man," the undertaker grinned as he helped Egan into the new shirt.

"Thank ye," Egan said in a small, subdued voice as tears splashed down his cheeks.

"Now wot is it that you need?" Mister Bixby asked.

"Me friend, Pitt, died in a chimney fire this morning," Egan started, choking back tears. "He gave me his shoes, the ones Missus Bixby give him."

"Those are fine shoes. He would have wanted you to have them."

"I don't know how to count, not everything," Egan blurted out.

Mister Bixby considered the statement. "Do you need help counting?"

"Yes, sir." Egan pulled the shoes from his feet and peeled back the worn padding.

"You need help counting the coins?"

Egan nodded, hugging the shoes to his chest. If the man took them, he would have nothing.

"I'm here to help you. I'm not going to steal from you."

Egan nodded and set the shoes on the embalming table.

"Well," Mister Bixby started, pulling the coins from the shoes. "This is a guinea. It's gentlemen's money and is worth a shilling more than a pound. You have two pounds here," he said, pointing to two silver coins.

"I need five guineas."

"I see. That's a large sum. Well, if you add a shilling to each of yer pounds, they equal a guinea." Mister Bixby set the guinea, pounds, and shillings to the side. "That's worth three guineas."

"That means I need just two more guineas."

"Aye. You have seven shillings, half a crown, sixteen pence, and seven farthings." Mister Bixby identified the different coins.

Egan looked at the undertaker expectantly. "How much is that?"

"Twelve pence equals a shilling. Twenty-one shillings equals a guinea. Half a crown is two shillings and a sixpence. Yer farthings equal one and three-quarters pence. Yer coins are worth a little over six shillings."

Egan became lost in the explanation. "How many shillings are in a guinea?"

"Twenty-one."

"Am I close to that many?"

"Not quite. To make a guinea, you need a shilling for each finger and toe you have, plus one. Do you have all yer fingers and toes?"

"Aye. I think so."

"Let me see yer hands first. One, two, three...". Mister Bixbey counted to twenty for Egan, pointing to each finger and toe as he counted. "Plus one more equals twenty-one."

"Now a shilling is twelve pence. One for each finger plus two."

Egan looked at his coins and then at his fingers.

"So I still need most of the two guineas."

"You do." Mister Bixby organized the coins and stacked them back into the soles of the shoes. "You shouldn't let anyone know you have these coins. There are thieves a plenty in London who wouldn't think twice about killing you for them."

"That's wot Pitt said too."

"If you need help counting, you can come to me."

"Thank ye."

"I know them shoes," Missus Bixby said from the doorway. She removed her bonnet and set her basket down on the embalming table. She searched Egan's eyes for an explanation.

"Pitt got stuck. The chimney, it was burning," Egan choked.

Missus Bixby collected Egan in her arms in a gentle hug as fresh tears flowed from his swollen eyes.

"He's in a peasant pit. I should have brought him here," Egan cried.

"There now, the good Lord blessed him with an early grave. There's a small blessin' in that, and there's naught much to be done about it now," Missus Bixby comforted.

Egan clung to Missus Bixby. Her arms felt like Mum.

CHAPTER XXXVI

"Get up, you!" Rory shouted.

Egan turned a lifeless gaze towards the back wall.

"Get up!"

"Egan, you have to get up," Will implored.

"No matter wot happened to Pitt, we gots to get started," Adam added.

"I don't know how to," Egan responded.

"Just like all days. We get our gruel and head out to the streets. Earn Master Armory's wages then scrounge extra for the belly. You gots to get up." Andrew's reasoning was sound and Egan knew a whipping waited for him if he stayed in the cellar, but it did not matter what happened next. It did not matter to Pitt anymore, so it did not matter to Egan.

"Egan, please," Iggy whispered.

Rory crossed the cellar, lifted Egan's head up by his collar, and smacked him across the face.

"No!" Tick yelled.

Rory turned and smacked Tick across the face. Then he returned to Egan and lifted him again by the collar.

"Get up," Rory's hushed voice was vile in Egan's ear. "I will not have any cheek. Pitt was too easy on the lot of you."

Rory retrieved his pail and tools and took his place at the front of the line. Egan pulled himself up, gathered his tools, and joined the back of the line. Rory glanced back at Egan with a depraved grin.

"Everyone brings me a tuppence tonight before paying Master Armory," Rory ordered.

The broomers acknowledged Rory's authority and followed him up the stairs. Will was second in line. Egan wished it were Will watching over him.

"Morning boys, I am so sorry about Pitt," Miss Clara's eyes were full of tears. "He was such a good soul."

She handed out the bowls of gruel and kissed each grimy head.

"I'll wash you up tomorrow," she said with a sniffle.

"Thank ye," Will said to Miss Clara.

Master Armory stamped into the room dressed in his formal sweeping clothes. He donned the black tailored suit only when sweeping an affluent estate house. Inspecting the broomers, he pointed to Tick, Egan, Adam, and Iggy.

"You four are with me this morning."

"Sir, I'm also at yer service." Rory stepped forward.

"I only need the smallest ones."

"Yes, sir," Rory responded, giving the others a stern look of warning.

"Are you the leader now?" Master Armory asked Rory.

"Yes, sir."

"You don't look fit for the job."

"I'm a better man than Pitt ever was," Rory answered.

"Bollocks. Pitt sold hisself to me. Two shillings for his pock-ridden father dying in a workhouse. Do you have those kind of balls?" Master Armory challenged.

Rory lowered his head.

"Do you?"

"No, sir." Rory clutched his fists.

"Do any of you?" Master Armory yelled.

The broomers bowed their heads, stunned by the revelation.

A man always pays his debts, Pitt had told Egan. Pitt would never sail the seas, ride a horse in the country, or breathe another day because he was too honorable to abandon an unjust obligation.

Egan seethed with anger. He balled his fists and flew at Master Armory in a rage, screaming and slamming his fists into the detestable man.

Will and Iggy tried to pull Egan away, but Master Armory pushed them back and picked Egan up around the waist. Egan's arms and legs flailed, trying to attack anything within reach. Master Armory flung Egan down the cellar stairs, retrieved his whip, and descended the stairs as Egan was lifting himself up.

"Bloody miserable wretch!" Master Armory yelled.

The whip cracked across Egan's chest. Egan cried out in pain and bent over to protect himself. Master Armory let the whip fly against Egan's back, ripping away his clothes and tearing bloody ridges through his flesh. When the whip sliced through the charred flesh on Egan's face, Egan saw Master Armory smile.

Egan cowered in the shadow of cruelty. Master Armory threw the whip aside and pounded Egan with his fists. He punched Egan in the face and then in the gut before picking Egan up by the legs and tossing him against the wall. With one final kick to the side, he swaggered over to the staircase.

"You bloody shite," Master Armory said in a dark, raspy voice. "That's less of a beating than you deserve, but I don't want to lose me investment. Be ready to sweep tomorrow."

With a satisfied smirk and a laugh that pushed a puff of air and snot through his nostrils, Master Armory climbed the stairs and locked Egan in the cellar.

Egan huddled in the corner of the cellar with his arms wrapped tightly around his bent knees. He feared to move, not even to seek the comfort of a bag of ash. Pain seared through his back and neck as blood trickled down from the gashes in his soiled and burned skin. As the shock began to fade, Egan's chest tightened with tears that ran uncontrollably down his face. He sobbed, releasing tears of regret and loss.

Surrendering to the bitter reality of his existence, Egan leaned his head against the wall only to relive Master Armory's savageness in his sleep.

When he woke, a dim light was shining through the cracks in the ceiling. It illuminated the cellar in an almost beautiful way. Egan's drowsy eyes watched the swirling dust as his heart searched for the resolve to pick up his body. Stiff and weary, Egan crawled to his bed of ashes. As he extended his body, his clothes ripped from his skin where the fabric had been soaked by blood. He winced as blood trickled anew from the crimson stripes across his back.

Egan hunched on his side. His fingers landed on an upturned stone at the edge of his sack. He flattened the burlap over its smooth form. It felt like a stone from the banks of the River Thames – smooth and worn down by the water.

This was Reeves' sack of ashes. It would belong to someone else when Egan was dead. Egan looked over to where Pitt had slept. Pitt's familiar form had disappeared. Rory had formed a new bed for himself using Pitt's ashes.

"It was me fault. I made him angry," Egan whispered to Pitt.

Egan shifted his feet and tried to find a comfortable position on his side. The coins were heavy in the shoes. Maybe he should give the coins to Master Armory. Maybe the coins would make Master Armory forgive him. Maybe he would apologize for hitting Egan. Maybe the coins would fix everything.

"No," Egan's voice stopped his thoughts abruptly. "I can't fix him," he spoke loudly in the empty room. Missus Winchester was right. Some people cannot be fixed.

Egan lifted himself up, unfolded the top of Reeves' sack, and dug his hand into the ash. He felt around for the stone, grasped it, and freed it from the ash. Tucking the ends of the sack back under, Egan opened his palm. It was not a stone. It was something encased in viscid soot.

Ignoring the blood dripping down his arms, Egan rubbed at the trinket with a frayed piece of burlap. His efforts proved futile. He needed water and the bristled broom he had deposited that morning in the narrow hallway above.

Egan gently lay back down on his sacks. He held the object between his palms and succumbed once again to sleep. His dreams at first were comforting. A family whose faces had been erased by time. There was love in the dream, comfort and warmth that twisted into Pitt's fiery chimney of death.

"I cannot move," Pitt had said.

"I cannot move," Egan repeated, awakening to muscles frozen in pain.

Egan's throat was raw from dehydration. His stomach ached from hunger. He limped up the stairs to find the door still locked. It was too early for the broomers to return.

"The pheasant is ready," a husky voice announced. Egan heard multiple sets of feet racing across the kitchen floor. Master and Missus Armory were being served dinner.

The thought of Master Armory eating his fill as if it were a regular day should have made Egan angry, but his anger was gone. His sorrow was gone. He was empty. He clutched the trinket between his palms, limped to his bed of ash, and prayed for a way out of the cellar. A way out forever. When the quest for comfort failed, Egan began singing Will and Tick's sweeping song. He made up verses for Pitt. Verses to remember Pitt. Verses to say farewell.

When the broomers trudged through the back door a few hours later, Egan slipped the trinket into his pocket.

Rory unlocked the cellar door and stamped down with an air of authority. The other broomers descended cautiously, looking to Egan and assessing his condition.

"Will," Miss Clara whispered.

Will went back to the top of the stairs. He returned with a glass of water, slice of bread, and wet washing cloth for Egan.

Will handed the glass to Egan. "Drink," he ordered in a soft voice.

Egan gratefully accepted the water and the bread. Will attempted to attend his wounds, but the blood had already scabbed and hardened. It was difficult to determine what was burned flesh and what the whip gouged.

"All right there, Egan?" Tick asked.

"No, you don't. No pity for that stupid foul git." Rory picked up Master Armory's discarded whip and looped it around his arm. "You best not anger me neither," he warned Tick.

Tick shrank from Rory's shadow and curled up on his sacks. When Rory turned his back, Iggy reached over and placed his hand lightly on Egan's back.

"Five guineas to freedom," Iggy whispered.

The next morning, Egan took his place at the end of the line.

"Don't forget you owe me a tuppence," Rory sneered. "Egan, you owe me four pence. Yesterday weren't no day off for you."

The broomers nodded obediently and climbed the steps. Egan's tools were waiting at the top of the stairs for him, as was Master Armory. Egan bowed his head respectfully, tensing his muscles in preparation for another thrashing. Mercifully, it did not come.

"Good. You know yer place. Naught wrong that a good whipping can't fix."

"Yes, sir," Egan replied meekly.

"Two shillings by nightfall," Master Armory ordered.

"Yes, sir."

"Out with you," Master Armory commanded.

Egan grabbed his tools and hobbled out the back door alone while the others ate their morning gruel. He was hungry, but the ache in his gut did not damper his relief to be out of the house.

Part Five
London, 1722

"[T]he master, who gives credit to his apprentice…is answerable for his neglect."

-Armory v. Delamirie (1722)

CHAPTER XXXVII

E gan tried to stretch his battered body on the walk to the Little Conduit. His left eye was swollen shut. His burned skin throbbed where the blackened wounds began to fester. The lashings and bruises from Master Armory overwhelmed his every step. Egan tried to ignore the pain and compensate for his strained movements with speed. He had work to do and did not have time to mope about.

The keeper at the conduit let Egan draw an inch of water from the cistern and pour it into his metal pail. Brewers, cooks, fishmongers, and other businesses would pay for their substantial use of the water, but Egan's request for a few drops was of little interest to the keeper's purse.

Egan looked around at the gathering crowd of sweeps. First light was approaching, and the road was getting crowded. He carried the water towards a quiet street and found a solitary doorway. The shopkeeper would not open for several hours, and Egan could work uninterrupted.

He retrieved the trinket from his pocket and swished it in the freezing water. Using the edge of his burlap sack, he scrubbed the soot from the object.

The slow process revealed more than a cheap trinket. A round red stone glistened from the center surrounded by three encircling rows of tiny white seed pearls in a gold casting. Two of the pearls were missing, but the pendant was exquisite. Egan thought of the ribbon Mum wore around her neck; it was the same red color as the large round stone.

Egan turned the pendant over in his palm. A golden clasp was fastened to the back, and a letter in ornate writing was engraved on the surface. Egan had seen jewels worn by the wealthy but had never held such a fine piece. He wondered how it found its way into Reeves' sack.

Egan's heart expanded in his chest, pumping blood in loud spurts that rang in his ears. He grasped the pendant tightly. This jewel had to be worth at least two guineas.

He cautiously looked around; the side street was still empty. He scrubbed the remaining soot from the pendant, wrapped it in his cleanest rag, and concealed it safely in his pocket.

Egan collected his tools and walked down the street, looking through windows into the shops. A goldsmith would buy the pendant from him. He could sell it and deliver five guineas to Master Armory before Rory could press him for a brass farthing. He would find Leadenhall Street and be a ship's boy by tomorrow morning.

"Looking for business, sweep?" a voice interrupted Egan's thoughtful planning. The words came from a shopkeeper who was opening a store across the street.

"No, a goldsmith," Egan replied, crossing the street to speak with the man.

The shopkeeper chuckled, "In the market for a golden crown? Or maybe a set of silver goblets fer yer dinner table?"

"No, sir, I was to sweep for a goldsmith this morning, but I don't remember where to find his shop," Egan lied. He bit his lower lip and waited for an answer.

"Closest to here is on Cheapside, just down the street there."

Egan looked down the street. Master Armory knew the merchants in this area.

"He weren't near here."

"There is Paul de Lamerie on Great Windmill Street. He's goldsmith to King George."

"I think that be his name." A second lie.

"He has a house on Great Windmill Street near the Haymarket. It's a good walk from here. Who is yer master? Do you sweep near the Haymarket often?"

"I sweep anywhere there's work. I'll be on me way. Thank ye, sir."

Egan hustled past the dark shops and disappeared around the corner.

"Great Windmill Street near the Haymarket," Egan repeated to himself.

Haymarket was a fair distance away. Egan had worked in the area between Holborn Road and The Strand a couple of times with Pitt, but he had never worked that far away on his own. It would take him at least an hour to walk there the way his body ached. It would be easier without his sweeping tools.

Egan glanced around, settling on the churchyard of a nearby parish. He placed his pail, brushes, ash sack, and wooden pole beneath a bush. The tools were hidden from the road but obvious from inside the gate. No one would be working in the churchyard in winter, and his tools should still be there when he returned in a few hours.

Free of his burdens, Egan moved quickly over Holborn Bridge and walked the distance of Holborn Road to St. Giles High Street and up Tottenham Court Road towards the Haymarket.

The Haymarket was a pleasant place. The air was fresher in this part of London, and most of the residents had some means of living. Egan admired the ornamental houses of eminent tradesmen that lined the streets. He passed the imposing King's Theatre, empty in the daylight, and approached the large carts in the middle of the street, laden with hay and straw brought in from the country for the winter-feeding of horses. He breathed in the fresh smell of hay and smiled at the nearby farmers.

Egan walked up the street, looking into shops and checking the cobblestone corners for a windmill to identify the right street. He studied the letters on a street sign and wished again that he could read. Around the next bend, Egan saw a large sign hanging from the side of a building. Yellow letters on its face pronounced the name of a business.

Egan approached the building and looked through the dirty, square windows. The small front room was empty. Egan opened the door, ringing the bell affixed to the door's molding by a curving strip of metal.

A young man appeared from a door behind the wooden counter.

"Get out you. No charity today," he waved at Egan to leave.

"I have business with Mister de Lamerie."

"You do, do you?"

"Aye, I want to see him."

"Well, come in then. I apprentice for Mister de Lamerie. Charles Greville at yer service."

Egan entered the shop warily. He could barely see above the long counter, behind which stood a small desk occupied by a set of scales and various tools.

"Where is Mister de Lamerie?"

"Working in the shop. No customers are allowed back there. I conduct his business here while he is working."

Egan retrieved the pendant from his pocket, unwrapped it, and held it up between his fingers. "How much would you give me for this?"

The apprentice's expression softened at the sight of the pendant. The red stone sparkled in the light sifting through the dingy windows. "Let me take a look." Charles held out his hand.

Egan hesitated.

"I can't offer a price if I can't inspect and weigh the jewel."

Egan reluctantly handed over the pendant.

Charles took the pendant and sat down at the desk. He picked up a round copper instrument and stared through the glass in its center. "Very nice. Good color. Good clarity. Who did you filch this from?"

"I didn't filch it! I found it."

"Yeah, and who lost it?"

"I don't know. Some noble lady I spec."

The apprentice stared at Egan through squinted eyes.

"I'll need to remove the stones for weighing."

"Remove the stones?"

"Take it out of the casting. The weight of the casting is separate from the price of the stones."

"All right, then," Egan said uncertainly.

In silence, the apprentice stood and took the pendant through the door behind the counter. Egan sat on a chair in the corner and waited for the sound of his feet to return. He leaned his head back, resting against the windowpane and looked about the shop.

The walls of the room were bare. Other than the sign outside that Egan could not read, nothing advertised Lamerie's work. Items fashioned from silver and gold were as good as money, which one did not leave on display in a public shop.

Egan let his thoughts wander back to his plans. He could almost imagine the sea air on his face. When he earned his way on a sailing vessel, he would return to find Mum and Kerrin. He had failed to take care of them when Da died. He would not fail them again. He and Pitt would work hard.

Pitt was gone. It did not seem possible, but Pitt was dead. Egan had made an oath that he would not sail the seas without Pitt. He would break that oath. Just as he had lied this morning, he would break his oath to Pitt. Lying and breaking promises, what kind of boy was he?

Charles came back through the door and sat down at the desk. Egan stood to watch over the counter as he balanced objects on opposite sides of the scale.

"Sir, it comes to three halfpence," Charles shouted through the open door towards the back room.

"Well, welcome young sweep," Lamerie greeted as he came through the back door. He wiped sweat from his brow with a rolled shirtsleeve. "It's not often we have climbing boys in the shop during casting days. Too hot for climbing to be sure."

Lamerie pulled a purse from his pocket and picked out three coins. "There's three halfpence for you lad."

"Three halfpence? It's worth at least two guineas!"

"It's not worth two pence," Charles said.

"Three halfpence is my price," Lamerie affirmed.

Egan drew himself towards the counter, confused with disbelief. The pendant should fetch a much better price.

"No, I'll keep it," Egan held out his palm.

Lamerie slipped the coins back into his purse, nodded towards his apprentice, and retreated to the back room.

Charles placed the empty casting on the desk. "There. Off you go."

Egan looked down at the empty casting on the counter.

"Where are the stones? I want the stones."

"Wot stones? You only brought in this worthless casting of brass."

"I want the red stone and the little white stones back!"

"I don't know wot you mean."

"You can't take them. They're not yers!" Egan shrieked.

"They're not yours either, you little thief!"

Charles's face twisted into a deceitful grin. "Who would believe that a climbing boy owned such a pendant? No one I know," he whispered.

"They're mine!"

"Wot's the problem here?" Bennett walked into the front shop.

"He took me jewels! I want them back!"

"Is that true?" Bennett asked.

"Of course not! Now get out before I bloody ruin yer other eye!" Charles yelled at Egan.

Egan's eyes filled with hot tears, his fury reignited from the day before. He grabbed the casting from the counter and ran out the door, slamming it with every ounce of wrath his broken body could muster.

Egan ran down Tottenham Court Road, releasing his anger as scabs painfully twisted and pulled from his body with the exertion.

If Egan told the constable, would the constable believe him? What if the constable thought he stole the pendant? He could be sent to Newgate Prison. Maybe they would cut his hand off.

By the time he arrived at the Holborn Bridge, Egan knew there was only one person that might believe him.

CHAPTER XXXVIII

"Runt, you're doing the Tyburn jig. Out with it. What heinous thing have you done now?"

"Inside me sack of ash was a jewel, a pendant."

The corner of Master Armory's mouth twitched. "Give it here."

"I can't. I took it to a goldsmith to sell to pay me debt," Egan confessed.

"Pay yer debt then." Master Armory held out an open palm.

"I can't. He said it were worth three halfpence, and I wouldn't take it. I wanted more, enough to pay me debt."

Master Armory pursed his thin lips.

"I said I'd keep it, not sell it, and he gave me back only the casting. He stole the stones from me."

Egan pulled the casting from his pocket and handed it to Master Armory.

"You were keeping this from me?" Blood rushed to Master Armory's face.

"I just found it." Egan cowered.

Master Armory stood and smacked Egan to the floor in one sweeping motion.

"I'm sorry! Please no!" Egan cried.

"How dare you! After yer lesson yesterday, you hid this from me?" Master Armory yelled.

"I didn't, sir. I didn't hide it," Egan pleaded.

"Wot is wrong now?" A woman's voice called out just moments before she walked into the study.

"The boy says he found this pendant." Master Armory held the empty casing out to the woman. "He tried to sell it and was robbed."

"What did the stones look like, dear? The ones that were in this casting?" the woman asked Egan.

"One was big in the middle, and wee ones were 'round it."

"What color were the stones?" she asked as her finger traced the elegant curves of the metal.

"The big one was red, and the others were round white balls."

"Were the stones clear?"

"The big red one was, but not the wee ones," Egan said.

"Daniel, the stones could be valuable. A ruby with seed pearls perhaps."

Master Armory snatched the casing from the woman's hand and inspected it. "There's an "E" inscribed on the back. Did you find it at the Edward's house, or Exter or Eplett? At a house with an "E" in the name?"

"No, it were in the ash I got from Reeves. But I found it. It's mine."

Master Armory began to lunge at Egan, but the woman stopped him.

"Of course, you dear boy," she purred.

"It's mine to pay me debt," Egan grew bolder.

"And you shall get the stones back, won't he Daniel?"

Master Armory looked at the woman and then down towards Egan. "Which goldsmith did you call on?"

"Mister Paul de Lamerie on Great Windmill Street."

"John!" Master Armory shouted.

The manservant bounded into the room.

"Hire a carriage."

"Yes, sir," he replied and was gone.

"Clara!" Master Armory barked. "Clara!"

Miss Clara scurried into the room. "Yes, sir?"

"Wash him up."

"Yes, sir. Egan, come with me. Come here now," Miss Clara beckoned.

Miss Clara pulled Egan into the kitchen and attacked him with a wet rag and a bar of soap. She was a bit rough around his black eye and the burned skin on his cheek. "I'm sorry, dearie. I know it hurts."

Egan could barely lift his arms to help Miss Clara pull off his tattered shirt.

"Oh good Lord Almighty," she whispered.

His body was a collage of blisters, welts, bruises, and lacerations.

Egan looked up at Miss Clara. "It was me fault."

"No dear, it weren't." Miss Clara looked towards the dining room before whispering, "Be careful not to make him cross today. Yer body needs to heal."

Egan nodded.

"Wash yer hands, and I'll be right back," Miss Clara instructed and left the room.

Egan scrubbed his blackened hands, but the soot was unrelenting. He resorted to using the wet cloth, now black with soot, to swirl black designs on his palms.

When Miss Clara came back, she glared her disapproval with his progress and set a bundle of clothes on the table.

"Yer filthy, but I guess yer cleaner than you were. It will have to do. Now shed to yer small clothes and get into these." Miss Clara pointed to the pile on the table.

The navy blue suit and white stockings looked like clothes for a child from a wealthy family, like those boys he had seen at the school.

"Don't waste time. The carriage will be here any moment."

Egan obeyed. When he had trouble trying to put the stockings over the knickers, Miss Clara dove in to help him dress.

"Miss Clara, who is that woman with Master Armory?"

"That's the Missus Armory."

"Is she nice?"

"Maybe so. I don't rightly know."

Fully clothed, the expensive suit hung over Egan's tiny frame.

"Where did you get these clothes?" Egan asked.

"Master Armory keeps this one set for when he needs to take a climbing boy somewhere looking 'spectable," Miss Clara answered as she patted down Egan's short, thick hair. "You need a head shave, but there's no time. Now go wait by the door."

Egan walked towards the kitchen door.

"No, dear. The front door."

"I should walk through the house?"

"Aye, go wait for Master Armory by the front door."

Egan peered into the hallway and cautiously walked to the front door. John was already waiting by the door.

A few seconds later, there was a knock. John answered the door as Master Armory descended from upstairs. He had cleaned himself up as well. He retrieved the empty casting from the study, slipped it into his drawstring pouch, pulled the strings tight, and roped it over his belt.

"Come," Master Armory ordered as he exited the house.

Egan followed him outside where a carriage was waiting. A footman held the door open, and Master Armory entered the carriage.

"Paul de Lamerie's shop on Great Windmill Street near the Haymarket," Master Armory told the footman.

The footman nodded and waited at the open door.

"Get in," Master Armory barked from inside the carriage.

Egan was hesitant. He had never ridden in a carriage before. Impatient, the footman grabbed Egan and lifted him inside. Egan sat on the seat opposite Master Armory as the footman shut the door and the carriage started a jaunty glide across the cobblestones.

Egan curled his hands under the edge of the cushioned bench, trying to remain seated as the carriage jarred across London. He held himself as stiff as possible, wincing in pain with each jolt. As exciting as his first carriage ride was, Egan wished he was walking instead.

Egan looked down at his new clothes. He looked at the fine carriage. He looked at Master Armory, who gave him a slight smile.

"Are you enjoying this ride?"

"Very much, sir," Egan responded.

Master Armory's eyes were lit with anticipation; he needed a good fight to liven his day. Egan felt a great amount of relief that he was no longer the subject of his master's aggression.

"When we get there, show me the man, and then keep yer mouth shut. Understand?"

"Yes, sir." Egan looked out the carriage window and watched the buildings and people disappear from their view. Traveling by carriage was thrilling, leaving no empty spaces for Egan to contemplate the confrontation ahead.

All too quickly, the carriage slowed to a stop in front of Lamerie's shop.

"Is this the shop?" Master Armory asked looking out the window.

"Yes, sir."

The footman opened the door, and Egan followed Master Armory down the metal steps.

Master Armory opened the shop door, which announced his arrival with the ring of the bell. The apprentice promptly appeared in the doorway behind the counter.

"Good day sir. How may I assist you?" Charles greeted Master Armory.

"Boy?"

The apprentice appeared confused until Egan stepped out from behind Master Armory. "That is him, sir, the one that took the stones."

Charles folded his arms across his chest defensively.

"I have business with Mister de Lamerie. Get him," Master Armory ordered the apprentice.

"I am his apprentice, Charles Greville at yer service. You can do your business with me."

"Get de Lamerie," Master Armory ordered.

Reluctantly, Charles retreated through the doorway. Moments later, Lamerie entered the room with the apprentice behind him, much as Egan hid behind Master Armory. This was a matter for the masters, not their boys.

"How many I be of service?" Lamerie asked curtly.

Master Armory retrieved the casting from his pouch. "Me boy brought you this pendant to appraise and sell. Instead of offering him a fair price, you stole the stones from him."

"I did nothing of the sort. Your boy is mistaken."

"It was yer apprentice!" Egan pointed at Charles.

Master Armory glared at Egan. Remembering his place, Egan stepped back.

"Yer apprentice removed and kept the stones. As his master, you are responsible for his actions," Master Armory asserted.

Lamerie pulled Charles towards the counter. "Have you done this thing?"

"The boy stole the pendant. He has no right to keep it."

"He found it, and it belongs to him," Master Armory pounded his fist on the counter.

"Your boy is a thief, and I do not conduct business with thieves," Lamerie countered.

"Yer reputation suggests otherwise," Master Armory accused.

"Get out!" Lamerie shouted.

"Did you beat me boy also? Look at his bruises," Master Armory grabbed Egan's chin and lifted his swollen eye for inspection. "Why else would you do that, except to steal from him?"

"I did not strike him!" Lamerie said.

"Not you, but yer apprentice did!"

"I did not touch him!" Charles was flummoxed.

"Get out before I call the constable!" Lamerie threatened.

"Return the stones or the constable will be coming for you!" Master Armory yelled.

"Out of my shop!" Lamerie shouted.

"I'll take this to the king!" Master Armory bellowed and exited the shop in a fury, the bell clanging spitefully behind him.

Egan obediently followed Master Armory back into the carriage. He shrunk into his seat and stared at Pitt's shoes. Master Armory's rage fumed as the blood rushed to his face.

The return carriage ride was long. The excitement of the earlier trip was forgotten as the silence stretched painfully under Master Armory's condemnatory stare.

When the carriage swayed to a stop, Master Armory bounded out of the carriage and into the house on Distaff Lane, opening doors for himself. Egan ran to keep up with his master's quick stride.

"Clara!" Master Armory shouted upon entering the house.

Miss Clara bustled from the formal dining room into the hall.

"Yes, sir."

"Watch him," Master Armory pointed to Egan. He left Egan with Miss Clara and entered his study where John was stoking the coals in the fireplace.

"Yes, sir. Egan, come," she waved her hand to beckon Egan.

Egan followed her to the kitchen. A bulky woman was pounding dough on the flour-covered table. She looked up and winked at Egan. He had never seen her before.

"Finish with him and get going on the potatoes," she instructed Miss Clara. He had heard that husky voice through the floor last night.

"Yes, mum. Egan, this is Missus McGivney, the finest cook in London."

"None of that now," Missus McGivney responded with a smile.

"Egan, change into yer sweeping clothes," Miss Clara directed.

Egan obeyed. It never occurred to him that Miss Clara took orders from anyone other than Master and Missus Armory. She was the only servant about early in the morning and late at night. As Egan dressed, Miss Clara retrieved potatoes from a wooden bin in the corner of the kitchen. She placed them on the edge of the table and began peeling the skins into an empty bowl.

Egan changed, folded the fine clothes into a pile on the floor, and headed for the back door.

"And where do you think yer going?" Miss Clara asked.

"To get me tools. I left them in the churchyard this morning, and I need to earn a day's wages before the others get back."

"Yer not going anywhere, not until Master Armory says so."

"But Miss Clara, I need to get me tools before they get snatched."

"Call John to go with the boy," Missus McGivney told Miss Clara.

She wiped her hands on her apron and left the kitchen to fetch John.

"Me son was a climbing boy for Master Armory," Missus McGivney smiled at Egan. "I remember scrubbing the soot from his face in this very kitchen."

"Wot was his name?"

"Elijah, named after his da and, of course, the prophet who prayed to God to send fire down from the sky," her eyes welled tears as she smiled.

"He was crushed when a chimney collapsed, but the fire never burned him. Wouldn't touch him on account of his name. The broomers called him Eli. Just Eli. He was a good boy," she said as she pounded the dough, rolled it into loaf-sized sections, and set it into two pans.

Miss Clara entered the room with John.

"Where are yer tools?"

"At the churchyard."

"Which one?"

"The one by Aldersgate."

"Christ Church, St. Anne and St. Agnes, or St. Botolph?"

Egan stared at John. He did not know the name of the churchyard.

"Do you remember how to get there?"

Egan nodded.

"Come with me then. We'll fetch his tools, and I'll bring him right back," John called back to the women as they exited through the kitchen door into the alley.

Egan led John to the Little Conduit, past the merchant street where he had cleaned the pendant, and up towards the churchyard.

"This is St. Anne and St. Agnes church," John said.

"Me tools are under that bush there," Egan pointed and ran to retrieve the pail, burlap sack, brushes, and pole that lay undisturbed under the brush.

Egan collected the items and rejoined John on the road.

"I have brothers about yer age. They will start sweeping for Master Armory soon," John said.

"Don't make them sweep," Egan quietly objected.

"Me family needs the money," John reasoned.

Egan looked up at John through his unbruised eye, "Please don't make them do it."

John shrugged, and they walked back to the house on Distaff Lane where Miss Clara gave Egan a piece of bread and sent him to the cellar.

CHAPTER XXXIX

E gan waited impatiently until the broomers came home. Andrew and Adam were the first down the cellar stairs.

"Yer face is clean. Is it washin day? Did I miss it?" Adam asked.

"Miss Clara got to me, and I washed meself too," Egan replied.

"Wot for?" Adam looked perplexed.

"Enough about washin. Did you see Rory getting his daily wage from us? If only Will or meself was in charge," Andrew scoffed.

"I want Will in charge. I don't want to take orders from you," Adam said.

"You already take orders from me," Andrew responded.

"But I don't listen."

"Yes, you do."

"Yer an arse," Adam pouted and headed for his sacks.

"Anyway, Rory's out there waiting for you, Egan."

Egan sat on his sacks and retrieved a tuppence from Pitt's shoe. He hated Rory but did not want trouble.

Iggy shuffled down the stairs and collapsed on his sacks. "All right there, Egan?"

"No. You?" Egan asked.

"How can it ever be right again?"

"Maybe it can be, Iggy. I found..." Egan began but was interrupted as Will loudly stamped down the stairs and hastily tossed his ash sack aside.

"Listen up you gits, Rory will come down soon, and we need to talk before he does," Will said.

The broomers got to their feet and approached Will.

"Where's Tick?" Andrew asked.

"He's down the street waiting to come back. Told him I needed a few minutes alone with you, and we knows Rory will wait in the alley for him. He's waiting for you too, Egan."

"Rory's a jackal," Iggy said.

"We needs to get rid of Rory," Will said.

"How?" Andrew asked.

"Don't know. Tick and me been thinking all day but come up with nuffink," Will responded.

"I'd almost give him five guineas to leave if I had it," Andrew said.

"Rory's got savings," Iggy interrupted. "He has a pouch around his waist underneath his shirt."

"Rory's a thief. I bet he has loads of coin," Andrew said.

"Let's steal it from him!" Adam shouted.

The others furiously hushed him.

"Trying to get us beat?" Will scolded.

"We don't hurt other broomers. That's wot Pitt said. We don't hurt other broomers never, not even Rory," Egan said.

"Well he's hurting me," Adam blurted out.

"He's just taking his share. Lots of head boys do. Egan is right. We can't hurt him. Not really," Will said.

"Wot do we do then?" Iggy asked.

Will placed a finger to his lips as footsteps were heard above.

"But I paid me tuppence," Tick protested as Rory followed him down the stairs.

Will whispered to the group, "Think of a plan. We meet tomorrow night again."

The broomers scattered and lounged innocently on their sacks.

"You were late," Rory said. His voice was harsh with authority.

Tick smiled and winked at Will as he walked to his sacks in the corner and dropped his burlap sack holding the day's collection of soot.

"Egan." Rory stood in front of Egan with his palm open.

Egan obediently placed the tuppence in Rory's palm.

"No broomer comes to the cellar without first seeing me. Understand?" Rory asked.

Egan nodded.

"Why are you wearing Pitt's shoes?"

"He give them to me," Egan said.

"Don't take the shoes, Rory," Will stood up.

"This ain't yer business," Rory snapped at Will. "What happened to Pitt's savings? I know he had savings. Probably more than any of us."

"Master Armory took his coins," Egan lied.

"He had a stash hidden in here I'm sure," Rory said. "I'll find it. Now to sleep all of you."

Egan walked to his sacks in Pitt's heavy shoes. He tightened the laces before lying down.

An uneasy quiet settled over the broomers. The days of lighthearted games and conversation before bed were over.

Egan waited several minutes and then whispered, "Iggy!"

Iggy rolled over to face Egan.

"I have sumfink to tell you."

"A secret?"

"Sort of. No one else knows."

"Wot is it?"

"Quiet!" Rory's voice splintered across the cold, damp room.

"I'll tell you tomorrow," Egan whispered.

CHAPTER XL

"Two shillings by nightfall," Master Armory ordered.

"Yes, sir," the broomers answered.

"Clara, the runt stays here," Master Armory said.

Egan looked up in surprise.

"I have business later and yer coming with me."

"Yes, sir," Egan replied.

Egan looked at Iggy, who nodded. The secret would have to wait.

"The rest of you get going," Master Armory barked.

As they left, Rory sneered at Egan.

"He stays right here," Master Armory repeated pointing at Egan.

"Yes, sir," Miss Clara promptly responded.

Alone in the kitchen, Miss Clara poured the leftover gruel into one bowl and handed it to Egan. Egan accepted the bowl with gratitude tampered with tremendous guilt.

"No use in it going to waste," she said patting his head.

Egan finished the gruel and licked each of the bowls clean. Still hungry, he sat in the corner and waited, listening to the quiet house begin to stir.

Miss Clara bustled in and out of the kitchen. John brought in buckets of water until he filled a large tub near the washbasin. He filled the kettle and set about helping Miss Clara cook breakfast. Egan watched in silent fascination as she arranged a large tray with tea, sausage, stewed tomatoes, baked beans, toast, and black pudding. It was a feast.

"Don't touch anything," she warned Egan as she carried the tray to Master Armory's study.

"Yer breakfast, sir," Egan heard her say.

"Get the runt ready," Master Armory ordered.

"Yes, sir," Miss Clara answered.

Miss Clara entered the kitchen with the pile of clothes he had worn the day before. She set the clothes on a chair, retrieved a wet rag, and beckoned to Egan.

"I washed yesterday."

"And yet yer still filthy," she replied, wiping his face. She pointed to the clothes. "Best get those on again."

Egan changed into the clothes, careful to follow the routine Miss Clara had established the day before. First stockings and then knickers. He carefully fastened Pitt's heavy shoes on over the white stockings and resumed his place in the corner. Miss Clara arranged another equally impressive tray and disappeared into the hallway. Egan heard her climbing the stairs. The second tray was for Missus Armory.

John left the kitchen through the back door and returned with large buckets filled with coal in each hand. He nodded to Egan and hurried into the hallway.

The sound of Miss Clara's feet echoed down the stairway and padded to the study.

Dishes clashed together softly.

There was a knock at the front door. The metal hinges groaned as the door opened.

"The carriage is here, sir," Egan heard John say.

Miss Clara entered the kitchen, took a few sips of tea from a cup on the table, and set about tidying the kitchen.

"Runt!"

Egan flew to his feet and answered the call. Master Armory and John were already outside when Egan caught up.

"Westminster Hall," John ordered the carriage driver.

Egan followed the men into the carriage and sat with John on the seat opposite Master Armory. It was a different carriage than yesterday, but it bounced over the cobblestones in the same rhythmic pattern. Egan's wee frame jostled about, but John's shoulder beside him kept him firmly seated.

The carriage stopped in front of the grandest building Egan had ever seen. Large spires extended into the heavens from brick walls with ornate and colorful windows. On the other side of the street, an equally ornate church matched the stature of the magnificent building.

Carriages and people bustled through the streets. Men with large wigs of curls and black suits engaged in hushed, but earnest discussions. Women in delicate dresses with elaborate skirts promenaded across the square. The site was overwhelming, its brilliance paralyzing. Egan hardly noticed John grasping his hand and pulling him towards the great hall.

"Is this King George's palace?"

"No, the king lives at St. James' Palace. This is Westminster Hall," John explained.

"Where they chop off heads?" Egan asked anxiously. No one had told him the purpose of this trip.

"No, that happens at the London Tower, that way," John pointed. "This is the seat of government, for Parliament and court. Mister Armory said we've come to find a solicitor to bring a case against Paul de Lamerie."

"So he can be sent to the Tower?"

John chuckled, "I don't think they would behead him for stealing from Master Armory, maybe for stealing from the king or a nobleman, but not from a chimney sweep."

Although he wanted his jewels back, Egan was comforted knowing that Lamerie's head was safe on his shoulders.

John pulled Egan towards the building, following Master Armory through the crowds. Egan gasped in delight as they entered Westminster Hall. The room was expansive, as tall as ever he'd seen. Artfully cut woodwork supported the ceilings and framed a great stained-glass window at the end of the Hall. Even Master Armory and John appeared taken with the elegance and enormity.

The hall was open and bright, separated only by bars of oak planks that defined sections of the room. People sat on benches inside the planks, facing imposing figures seated above on a raised dais at each end of the hall. Many more people stood crowded around the proceedings or in small groups scattered around the room. At the south end, an empty marble chair was positioned higher than the entire hall.

"Is that the king's chair?"

"I think so," John said.

"Wait here," Master Armory growled.

"Yes, sir," John responded.

"Yes, sir," Egan echoed.

John and Egan stood back and waited as Master Armory approached a group of gentlemen. They conversed a few brief moments and then directed Master Armory to another section of the hall. Master Armory headed where they had indicated.

Egan watched the people and listened to the conversations around him, enamored with the complexity of affluent figures of various stations. He heard voices he didn't recognize speaking languages he didn't understand. The court was a social affair with few signs of business taking place.

"Is that Daniel Defoe?" Egan was immediately alert when he heard the words.

"Who?" the response.

"The man who wrote Robinson Crusoe."

Egan's ears perked up as he moved closer to the voices. Was Robinson Crusoe here at court?

"Why of course, that is him."

"Why is he at court?"

"I am not aware of his circumstances," was the answer.

Egan stepped up to one of the men and pulled on his coat. The man was quite startled; it was his companion that spoke.

"Wot is it young squire?"

"Which one is he? Robinson Crusoe?" Egan asked.

The men chuckled. "The one with the scarlet cravat and cane. Off to himself just there. Do you see him?"

"Yes, sir. Thank ye," Egan answered, already stepping towards the man they identified.

Egan approached with cautious admiration.

"Are you Robinson Crusoe?" Egan asked.

Defoe looked down at him.

"I am not, but I am, shall I say, acquainted with him," he answered.

"Sir, is he real?"

"Crusoe?"

"I know Crusoe is real, me Da told me about him, but wot about Friday?" Egan asked.

"Come, Egan," John approached, "Me apologies sir," John said with a slight bow.

"No apology is required. I am genuinely interested in the boy's question." Defoe captured Egan's eyes with an intense look.

"Friday is as real as Crusoe, my lad," he answered.

"Did Friday really save his father?"

"He did. Do you have a father to save?" Defoe asked him.

"Me Da died at sea, but I lost me Mum and sister."

"You lost them?"

"In Southwark or London somewhere, I don't know where they are."

"Courage and faith my boy," Defoe laid his hand on Egan's head. "You will find them, and save them you must."

"Thank ye, sir. I will."

Defoe nodded towards Egan and then blended into the crowd at court.

"He knows Robinson Crusoe," Egan whispered to John, pure exhilaration sparked from his eyes.

Egan was still chuffed as nuts when Master Armory approached them.

"Mister Hackney, this is me servant, John, and me apprentice boy," Master Armory introduced them.

"Phillip Hackney, solicitor," Mister Hackney introduced himself and shook their hands.

"Egan Whitcombe, yer honor," Egan said.

Master Armory glared at Egan with a stern warning.

"Well, Egan, I hear you have a story to tell me," Mister Hackney stated.

"I just met Robinson Crusoe's mate!"

"About the pendant, boy," Master Armory reminded.

"Perhaps we should seek some privacy in the gardens," the solicitor suggested.

Master Armory agreed, and the solicitor led them from the hall, down the corridor, and out into the crisp winter air. The gardens were iced over and brown, but Egan could imagine how impressive the summer landscape would be.

Egan looked up at the solicitor and studied the bald patch on his head, from which small stray hairs stood up at all angles. Egan wondered why this man was not wearing a wig as the others did at court. The man squinted through glasses perched on his nose and smiled at Egan.

"I am most interested in your story, young chap," he pointed a knobby finger towards Egan's nose. Leading the group towards a vacant bench, he sat and waited for Master Armory to join him. John and Egan remained standing.

"Start from the beginning, and tell me only the truth. How did you get the pendant?"

Egan repeated the events, beginning with the finding of the pendant in Reeves' sack and ending with Master Armory's confrontation with Lamerie.

"And how did you get a black eye?"

Egan hesitated and looked towards Master Armory, although he already knew a warning was in his eyes. "I fell down the stairs."

"I'll make sure he is more careful," Master Armory interrupted.

Mister Hackney gave a stern nod in Master Armory's direction before continuing. "And how much did Mister de Lamerie offer you for the pendant?"

"Three halfpence."

"Did you take it?"

"No, I told him I'd keep it."

"Did you accept any money from him?"

"No, I didn't take any money from him," Egan stated.

"Why were you trying to sell the pendant?"

"I wanted five guineas to pay me debt. The casting is worth three halfpence. I need lots more than that."

"I'll do my best to get the jewels back for you." The solicitor smiled winked at Egan. "I'll bring your claim, Mister Armory."

"Very good," Master Armory responded, shaking the solicitor's hand.

"It's an action in trover, which may be brought directly to the King's Bench by bill. As Mister de Lamerie resides in Middlesex County, he is already subject to the king's jurisdiction, and no writ of trespass is required to take him into custody should he fail to appear in court," the solicitor said.

Master Armory nodded but appeared uncertain.

"I will also look into Mister de Lamerie's business dealings for additional leverage."

"Very good," Master Armory stated.

"I will write to you when the case is scheduled. In the interim, I can be reached at Gray's Inn," Mister Hackney said.

"Very good," Master Armory repeated.

"Your boy shall have justice, Mister Armory."

CHAPTER XLI

R ory was poised to attack when he came down the stairs that evening.

Egan was waiting with a tuppence from Pitt's shoe, anticipating Rory's reaction. Egan held out the coin to Rory, but Rory smacked Egan's hand, sending the tuppence flying across the room.

"I don't want yer coin. Why didn't you sweep today?" Rory grabbed Egan by the collar of his ragged shirt.

The broomers gathered around to listen, except Adam who was looking for Egan's coin, which he promptly found and hid in his pocket.

"Let me go," Egan squirmed. "Let me go, and I'll tell you."

Rory pushed Egan onto the nearest sack of ashes. "I'm listening."

"I found sumfink, a pendant with jewels, and then the jewels were stolen from me. Master Armory couldn't get them back neither, but the solicitor will."

The broomers looked confused.

"Jewels? Wot kind of jewels?" Will asked.

Egan told the broomers about the pendant, the apprentice, Mister de Lamerie, the solicitor, Westminster, and every detail he could think to tell. The story captivated the broomers; even Rory was interested in the smallest of details. Egan had to repeat himself and vow that he wasn't lying.

"And I met Robinson Crusoe's friend! He told me Friday was real and that someday I would save Mum and Kerrin, and he had really big hair like most everyone else, and he had a cane."

The broomers stared at Egan in amazement.

"Did he try to eat you?" Tick asked warily.

"No. Why would he try to eat me?"

"Robinson Crusoe had friends that ate each other."

"Those weren't his friends. Friends don't eat each other," Will said.

"But they did eat each other." Tick was adamant.

"How much are the jewels worth? Enough to buy yer freedom?" Rory asked.

222 | A. M. WATSON

"Maybe."

"And Master Armory is going to get them back for you?" Rory asked.

"No, but the solicitor will. He said so."

"Will you be sweeping tomorrow?" Rory's face contorted in envy.

"Aye. I don't have me five guineas until I get the jewels back and can sell them."

"When you get the quid, I gets a guinea of it. Off the top, before you gets yers," Rory demanded.

"Is that all you need? One guinea and you'll have five?" Will asked Rory.

"Like I'd tell you," Rory snapped. "Egan, you hear me? One guinea is mine off the top."

"Twig," Egan agreed, hoping the stones were worth at least three guineas.

"And you still owe me a tuppence every day."

"Twig. I had a coin for you from me savings."

The broomers looked in the direction the coin flew and found Adam shifting on his sacks.

Andrew held out his hand, "Give it here."

"But I found it!"

"You can't find sumfink that was never lost," Andrew retorted. "Give it here."

"But its Egan's tuppence."

"Well then, give it to Egan," Andrew ordered.

"I was giving it to Rory," Egan said.

"Rory said he didn't want it. If Egan doesn't want it neither and I found it, then it belongs to me," Adam whined.

"Adam!" Andrew scolded.

Adam threw the coin at Andrew, who picked it up and handed it to Rory.

Egan smiled and lay down in his ashes. A weight was lifted from his chest.

"Was that the secret?" Iggy whispered across to Egan.

"Aye."

"So yer leaving?"

"After I find me Mum and Kerrin, I'll get a job on the first ship I can."

"Oh," Iggy looked lost.

"The real secret is that I'm taking you with me. I only need two guineas for me and one for Rory, anything else will be for you."

"Why me? I ain't done nuffink for you," Iggy said.

"Because Pitt would have chosen you, and I can't leave you behind."

"I only have seventeen bob and a haypenny for savings."

"If we keep earning, it will be enough," Egan stated more confidently than he felt.

"Do you mean it? About taking me?"

"Aye. Yer me friend, Iggy."

The cellar grew quiet as the other broomers settled in for the night.

"It matters you know," Iggy whispered.

"Wot?" Egan asked.

"The good things. When Pitt was here, he did good things for us. Those good things mattered."

"Those good things did matter."

"Saying you'll take me, even if you somehow can't, that matters too," Iggy whispered.

CHAPTER XLII

Despite Master Armory's absence, the broomers headed to the streets in a melancholy mood the next morning. Egan's riveting story starkly contrasted with their unchanged circumstances. The same dreary streets greeted them with the same demanding urgency of earning coin before the day dissipated into night. Even Rory seem subdued; he forgot to remind them of their daily obligation to him.

Trudging along, they heard John running to catch up with them.

"Hold up," he yelled in a hushed voice.

"Miss Clara sent us out," Rory defended them against whatever accusations may come. "Master Armory was not up yet."

"Yer not in trouble," John said.

The broomers relaxed.

"Egan, yer to come with me."

"He works same as us," Rory objected.

"Shall I tell Master Armory that you defy his orders?" John challenged.

"No, sir. Let's go broomers. We have work to find," Rory spat on the pavement and glared at Egan before turning away.

The other broomers shrugged and followed Rory down the alley.

Egan followed John back to the house. Steps away he could hear Master Armory yelling at Miss Clara.

"Wot if he was picked up by nabbers!"

"Me apologies, sir, I...," Miss Clara cried.

"Or killed!"

"I didn't think to ask you..."

Master Armory yelled and threw a bottle across the room. The pieces of glass shattered against the wall as John opened the door.

"Disloyal wretch!" Master Armory yelled and backhanded her across the face.

Miss Clara crumpled to the floor.

"He goes nowhere!" Master Armory shouted. "He doesn't leave this house!"

"Yes, sir," John answered.

Master Armory stormed out of the room, overturning a chair in the corner.

Egan ran to Miss Clara and hugged her around the neck. "Miss Clara, are you hurt?"

"No. I just need a moment to get on me feet."

John swept up the broken glass and returned the chair to its corner.

"All is set right now," he spoke softly as he helped Miss Clara get up and led her to the chair.

She wiped her eyes with trembling fingers and tried to smile at Egan. "Yer to help me in the kitchen today. How's that sound?"

"This is me fault."

"No dearie, don't you think that," Miss Clara kissed Egan's forehead and hugged him close. "Don't you dare think that."

"Why can't I leave?"

"If you don't stand witness, Master Armory will lose the case. He's just worried sumfink might happen to you. Until the trial, you can help us around the house. It will be nice to have two extra hands," John said.

"And we can get to know each other better," Miss Clara smiled through lingering tears. "Let me get breakfast ready, and then I'll put you to work. Sound good?"

Egan nodded and tried to smile for Miss Clara.

"Where's Missus McGivney?"

"She does washin in the morning and comes in for the noon meal. I cook and serve breakfast by meself. I expect Master Armory can only afford John and me, but the Missus insists on having a cook too."

"I like Missus McGivney."

"Everyone likes a good cook," Miss Clara winked at Egan. A single tear flicked towards him from her damp eyelashes.

The inside work left Egan little time to think. He emptied and cleaned chamber pots, shined Master Armory's shoes and brushed his suit, peeled vegetables, scrubbed floors, and washed dishes. Once a week he helped Miss Clara with the washing. He stirred clothing in a large tub they filled with hot water and then scrubbed and squeezed the water out of each piece before hanging it to dry. The sweaty work left him exhausted. Sometimes he fell asleep before the broomers joined him in the cellar.

Master Armory left the house several times to meet the solicitor, but without Egan. Used to wandering the streets of London looking for work, the walls of the house closed in upon him.

Sensing his restlessness, Missus McGivney decided to teach Egan to cook. He stood on the kitchen chair and measured and stirred mixtures of eggs, milk, dried fruit, and spices, which were poured over stale bread to make a pudding. He learned to knead bread and roll out dough for pies. When he was getting under her feet, Missus McGivney sent Egan with John outside into the alley to cut the head off a chicken and pluck its feathers, which Egan found fascinating and sickening at the same time. The chicken's skin seemed to stretch in strange directions and then snap back when the feathers were pulled free. Egan decided that chickens looked better with feathers and heads.

Egan ate dinner with Miss Clara, Missus McGivney, and John before the other broomers got back from the day's work. They never ate the rich foods or portions that Missus McGivney fixed for Master and Missus Armory, but after a week of regular meals, the constant pain in Egan's stomach subsided.

It was like summer, except he was the only one at St. Olave's while the other broomers continued to starve in the cellar. Egan hid bread from his meal in the folds of his shirt when the adults were not looking and delivered it to hungry broomers each evening. His thoughts were constantly on their turmoil.

"How's the special boy? The fragile house servant?" Rory taunted him in the evenings.

"Wot's it like up there all day?" Will asked, ignoring Rory.

"Yer clothes are clean. Did Miss Clara wash yer clothes?" Adam asked.

"Wot did you eat for dinner?" Andrew always wanted to know.

"Has Master Armory got the jewels back yet?" Iggy inquired.

Egan learned to deflect most questions and tell them about the work he did all day. It did not matter. Rory was always mean, but after a few weeks, the others also began to resent his good fortune. Unspoken envy stretched through the space between them.

"I wish I had half yer good luck," Will admitted one evening.

Things had changed. It did not matter how many slices of bread Egan gave them; the broomers envied his position. Egan longed for the way things had been. He was a broomer. He was one of them. And yet, he was not. The day of court could not come quick enough.

CHAPTER XLIII

The next morning Master Armory instructed Miss Clara to make Egan presentable. Egan quickly stripped down in the kitchen, excited to finally be going to court. If the solicitor got the jewels back for him, Egan, hopefully Iggy, and regrettably Rory, would finally be free.

But it was not the day for court. Rory was waiting with Master Armory at the front door. He grinned shrewdly at Egan. This was wrong. Whatever was happening, it was wrong.

Egan followed Master Armory obediently; trepidation filled his thoughts as he walked out to the main street for the first time in more than a month. It was a gloomy day, but winter was receding. Spring would arrive soon.

"Don't you look grand," Rory commented in a low voice as Master Armory walked ahead. "Wot you scheming?"

"I'm not scheming nuffink."

"You don't belong in them clothes. I'll remind you of yer place when all this is over." Rory's voice held a warning.

"When this is over I'll be gone and so will you."

"You'll be gone like Pitt is gone," Rory jeered.

"Pitt was better than you," Egan said, wanting to hurt Rory.

"Better watch yer tongue, you won't be safe much longer."

"Runt," Master Armory called.

Egan caught up to Master Armory and walked by his side. Egan hated Master Armory and loathed every second of his company, but he was far too close to freedom to disobey.

Master Armory led Egan towards Whitechapel as Rory disappeared into the crowd behind them. Egan looked about as the streets grew more destitute and the people more desperate. He felt ashamed to be parading about in fine court clothes. He belonged here, in this poor street, struggling to survive. Yet he had eaten two meals every day for weeks.

"Are you Daniel Armory, the sweep?" a woman approached them holding a tiny hand in each of hers. The boys were gaunt with hunger.

"I am."

"These are me sons, looking to apprentice."

Egan caught his breath.

"How old?" Master Armory questioned her.

"Six and almost five."

"Has either one been sick in the last year?"

"No, sir. You do take care of yer boys, don't you?" she pleaded.

"I take great care. Look at this here lad. Clean, clothed, fed. He is well looked after and is learning a trade to build a respectable future."

Egan was there to deceive. He began to shake. These boys were so wee, smaller than he. She was selling them, just like Mum sold him.

"Ten shillings," Master Armory offered.

"They be fine boys, sir."

"Ten shillings is me price. I'll be giving yer sons a home and teaching them a trade. You should be paying me to take them."

Egan pulled his eyes from the children, who were just beginning to understand the scope of the transaction.

"Ten shillings," Master Armory held out the coins in the palm of his hand.

The woman accepted and pushed her boys towards Master Armory.

"Mum?"

"He is yer master now. Go with the gentleman."

"Mum, I don't want to leave you," the older boy began to cry.

"Mum no!" the younger boy screamed as his mum turned and ran away.

Rory appeared and grabbed one boy by the neck while Master Armory held on to the other.

Egan relived his own terror and remembered the beating he received that dreadful day. He remembered Pitt's voice, convincing him that there was hope. Rory would give these boys fear, not hope. They were infants at the mercy of two vindictive and malicious masters.

"Boy, hold him," Master Armory ordered Egan to grasp the younger boy. Egan obeyed, hating himself.

"Calm yerself," Egan whispered in the boy's ear.

The boy didn't listen. He continued to struggle as Master Armory bound his hands with a bit of rope and tied him to his brother.

"Let me go!" the older boy shouted.

Master Armory responded by kicking the child to the ground. The force of his fall pulled his brother down on top of him. The children wailed, igniting Master Armory's wrath. He struck and kicked each boy until they bled.

"Rory, ready them for work," he ordered and began walking away.

"Runt!" he yelled at Egan, who stood fixed with horror. Master Armory's voice held a warning. Feeling like a traitorous wretch, Egan ran submissively to Master Armory's side.

CHAPTER XLIV

A ring of the bell announced a visitor to the shop, the first that week.

"Bennett? Will you see to the front?" Lamerie asked.

"Yes, sir." Bennett set down the pad of compressed wool beside the silver plate and walked through the door to the shop.

"How may I be of assistance?" Lamerie heard the apprentice say.

"I wish to see Mister Paul de Lamerie," a gruff voice stated.

Lamerie stood and met Bennett at the door.

"I'll handle this," he told the apprentice.

"How may I be of assistance?" Lamerie asked the man standing in his shop.

The man was attired in formal livery and holding a sealed letter.

"Are you Paul de Lamerie?"

"Aye, I am."

"Paul de Lamerie you are hereby summoned to the King's Bench on Wednesday next to defend yourself in an action of trover concerning stolen jewels from a pendant, such action is brought by Mister Daniel Armory on behalf of his young apprentice Egan Whitcombe. Should you fail to appear, the king's soldiers will arrest you and take you to Marshalsea Prison to await a new trial date. Sir, your summons."

The man handed Lamerie the sealed letter and exited the shop.

"Sir? Is this about Charles?" asked Bennett.

"Aye."

"Do you think Charles took the jewels as that boy said?"

"He must have. Have you seen him?"

"No, sir. Not since that day."

CHAPTER XLV

The solicitor's letter finally came. Their bill of trover was to be heard by the King's Bench on the next Wednesday.

Egan was relieved that the waiting would end but terrified that the solicitor might not get the jewel back. If Rory was right, there was hell to pay when this respite was over.

Rory was training both new boys, Jacob and Jude. The boys cried every night in their sleep. His tears had been from the pain of losing his family; their tears were from Rory's cruelty. Burn marks appeared on their faces and hands the first few days of sweeping.

Pitt had protected Egan from harm. Rory was abusing Jacob and Jude to prove that he was in charge.

In the mornings, Jacob and Jude lined up behind Egan. There was no joy in his promotion, only pity for those behind him.

"Five guineas to freedom," Egan whispered to them.

Neither responded.

Egan kept himself occupied with chores. One afternoon, he hauled water from the conduit with John for Miss Clara, just like they did on wash day, but it was not wash day.

Miss Clara heated the water up and began filling the wash tub.

"Wot's the tub for?"

"For washing."

"It's not washing day. "Wot are we washing?"

"We are washing you."

"Me?"

"You are going to court this week and better be presentable."

"I haven't swept for weeks. Most the soot has fallen off already," Egan reasoned.

"Only from yer hands. The rest of you looks like you swam in a coal bin. Now shed yer clothes and get in."

"I can go down to the river to wash."

"And how cold do you think that be this time of year?"

"But that's boiling hot!" Egan pointed to the steam drifting above the tub.

"Most of the water has cooled. It's just hot enough to get all the soot from yer skin."

"River water works good too. We did it last summer."

Miss Clara's patience waned. "Get into the tub so I can wash you."

"Can't I use a cloth instead?"

"No."

"That will burn me. I don't want to burn, Miss Clara."

Miss Clara knelt next to Egan and looked into his fearful eyes. "I would never make you get into water so hot it would burn you." She unbuttoned the cuffs at her wrists and rolled up the sleeves of her blouse. She draped one arm into the tub and calmly swirled the water through her fingers.

"Rich people bathe in hot tubs. It's a luxury." She withdrew her hand and laid it gently on Egan's shoulder. "See? Hot but not burning."

Egan nodded.

"Now get out of yer trousers and small clothes and get into the tub. I'll fetch the soap."

Egan removed his clothes and stood anxiously at the edge of the tub. He dipped his toes cautiously into the water before coaxing himself into the tub. He stood naked and shivering with his feet in the water.

Miss Clara called out from the hall, "Make sure yer head gets wet too."

Egan reluctantly lowered himself into the warm water and patted his head with his wet hands.

"How is it now?" Miss Clara emerged with a scrub brush and a lump of soap.

"Not burning."

"Good. Now lean back and get yer head wet."

"It's wet," Egan said, patting his head again with wet hands.

"Not enough." Miss Clara leaned him back and started scrubbing his head with soap.

Egan tried to object, but Miss Clara was far too efficient. She scrubbed his head and worked her way down his face to his neck and shoulders. She sat him up and scrubbed him down, careful with the areas of his skin that had scabbed over and were still sensitive to touch.

"Yer skin is healing nicely, and yer bruises are all yellow now."

"It don't hurt much no more."

Missus McGivney arrived just as Miss Clara finished scouring Egan's feet. She looked at the drenched boy and chuckled.

"I'm clean enough now," Egan protested.

Miss Clara responded by starting all over again.

"Yer ears are still dirty," she said, decisively circling the scrub brush behind his ears and pouring bowl after bowl of water over his head.

"I'm sure rich folks don't bathe like this," Egan complained.

"Rich folks ain't as sooty as you are."

"Or as stubborn," Missus McGivney added with a laugh.

Miss Clara did not stop until Egan's skin was scrubbed to a reddish pink and the water was pitch black. She made Egan soak a few extra minutes while she trimmed his shaggy hair with a razor and drowned him with one last bowl of water.

Finally, Miss Clara allowed Egan to stand up, and she wrapped him in a large blanket to dry off.

"You look dashing, young man! How do you feel?" Miss Clara beamed.

"A bit sick," Egan confessed.

"Oh shush. Washing only makes you sick if you do it too often," Miss Clara said, rubbing Egan's head with the blanket.

Miss Clara dressed Egan in a clean nightshirt that was several sizes too big and sat him at the table for bread and soup.

"It's an early night for you, young man," Missus McGivney said.

"Yes, mam," Egan replied as he headed for the cellar.

"No you don't. I didn't scrub you head to toe only to have you roll in ashes all night," Miss Clara objected. "Come with me."

Miss Clara led Egan up the stairs to a small empty room on the third floor. He had never been upstairs.

"You'll sleep here tonight," Miss Clara nudged Egan into the room.

"Where?"

"In the bed, of course."

Miss Clara pulled back a quilt, "Get in you."

Egan slowly climbed into the bed and allowed Miss Clara to arrange the blanket around him.

"Do you have kids, Miss Clara?"

"No, why?"

"Yer like me Mum."

"You miss her, don't you?"

Egan nodded.

Miss Clara kissed Egan on the forehead. "Sweet dreams. In the morning, yer to dress in the nice clothes. They're folded on the chair in the corner."

Egan nodded. "Miss Clara?"

"Yes?"

"I've never slept in a bed. Wot if I fall off?"

"The floor will wake you up. Good night, dearie," she whispered and closed the door.

Part Six
Westminster, 1722

"[C]hildren should be considered free agents for wage bargaining purposes."

-James Maitland, 8th Earl of Lauderdale (Arguing in the
House of Lords against any restraint on the practices
of the masters of chimney sweeps.)

CHAPTER XLVI

"The King's Bench is now in session. Chief Justice Lord Pratt presiding," a clerk of the court bellowed from his desk supplied with several quills, an inkpot, and paper.

The chief justice entered the room and sat at the table on the raised dais. The large marble throne was elevated behind him. The symbolism was clear; this man spoke with the authority of King George.

The audience sat. The chief justice organized his papers upon the table, unconcerned with the litigants anxiously waiting the trial. A long brown wig of curls set on his head, falling forward over his shoulders and onto his scarlet judicial robe. Bronze fur lined his garment, and an ornamental chain crossed his ample girth.

Egan sat on a bench beside John and studied his surroundings. Master Armory and Mister Hackney sat at a table in front of them. Mister Hackney wore a gray horsehair wig that covered his balding spot. Paul de Lamerie and two other gentlemen were at the table directly adjacent to them. Twelve men in various styles of dress sat on benches to the side. Egan guessed they were noblemen. People of society filled the hall, taking available seats on benches and milling throughout the open chamber. Even on his second visit, the exquisiteness of Westminster Hall impressed upon Egan a silent reverie of awe.

The chief justice signaled a clerk with a slight nod of his head.

"The King's Bench will hear Armory verses de Lamerie, a bill of trover concerning a jewel of uncertain ownership," the clerk announced.

"God save the king," Chief Justice Pratt announced, pounding a gavel on the desk.

"God save the king," the audience echoed.

"God save the king," Egan said a little late.

"The plaintiff may present its claims," Chief Justice Pratt ordered.

Mister Hackney stood and addressed the court.

"My lord," Mister Hackney bowed to the chief justice. "Distinguished members of the jury," Mister Hackney bowed to the twelve men sitting apart to the side.

"The plaintiff is a mere chimney sweeper's boy who was robbed by Mister Paul de Lamerie, a goldsmith of great wealth who is unscrupulous in his business dealings."

Mister de Lamerie held his chin high with a disgusted look on his face.

"The plaintiff found a pendant and took it to Mister de Lamerie's shop to sell, whereupon Mister de Lamerie's apprentice removed the precious ruby and pearls from the pendant's casting and offered the boy three halfpence. The boy refused and demanded the jewels to be returned, yet Mister de Lamerie and his apprentice were determined to rob from the boy and retained the stones for themselves.

"My first witness is the plaintiff himself, who will recount the events of the theft for the court," Mister Hackney waved for Egan to join him. "The plaintiff calls Egan Armory to testify."

Egan grimaced. He was Egan Whitcombe. But the smile on Mister Hackney's face prompted his immediate forgiveness. It was a simple mistake. Mister Hackney led Egan to the open space between the litigant tables and the clerk's desk.

"Stand here," Mister Hackney instructed. Egan fixed Pitt's shoes on the exact place Mister Hackney had indicated and looked up to the chief justice without lifting his chin.

"There is no need to fear," Chief Justice Pratt spoke softly.

The clerk approached Egan with a large Bible. Egan stared at it.

"I don't know how to read."

Murmurs of amusement rippled through the jury and the surrounding audience.

"Place your hand on the Bible," the clerk commanded.

Egan obeyed, placing both hands on the large book.

"Do you swear to tell the truth, the whole truth, and nothing but the truth, so help you God?"

"I will tell you the truth."

"Do you swear to tell the truth?"

"Yer not supposed to swear, me Mum said so."

"Do you promise to tell the truth?" the clerk revised the statement.

"Yes, sir, I promise I will."

The clerk looked up at Chief Justice Pratt with a questioning expression.

Chief Justice Pratt nodded, and the clerk walked back to his desk with the Bible.

"Please tell your name to the court," Master Hackney instructed.

"Egan Whitcombe."

"What is your occupation?"

"I don't think I have one of those."

Amused murmurs ran through the court.

"What do you do every day?"

"Oh, I be a broomer. A climbing boy for Master Armory."

"Son, where did you find the jewel?" Mister Hackney asked.

"It was in Reeves' sack of ashes. I thought it be a rock."

"Who is Reeves?"

"He was a broomer."

"He worked for Master Armory?"

"Yes, sir."

"Did you know Reeves?"

"No."

"How did you get Reeves' sack of ash?"

"When Master Armory bought me from me Mum, I got Reeves' ashes to sleep on."

"I see. Why did you take the pendant to Mister de Lamerie's shop?"

Egan looked down at his feet, ashamed and nervous to tell the truth.

"The court requires an answer," Chief Justice Pratt stated sternly with a slightly raised voice.

"I wanted to sell it," Egan admitted in a wee voice.

"Did Mister Armory tell you to sell it?" Mister Hackney asked.

"No, sir."

"Did Mister Armory know you had the pendant?"

"No, sir."

"What were you going to do with the money?"

"Get a potato from the Missus Winchester."

"And?"

"Get potatoes for the other broomers."

"What were you going to do with the money?" Chief Justice Pratt interrupted.

"I, I, I was going to pay me debt to Master Armory. Five guineas buys me freedom."

"I see," Chief Justice Pratt said.

"Then pay the other broomer's debt, at least Iggy's if I had enough. Then I would find me Mum and sister, then go to sea as a ship's boy, then buy me own ship, and then be a tobacco farmer in the Americas."

Chief Justice Pratt grinned, and quiet laughter spread throughout the court.

"I felt rich with the pendant in me pocket. I knew it were pricey 'cause it were so beautiful. But when the apprentice took the stones, I had to tell Master Armory. He thought I hid the pendant from him."

Chief Justice Pratt studied the boy.

"Continue the questioning," he ordered the solicitor.

"At Mister de Lamerie's shop, why did you give the apprentice the jewels?"

"He said he needed to weigh it and that he would give me a price for the casting and a price for the stones."

"What price did he offer?"

"Three halfpence."

"Did you accept the money?"

"No. Mister de Lamerie held the coins out to me, but I didn't take them. I asked for the pendant back."

"Did Mister de Lamerie return the pendant to you?"

"No, well sort of. The apprentice gave me back the empty casting, but wouldn't give me back the stones."

"Describe the stones for the court," Mister Hackney asked Egan.

"The big stone in the middle was a ruby and the little stones surrounding it were seed pearls. It were dusty gray from ash, but I washed it up good."

"What else can you tell me about it?"

"The little pearls were in three rows around the ruby," Egan answered, swirling imaginary circles in the space in front of him with his hands, "and the back was carved with a letter."

"Solicitor, does the plaintiff have the pendant casting?" Chief Justice Pratt asked.

"Yes, my lord," Mister Hackney answered.

"Bring it to me."

Mister Hackney obeyed, bowing his head in respect as he approached the bench. He placed the casting in front of Chief Justice Pratt and stepped back. Chief Justice Pratt examined the pendant casting. The parties waited in silence.

"Continue," the chief justice ordered.

"When Mister de Lamerie would not return the stones, what did you do?" Mister Hackney asked.

"I ran and told Master Armory, and he took me back to Mister de Lamerie's shop in a carriage. It was me first ride in a carriage. It was bumpy all the way to the Haymarket."

"Then what happened."

"The apprentice wouldn't give Master Armory the stones, so Master Armory argued with Mister de Lamerie, but he wouldn't give them back either. Then we came to Westminster Hall, and I met Robinson Crusoe's friend."

The crowd chuckled.

"You met Daniel Defoe, who wrote Robinson Crusoe," Mister Hackney corrected.

"He wrote him a letter?"

"Something like that, but that is not relevant to this case. Do you know how to read?" Mister Hackney asked.

"No, sir."

"If you had the wealth of the pendant, would you go to school and study to be a cleric of the church or a barrister of the law?"

"No, I would buy a ship and become a tobacco farmer," Egan responded. Maybe Mister Hackney did not hear him before.

The crowd laughed, and Mister Hackney quickly abandoned his misguided strategy.

"My questioning is finished," Mister Hackney informed the chief justice.

"Defense, your witness," Chief Justice Pratt ordered.

Mister de Lamerie's solicitor stood and approached Egan.

"How old are you, boy?"

"I don't know. About eight, I guess."

"I see. Boy, have you been properly taught in the ways of our Lord?"

"Yes, I've met two preachers and slept in a cemetery."

The audience roared with laughter. The gavel smacked against the table, silencing the gathering.

"Who did you take the pendant from?"

"I didn't take it, I found it."

"Did you find it in someone's house?"

"No, I found it in Reeves' sweeping ashes."

"Did your master tell you to say that?"

"No, that is wot I told him."

The audience laughed nervously, uncomfortable with the solicitor's attack on the boy.

"Tis apparent that this child has little religious instruction concerning the telling of lies. His word is not a lawful form of testimony when given to advance his master's wellbeing," the solicitor informed the court. "However, I will continue my questioning to prove an important fact in this case."

"Boy, who removed the stones from the casting?"

"Mister de Lamerie's apprentice."

"Is the apprentice here in this hall?"

"I don't see him."

"Did Mister de Lamerie ever see the stones?"

"I don't know," Egan answered truthfully.

"Did Mister de Lamerie take the pendant from you?"

"No."

"From the child's own mouth, Mister de Lamerie himself did not remove or retain the stones from the pendant. No further questions, my lord." The solicitor returned to his seat by Mister de Lamerie.

"You may return to your seat," the chief justice told Egan.

Egan looked up at Chief Justice Pratt, who pointed to the bench behind Master Armory.

"I'm all done?" Egan asked.

"Do you have something else to tell me?" Chief Justice Pratt asked.

"No. I told you everything that happened," Egan said.

"Then you are done. You may go sit with your master."

Egan nodded and walked back towards his seat beside John.

"Next witness plaintiff," Chief Justice Pratt called.

"My next witness will establish the value of the stolen jewels. The plaintiff calls Mister Charles Delmont, a goldsmith, to testify," Mister Hackney stated.

The clerk approached Mister Delmont with the Bible.

"Do you swear to tell the truth, the whole truth, and nothing but the truth, so help you God?"

"I do," Mister Delmont answered.

"Was that wot I was supposed to say?" Egan whispered to John.

"Shush," John whispered.

"Mister Delmont, please state your name and credentials for the court," Mister Hackney requested.

"My name is Charles Franklin Delmont. I was born in Surrey and apprenticed the goldsmith John Fortner Epallet of London. I own a shop in Southwark off Tooley Street and am a member of the Worshipful Company of Goldsmiths with a registered mark."

"Impressive standing, Mister Delmont," Mister Hackney acknowledged. "Have you had the opportunity to study the plaintiff's pendant casting?"

"I have."

"What were your findings?"

"The pendant was finely fashioned, suggesting a master craftsman, around 1714 to 1715. The casting is solid gold. The gold is worth two pounds, three shillings, and a sixpence."

Egan sat up straighter in his seat. Even if he didn't get the jewels back, the casting was worth over two pounds! He tried to remember how many pounds equaled a guinea.

"And what of the stones?"

"The tiny crevices could have held chips of diamonds; however, from the plaintiff's description, I find that the small round stones were seed pearls."

"And the main stone?"

"The plaintiff described the main stone to me, stating that it was red. The gem could have been a garnet, bloodstone, or ruby. I propose it to be a ruby, for a casting this valuable would be fashioned only for stones of like value and the finest water."

"Please explain the term 'finest water' to the court."

"Gemstones are classified in terms of transparency, luster, and brilliance. Stones that are very transparent are considered to be of the finest water while those that lackluster and brilliance are of second or third water."

"How much, in your expert opinion, are the missing stones worth?"

"The seed pearls are of minimum value, just over a pound, but the ruby would be valued from thirty to fifty pounds depending on its water."

The audience gasped. Egan jumped up from the bench in surprise. John immediately pulled him back down.

"No further questions, my lord," Mister Hackney returned to his table.

"Your witness," Chief Justice Pratt offered Charles Delmont for cross-examination.

Mister de Lamerie's solicitor stood and approached the witness.

"Mister Delmont, did you at any time examine the stones?"

"No."

"Could a cheap, but well-cut, garnet have been placed in the casting?"

"Yes, although unlikely due to…"

"No further questions, my lord," the solicitor interrupted.

"You are dismissed Mister Delmont," Chief Justice Pratt stated. "Next witness?"

"The plaintiff's next witness will testify to Mister de Lamerie's dishonest business dealings. The plaintiff calls Mister Robert Sarjeant of the Worshipful Company of Goldsmiths."

The clerk approached Mister Sarjeant with the Bible.

"Do you swear to tell the truth, the whole truth, and nothing but the truth, so help you God?"

"I do," the man stated.

"Mister Sarjeant, please state your name and credentials for the court," Mister Hackney requested.

"I am Robert Sarjeant. I was born in Whitechapel and apprenticed to William Robbins. At sixteen, I entered my first mark and now direct the assay office for the Worshipful Company of Goldsmiths."

"Mister Sarjeant, have you been involved in the regulation of gold and silversmiths?"

"Yes, sir."

"In what capacity do you serve?"

"Every ounce of silver or gold marked by a goldsmith is taxed, the silver being the same standard as coined currency. If coins are clipped, or if the silver is fashioned into hollow objects weighted by another less valuable metal, the value of the currency is diminished. I review the items produced by gold and silversmiths with registered marks and assess the tax upon the item."

"What happens if the regulations of the crown are not obeyed?"

"The goldsmith is brought before the court and fined subject to the indiscretion. A goldsmith can lose his mark and place in the Worshipful Company of Goldsmiths for repetitive violations. He may be deemed unworthy of the trade."

"Has Mister de Lamerie ever been disciplined by the court for such actions?"

"Yes, on numerous occasions."

"Please enlighten the court with the specifics."

"In 1714, Mister de Lamerie failed to have his work hallmarked in an attempt to avoid taxes. He was fined twenty pounds. In 1715, he took work from a French goldsmith and had it hallmarked as his own, thus allowing unregistered goldsmiths to sell work illegally. He was charged again in 1716 for the same indiscretion. In 1717, he illegally changed his mark and then was suspected of selling large quantities of unmarked silver plate. He was not charged with that offense."

"And why was he not charged?"

"The purchasers of the items required discretion in the matter."

Members of the audience looked at each other.

"Your witness," Chief Justice Pratt advised the defense.

Mister de Lamerie's solicitor stood and approached the witness in a confident, brazen manner.

"Mister Sarjeant, to your knowledge has Mister de Lamerie been charged with any indiscretions since his days as a youth?"

"No, he has not."

"Are you aware that Mister de Lamerie is the goldsmith to King George?"

"I am aware of that fact."

"Are you aware that he has served the King since 1717?"

"I am."

"Are your statements against Mister de Lamerie in any way accusing His Majesty the King of violating his own law?"

"No, sir. I would not assert any such statement."

"I did not think you would. No further questions, my lord."

"You are dismissed Mister Sarjeant," Chief Justice Pratt stated. "Next witness?"

"The plaintiff calls Daniel Armory."

The clerk approached Master Armory with the Bible.

"Do you swear to tell the truth, the whole truth, and nothing but the truth, so help you God?"

"I do," Master Armory stated.

"Mister Armory, please state your name and credentials for the court."

"Me name is Daniel Armory. I was born in Whitechapel and apprenticed a chimney sweep. Me profession is chimney sweeping. The boy that the jewel was stolen from, he belongs to me. The boy is me property. By law, anything he has or acquires is rightfully mine."

"By law, you are correct. However, would you let this boy have his freedom if he paid his debt to you? The five guineas the boy mentioned?"

"Yes. Them are the terms for all of me boys. I need to be repaid for the cost of taking them in and feeding and clothing them, times being tough as they are."

"Mister Armory, do you take responsibility for the actions of your climbing boys?"

"Yes. They sometimes get in trouble or don't do their work, and I must correct their behavior. If something goes wrong, I fix it for me customers."

Egan considered the words. Master Armory almost sounded sincere.

"No further questions, my lord." Mister Hackney returned to the table.

"Your witness," Chief Justice Pratt stated.

There was a slight pause as Mister de Lamerie and his solicitor exchanged a few hushed words. The solicitor stood, adjusted his coat, and approached Master Armory.

"Did you ever see the pendant covered in ash?"

"No."

"Did you see the sack that your boy found it in?" The solicitor emphasized the word 'found' in an exaggerated fashion.

"No, I did not."

"Did you see the stones that were supposedly in the casting?"

"No, the boy told me about the stones after Mister de Lamerie took them from him."

"How do you know your boy is not lying?"

"He's a good boy," Master Armory became defensive. "He doesn't lie."

Egan lifted his eyes to the King's Bench, as if in confession. Master Armory's assertion was itself a lie. Egan had lied more than once the day he tried to sell the pendant. Master Armory did not know Egan had lied, but surely the chief justice would know that he had lied. Judges could just tell.

"Let it be known that the boy's master never saw the jewels and that the boy never lies," the solicitor announced to the court. "No further questions, my lord."

"You are dismissed Mister Armory," Chief Justice Pratt stated. "Next witness?"

"The plaintiff rests its case," Mister Hackney announced.

"The court shall recess and reconvene after tea," Chief Justice Pratt stated.

CHAPTER XLVII

"Come, darling child," Missus Armory held out her hand to Egan.

He placed his hand listlessly within hers and allowed her to parade him about the hall.

"This is me boy, the one who found the jewel. Naughty of him to attempt to sell it, of course, but is he not a dear?" Missus Armory cackled. "I've been so distressed that such a crime was committed against one of our own. Paul de Lamerie ought to be ashamed."

Egan looked up at Missus Armory as she chatted away. She did not glide across the floor as the other women did; her wig bounced as she walked. Egan felt no warmth in her presence. He wished it were Mum holding his hand. Mum used to hold his hand and sing a song about his fingers. Egan could not remember the words. A familiar ache settled in his stomach.

He was tired of the charade and tired of waiting for a resolution. It was true that the stones had been taken from him, but it was not true that he was a treasured member of the Armory family. If he stepped out of line at court, he would not live to see the next morning. And if the jewels were not returned, Egan would be sent back to the cellar.

The remarks of "precious child" and "such a dearie" fell flat on his ears. Women like these never noticed broomers on the streets. They only cared for him because of his clean skin and fine clothes. No one helped him when Pitt died. No one cared for Pitt or called him a "dear child." Egan could not hide his disgust when Missus Armory pinched his cheeks and called him her "sweet fire imp."

From the crumbs on Master Armory's lapel, Egan guessed that he had missed tea when Missus Armory was introducing him to court.

Chief Justice Pratt returned in a timely fashion, and the proceedings began. Egan was tired and hungry. He leaned up against John's shoulder as the defense presented its case. Mister de Lamerie's mentor, Pierre Platel, testified to Mister de Lamerie's excellent work and stated that Mister de Lamerie established the standard for professionalism. Another goldsmith explained the common practice of presenting substandard jewels in high-quality castings to deceive society as to their worth. Bennett Bradshaw, an apprentice for Mister de Lamerie, testified that the apprentices frequently weigh empty castings and purchase the gold from selling parties.

Mister Hackney did not cross-examine any of the witnesses but instead consoled Master Armory with hushed comments.

"Next witness," Chief Justice Pratt ordered.

"My lord, the final witness is the defendant himself. The defense calls Paul de Lamerie," the solicitor announced.

Egan sat up, intent on listening to every word.

The clerk approached Mister de Lamerie with the Bible.

"Do you swear to tell the truth, the whole truth, and nothing but the truth, so help you God?"

"I do," Mister de Lamerie stated.

"Mister de Lamerie, please state your name and credentials for the court."

"I am Paul de Lamerie, goldsmith to King George. I came to London as a babe and was apprenticed to Pierre Platel at age 15. I registered my mark with Goldsmiths' Hall in 1713, and have established a business creating exceptional pieces, many of which are enjoyed by the king and ranking members of society."

"Mister de Lamerie, do you contest the facts testified to by the boy? That he brought a pendant to your shop and the stones were removed by your apprentice?"

"I see no need to contest those facts," Mister de Lamerie replied.

Murmurs of confusion and surprise moved through the audience.

"Please entertain the court with the events of that day."

"I was molding a silver plate when one of my apprentices informed me that a boy was at the shop to sell a brass casting. I instructed him to weigh and purchase the brass from the boy. My apprentice went to the front room, weighed the casting, and called to me that it was worth three halfpence."

"This testimony is consistent with that of the plaintiff. Please continue," the solicitor said.

"I collected my purse and prepared to pay the boy three halfpence. He refused, requesting the casting back. I instructed my apprentice to do so and returned to my work. Several hours later, Mister Armory arrived at the shop, accusing me of stealing from him and beating his boy."

"Beating his boy?"

"The boy was bruised and had a large burn on his cheek. One of his eyes was black and swollen, and he walked as if he had been beaten."

"My lord, if it so please the court, I call your attention to the fact that at no time during this trial has Mister Armory accused Mister de Lamerie of striking the plaintiff's boy."

"So noted," Chief Justice Pratt stated.

The solicitor continued. "Did the plaintiff tell you that he was the owner of the jewel?"

"No, he stated that his boy found it."

"Did the plaintiff specify who took the stones?"

"Yes, the boy stated that my apprentice took the stones from the pendant."

"Mister de Lamerie, do you have the stones in your possession?"

"No."

"Did you ever have the stones in your possession?"

"No. I have not."

"Did you ever instruct your apprentice to remove the stones?"

"No."

"Did you ever instruct your apprentice to sell the stones?"

"No."

"Mister de Lamerie, when did you realize that your apprentice may have stolen the stones from the plaintiff?"

"When I was summoned to court."

"No further questions, my lord," the solicitor returned to his table.

All eyes were on Mister Hackney. He stood, adjusted his coat, and began.

"Mister de Lamerie, do you claim ownership of the jewels removed from the pendant?"

"No. I do not."

"The apprentice, the servant you own that…"

"I am offended by that allegation. I do not keep slaves as does Mister Armory," Mister de Lamerie interrupted.

"Mister Armory apprentices boys the same as you," Mister Hackney stated.

"There is a great distinction between us. Mister Armory claims his boy is property. My apprentice is his own man."

"Apprentice or servant or slave, you are responsible for his actions. Are you not?" Mister Hackney challenged.

"I am not answerable for his actions. He is responsible for himself!" Mister de Lamerie shouted.

"You are answerable for his neglect!" Master Armory stood and shouted at his opponent.

"You are answerable for your neglect! Your boys are no better than slaves. You deliberately killed one last month by sending him into a burning chimney!"

"That was an accident!"

"Accident! You murdered that boy!"

"Order!" Justice Pratt commanded, smacking his gavel down on the table and glaring at the parties. "Solicitors, control your clients!"

"Apologies, my lord." Mister Hackney bowed to Chief Justice Pratt.

"You may finish your questions in a sophisticated manner."

"My lord, I have no further questions." Mister Hackney bowed again and retreated to the plaintiff's table.

"Mister de Lamerie, you may return to your seat," Chief Justice Pratt stated. "Solicitor?"

Recovering from the spectacle, Mister de Lamerie's solicitor stood and reasoned with the court. "My lord, distinguished members of the jury, the plaintiff brings an action of trover, an action to recover wrongfully taken personal property. The action against Mister de Lamerie should be dismissed for two reasons. First, in the plaintiff's own words he found the jewel. Only the owner of a thing has the property rights to maintain an action in trover. As a finder, the boy does not have requisite rights to bring a lawsuit."

"Second, this action for wrongful taking, whether true or untrue, is not rightfully charged against Paul de Lamerie. He did not take the stones, and he cannot return the stones. The responsible party is not even in this hall. Mister de Lamerie is an honorable man. Had he discovered any fault on his behalf, he would have already compensated the plaintiff.

"This case was brought in error and should be dismissed," the solicitor concluded.

Chief Justice Pratt directed his attention to Mister Hackney, "How do you respond?"

Mister Hackney stood, pressed his fingers together in front of his chest, and conveyed a composed and thoughtful speech.

"Tis true that the boy is a finder. However, a finder has better rights to property than a subsequent thief. If the true owner of the jewel is present, let him speak now so that his property may be returned."

A silence fell over Westminster Hall. No one stepped forward to speak.

"However, if the true owner is unknown, I offer that the boy has better rights as a finder than anyone else in this great hall. He is only a finder, but he still has the right to maintain this action of trover."

"Mister de Lamerie selects and trains his apprentices to act on his behalf. His apprentices conduct business in his shop. They are not free to act on their own behalf until their training is complete and they register their marks with Goldsmiths' Hall. Mister de Lamerie is responsible for them just as Mister Armory is responsible for his wee boy, the boy who wants to be a tobacco farmer. Mister de Lamerie's apprentice stole from Mister Armory's apprentice. The action shouldn't go with impunity, not when Mister de Lamerie is responsible for what occurs in his shop."

Mister Hackney bowed respectfully and returned to his seat.

Chief Justice Pratt's intense stare shifted between Master Armory and Mister de Lamerie. His eyes spoke fervent rebuke upon both parties. An unnatural silence filled the entire hall.

"Does another lay a claim to this pendant? Is the true owner present to contest this boy's possession?" Chief Justice Pratt's voice cut through the silence.

No one moved.

No one spoke.

A tense silence filled the hall as Chief Justice Pratt studied the audience and then the parties. He looked towards the jury and then to Egan.

The moments stretched the uncomfortable quiet.

When Chief Justice Pratt spoke, his deep voice echoed throughout the hall, commanding attention.

"On behalf of His Majesty King George, I hold that the finder of a jewel, though he does not by such finding acquire absolute property or ownership, has such a right as will enable him to keep it against all but the rightful owner."

"As a true owner has failed to claim lawful possession of this pendant, the boy may maintain this action in trover."

The court clerk quickly scratched a quill against the paper, recording the decision.

"On behalf of His Majesty King George, I hold that the action well lay against the master, who gives credit to his apprentice and is answerable for his neglect," Chief Justice Pratt glared at Mister de Lamerie.

"Distinguished members of the jury, unless Mister de Lamerie produces the jewels and shows them not to be of the finest water, you should presume the strongest against him. The measure of damages shall be the value of the best jewels that would fit in this casting," Chief Justice Pratt stated.

"My lord," Mister de Lamerie stood in appeal, "The most valuable stones that fit into that trinket would be rare diamonds. Is that not too great a price?"

"The price of deceit is always great," Chief Justice Pratt's fierce stare was as unwavering as his voice. "Mister de Lamerie, can you produce the stones for the court?"

"No, my lord. I cannot."

"Clerk, administer the oath," Chief Justice Pratt ordered.

"Members of the jury, stand and repeat after me," the clerk instructed.

The jurors stood. Egan listened as each phrase was repeated by the jurors.

"I swear by almighty God,"
"I swear by almighty God,"

"that I will faithfully try the defendant,"
"that I will faithfully try the defendant,"

"and give a true verdict according to the evidence."
"and give a true verdict according to the evidence."

Chief Justice Pratt slammed down his gavel, casting an austere silence over the courtroom. "The jury shall deliberate on the value of the jewels."

The litigants and onlookers stood as Chief Justice Pratt exited the hall, followed by the members of the jury.

Egan sat on the edge of the bench. The casting was worth over two pounds. He had more than three guineas in his shoes. If the jury announced that the stones were worth any amount over three guineas, he could pay Rory and then pay his debt. With eight, he could pay Iggy's too. Then he would find Mum and Kerrin and then walk to Leadenhall Street to find a position on a ship.

The court reconvened twenty minutes later under a veil of nervous anticipation. The jury arrived first, taking their place to the side of the dais. Everyone rose to their feet in respect as Chief Justice Pratt entered the hall and approached the bench.

"Has the jury reached a decision?"

A juror in the front corner stood and bowed to Chief Justice Pratt.

"We have, my lord."

"Members of the jury, what sayest thou?"

Egan brought his fists to his temples and bunched up his tiny body in anticipation. "Eight guineas," he whispered. "Please be eight guineas."

"Mister de Lamerie is hereby ordered to pay the chimney sweep's boy damages of fifty pounds within a fortnight or be taken into custody at Marshalsea Prison until such time as the debt is paid."

Egan's mouth dropped in a gasp. Fifty pounds! That was much more than he needed.

The audience erupted into a mingled roar of objection and approval.

Master Armory grinned and shook Mister Hackney's hand.

"A fair sum," Mister Hackney acknowledged. "A fair sum."

"God save the King," Chief Justice Pratt announced and slammed his gavel against the desk.

"God save the King," echoed around the room, and Chief Justice Pratt stood. His eyes found Egan, and his expression softened for a moment before he exited the hall.

The King's Bench was adjourned.

CHAPTER XLVIII

"Fifty pounds! Well done boy!" Men were patting Egan on the head and shaking his hands. "You can be a tobacco farmer after all," they laughed.

"Triumphant trial, Hackney, you old codger! One for the history books!" Nobles, solicitors, barristers, and members of society congratulated Mister Hackney.

Egan's head swam as the decision was discussed and debated around him.

"Do you like sausage, my boy?" Mister Hackney asked Egan.

"Yes, sir. I really do, sir," Egan answered.

"To the Red Lion to celebrate," Mister Hackney announced. The pub, patronized by the members of the Inns of Court and Parliament, commemorated Mister Hackney's achievement with plates of bangers and mash. It was the most delicious meal Egan had ever eaten, and he licked his fingers thoroughly when his plate was empty. Mister Hackney then ordered Egan sticky toffee pudding, which was the most delightful thing he had ever tasted.

It appeared that everyone in the Red Lion had been at court that day. People recited the arguments and spoke about the reaction of the crowds and Chief Justice Pratt's shrewd stare. A few fellow solicitors argued with Mister Hackney over points of law, arguments that would have made his case stronger, and tactics to remember for the next trial. Egan watched in awe as Mister Hackney again argued that the jewels belonged to Egan.

Several hours later the pub emptied and the victorious party headed out, walking across The Strand. With mutual wishes of much success and good health, Mister Hackney split off onto Holborn towards Gray's Inn. Master Armory and Egan continued towards Fleet Street.

It didn't take Master Armory long to settle on a pub to continue his celebration.

"I'm free to go then?" Egan asked Master Armory as they approached the pub.

"Tomorrow, me boy, business is for tomorrow," Master Armory cheered a loud greeting to the already drunken patrons as he entered the pub. He ordered a pint and lifted it to the ceiling. "To the King's Bench!" he yelled. The pub crowd cheered and drank with him.

Master Armory emptied flagons of ale, danced with barmaids, challenged other men to fight, and bragged about his victory at court. He retold the events to anyone who would listen and promised the barkeep extra coins for continued hospitality.

As the revelry continued, Egan realized that Master Armory was not going back to the house on Distaff Lane until morning. He longed to see the other broomers but was afraid to leave the pub, so he curled up underneath a table and fell asleep. His dreams were a confused muddle of bricks, soot, men shouting, jarring carriage rides, and people at court. His mind was too shattered to reach for the fading memories of his family. The restless slumber left him tired and confused when Master Armory shouted to wake him.

"Get up, runt," he barked, kicking the bench away from the table.

Egan slowly opened his eyes, remembering his surroundings. He was at a pub. It was morning. The jewels were worth fifty pounds.

Egan followed Master Armory as he stumbled out of the pub. He reeked of spirits.

"A grand victory. I defeated Paul de Lamerie, a sting he'll not forget. You can't cheat me!" he shouted into the quiet morning.

Egan followed Master Armory past the road to Distaff Lane. He was drunk and confused, but Egan was too cautious to suggest they turn around. They traveled along Thames Street until it became apparent where Master Armory was taking him.

"Are we going across the bridge to Southwark?"

"Yes," Master Armory muttered.

Master Armory was taking him home. But Jacob's Island was not his home anymore. Egan did not know where to find his home.

"I need to go back for Iggy. He gets five guineas, and Rory gets one."

"I'll see to it," Master Armory slurred.

"And all the broomers get potatoes, even the new ones."

Master Armory grabbed Egan by the neck, "I said I'll see to it," he spat in Egan's ear.

Egan recoiled and silently followed Master Armory across the bridge. He would follow Master Armory to Tooley Street, visit Mister Carrington and Curator Whalley, and then go back to meet Iggy that evening. The coins in his shoes would take care of them until they found a ship to work on.

The London Bridge bustled with morning activities and carriages trying to pass before the crowds slowed traffic to a crawl. Master Armory grunted at people who slowed his progress, although he was the one swaying from ale. Egan followed obediently, excited that he was almost free.

When they exited the gate at Southwark, Egan wanted to run until Master Armory was a distant memory. Instead, he walked obediently towards Tooley Street, not wanting to incur a parting jab.

"I'll be on me way then," Egan declared near St. Savior's Dock.

"Yer not going anywhere," Master Armory grabbed Egan's arm and dug his fingers into the thin flesh.

"Let me go! You have me fifty pounds!" Egan shrieked.

"You are me property, boy, so all of your property belongs to me. You never had fifty pounds. You never had five guineas."

"It's a lie? Five guineas to freedom? It's a lie?" Egan cried.

"You'll never get five guineas that aren't already mine."

"Do the other broomers know it? That it's a lie?"

"No. That's why you'll never see them again," Master Armory hissed, dragging him towards the dock.

"You there, dockworker. Is there a ship heading to the Americas? I have a boy to sell."

Egan struggled to free himself from Master Armory's grip. "I paid me debt! You can't sell me to the nabbers."

"I am interested in the boy," a voice behind them stated.

"I'll not take less than five guineas," Master Armory confronted the man. "That's wot he owes me, five guineas."

"How does he owe you such a sum? Did he steal it from you?" the man asked.

"No, he's my property, and five guineas is his price."

"How can one man really own another?"

"The law says so. The law judged me, and I won!" Master Armory spat.

"Maybe so," the man responded, "but will you win when God judges you?"

Master Armory tightened his grip on Egan and stared at the man. "The boy is mine, and five guineas is me price," he said.

"Done," the man agreed. "Rudgar!" he beckoned to his companion. "Take this boy aboard."

"Aye, captain," the man grabbed Egan's other arm and dragged him down to the dock.

"No, I paid me debt," Egan screamed as the man's strong arms grasped him about the waist. "No! I paid me debt!"

Rudgar secured Egan's flailing arms, hoisted him across the gangplank, and set him down inside the belly of the ship. Egan's fists pounded the man, but his large body blocked the exit.

"Yer not a slave, boy," Rudgar bellowed.

Egan struggled to escape, but Rudgar was strong and had a firm grasp of his shoulders.

"This is not a slave ship. Yer not going to the Americas. Yer not a slave," Rudgar repeated.

Egan surrendered in a torrent of tears.

"I paid me debt," he whimpered.

"I'm sure you did," Rudgar replied.

"But Master Armory sold me."

"Captain Andover doesn't trade slaves. He bought you to keep you from becoming one."

"Then wot am I?"

"A ship's boy I suppose. Yer a bit wee for anything else."

Egan's desperate eyes looked up at Rudgar.

"I'm a ship's boy?"

"It's the captain's call, but I'm not sure wot else you would do for. Will you let me show you 'bout the ship?"

Egan nodded, wiping his tears. He took hold of Rudgar's rough hand, which surprised the weathered sailor.

"Me Da was a sailor," Egan told the man between sniffles.

"Was he now?"

"He died at sea."

"Me father died at sea too, when I was about yer age."

CHAPTER XLIX

The Ademption, a merchant vessel, easing its way through the English Channel, became Egan's home. He had been assigned a rope hammock and a shelf for his belongings on a lower deck, although, he had no belongings to store. Everything was new and exciting. His Da had been right. Egan was a true Irishman. The sea called to him.

Egan was eager to learn his role aboard the ship and the language of sailing. Directions were renamed fore, aft, larboard, and starboard. Below deck, Egan couldn't figure out which direction he was facing or where the ship was sailing. He was tumbled about more than once by the constant erratic swaying of the waters. Sailors told him that he didn't have his 'sea legs' yet.

He had yet to meet the captain but looked up at the helm to watch him whenever he had a spare moment. His new master wore a stern, serious expression. He yelled out orders with controlled authority.

The captain and the other officers had sleeping quarters on the deck. He was instructed never to disturb them unless he was asked specifically to report for duty or deliver a message. If Egan disturbed the officers, they would throw him overboard. The warning came with a lighthearted tap on the head; still, Egan believed it might be true.

When Egan was instructed to go to mess, he looked about for what he was supposed to clean.

"Down to the mess deck," the sailor repeated, pointing to the hatch.

Egan obeyed and realized he was being sent to supper. He sat on the floor away from the table waiting for the sailors to eat, assuming the scraps would be for him.

"Wot you doing boy? Yer one of the crew. Sit." Rudgar patted the bench next to him.

Egan tentatively stood up and took a seat beside the weathered seafaring man. The sailors helped themselves to the food, passing square wooden plates up and down the table. Egan sat back and watched.

"Sick to yer stomach then?" Rudgar asked.

"No, sir."

"Then you need to eat." Rudgar placed a cut of salted meat, boiled potato, and biscuit on Egan's plate.

"That's all for me?"

"Aye, eat up."

"A sailor needs meat on his bones," said the sailor across the table.

Egan devoured the food with appreciative exhalations, much to the amusement of the sailors.

"He coos like a wee babe," one laughed.

"Aye. Skinnier than a babe too."

It didn't bother Egan. The sailors had teased him since he boarded the ship, but there was no malice in their words. After the teasing came help with chores and lessons on fastening knots. He was called "monkey" right before a sailor taught him to climb through the ship's arrangement of masts, spars, and yardarms. When Egan realized "monkey" was the name of a wee cannon, he swelled with pride. He never figured out what "son of a biscuit eater" meant, but was fascinated by the training that followed. And now, they were sharing their supper with him, and he sat at the table like a real sailor.

"Wot be yer name, boy?" a sailor asked.

"Egan Whitcombe, sir," he garbled with a full mouth.

"That's too much of a name for the sea. Wot shall we call you?"

Pitt had asked him the same question. Now Egan had a different answer.

"Me Da was called Whit when he was at sea. I'd like that too."

"Whit be a grand name for a sailor," Rudgar said.

"Tis, aye sir."

"It's aye aye at sea, boy," Rudgar said.

"Aye aye, sir."

"No, a loud 'aye aye' with all yer gut."

"Aye aye!" Egan shouted.

"Aye aye!" the sailors around the table echoed.

"Much better," Rudgar said.

"Can you sing?" a rugged voice at the other end of the table asked.

"A little," Egan answered.

"Favor us with a song."

"I know but one, and it's not fit for sea."

"Up on the table!" the sailor yelled.

Rudgar nudged Egan off his seat and onto the table. Egan positioned his feet around the empty plates and looked at the crew.

"Sing, Whit!" they cheered.

Egan began to sing Will and Tick's song, his voice raspy from the coal dust that coated his lungs.

"Sweeping chimneys keeps them neat,
Sweeping's best in summer's heat,
Come winter night when all is cold,
No trouble you'll have with smoking coal.

Scrape yer chimney and scrape it good,
Scrape it so you can burn coal or wood,
If you sweep in summertime,
In winter's chill, it will burn just fine.

Chimney fires burn so bright,
Casting off such dreadful light,
Get yer chimney cleaned all round,
Before a fire burns yer house down.

Up yer chimney he'll climb to fire,
Beat it down with crippled arms 'til he tires,
For in hell he's sure to burn,
A victim of his master's scorn.

For no one cries for the poor dead sweep,
Except for those that come to reap,
And those mates who search for sky,
That never meant for him to die.

Farewell, me friend, fare thee well.
Farewell, me friend, fare thee well."

There it was. Pitt's last benediction. Egan hoped Pitt was with Da, two ghosts following him upon the waters, sailing with Egan as they had promised. Maybe Reeves was with them too.

The sailors were solemn. It was not the cheerful song they had expected.

"You need a new song," Rudgar said, pulling Egan down from the table.

"I would not dishonor yer song with another tonight, but I'll teach you a new song on the morrow," the sailor at the end of the table promised.

"Aye aye, sir," Egan mustered his strongest voice.

"Yer father would be proud of you," Rudgar said, ruffling Egan's hair.

CHAPTER L

By the end of his second day aboard, Egan was sliding down ladders to the lower decks and standing tall and firm as the ship plunged through the waves. He had yet to understand his place on the ship or remember all his chores, but he scrambled about giving it his best effort. He was to help the cook in the galley, but he should not call it a kitchen. He was to carry messages between the officers and sailors, but not repeat any of the unusual words he heard. Such words could be vulgarities that he did not yet understand. He was to fasten sails and ropes and check that each line was taut, but not get in the way of the sailors working on deck.

Egan was awed by the sea, the crashing waves, the fresh air, the salty mist, and the wildlife. Egan saw birds dive towards the water; some were rewarded with a wriggling fish to crush in their beaks or pierce with their talons. Egan kept a vigilant watch for sea monsters, which he figured was part of his job. It was well known that evil things lurked in the water.

As he worked, Egan worried over Iggy and the other broomers and wondered what was happening in the cellar. He thought of Mum and Kerrin and the day he would return to find them. Egan pushed Master Armory from his thoughts. Master Armory no longer mattered. Egan belonged to the captain now.

"You, ship's boy!"

"Aye, sir?" Egan dropped a wet brush into the bucket of soapy water and stood.

"The captain called you to the bridge," the sailor's raspy voice was firm.

Egan's breath caught in his throat.

"Well, don't stand there, get moving!"

Egan ran towards the ladder and clambered up as quickly as his shaking legs allowed. On deck, he realized that the ship had changed directions, and he had to look both ways to find the helm. Once oriented, he ran across the deck and up the stairs to the helm where Captain Andover stood by the ship's wheel.

"Egan Whitcombe, sir," Egan announced in the strongest voice he could muster.

"Welcome aboard young man."

"Thank ye."

"We did not have time to speak earlier. I am Captain Andover. You shall call me Captain Andover, captain, or sir."

"Aye, sir...captain, thank ye."

"Well, Egan Whitcombe, what name do you go by?"

"I'd like to be called Whit, like me Da. He was a good Irishman. At sea, his mates called him Whit."

"Your father was a sailor?"

"Aye. He died at sea. I want to die at sea too."

Captain Andover studied Egan. "Very well, Whit, I hope you are worthy of being part of my crew."

"I am, sir. I'll show you I am."

"It will not be easy. I expect my crew to act bravely against tempests but also to be fair and honest in all their dealings."

"I will be just so."

"Whenever we dock and business is done, you will receive wages. After that, you may leave the ship or, if you prove yourself, I will hire you on for the next sailing."

"Wages, sir?"

"Every man aboard gets paid for his work."

"And I give it to you to pay me price?"

"Your price?"

"Wot you paid Master Armory."

"I did not buy you. I thought Rudgar explained that."

Egan lifted his head to look into the captain's eyes. The captain did not turn away or mock him.

"You paid me debt to Master Armory."

"He was selling what is unjust to own."

"I will repay me price. Take me shoes."

Egan pulled Pitt's shoes from his feet and held them out to the captain. "There are coins, me savings, over three guineas be in the soles."

"As long as I live, no slave will be transported on this ship, and only free men serve on my crew," Captain Andover stated firmly, lowering Pitt's shoes with the palm of his hand.

"Sir, me debt," Egan whimpered.

"You have no debt," the captain replied firmly.

"But me price..."

"Has been paid."

Egan dropped Pitt's scuffed shoes to the deck.

"You owe me nothing except to obey commands and work hard while you are part of my crew."

"I will," Egan choked, his voice wavering uncontrollably. Egan's knees buckled. He grasped his face in his hands and fell to the deck in anguish. Through guttural cries of horror, Egan released the fear, anger, bitterness, and sorrow that had held him captive since the day the Earnest Vesper came down the River Thames without Da aboard.

James Selvey, the first mate, approached the helm.

"Captain, shall I take the boy below? Rudgar will teach him proper behavior."

"No, Selvey. He needs no discipline."

"Sir?"

"Let the boy cry. Those who have known the brutality of bondage weep when they are made free."

Egan lay on the deck until his soul was drained of its misery. When the fresh, sea air revived his senses, he looked to find Captain Andover standing at the helm, intently steering the ship through the choppy waves with a quiet and commanding reserve.

What could he say to the captain to excuse his behavior? He should have been overwhelmed with the gratitude he now felt.

Egan wiped the tears from his face and tied Pitt's shoes back onto his feet. The coins slid into place beneath him.

"Selvey, the leech line is loose on the fore t'gallant sail," the captain bellowed.

Egan jumped to his feet and looked up to find the edge of a sail fluttering in the wind.

"I'll secure it, captain, sir," he offered.

"It's a fair distance up."

"I'm a climbing boy."

"You were a climbing boy. Don't forget who you are now."

"Aye aye, sir."

"Can you tie a figure-of-eight knot tight enough to hold against the wind?"

"Aye aye, captain. Rudgar showed me how."

"Very well, Whit. Climb and tighten the leech line of the fore t'gallant sail."

"Aye, aye, captain!" Egan ran to the main topgallant mast and began to scramble up, using his arms to heave him upwards and his legs to anchor his progress.

When he reached the foot of the topgallant sail, Egan pulled himself onto the wooden yard and grasped the thick rigging rope that held the shape and position of the sails. The loose corner of the sail flapped in the wind at the end of the narrow wooden beam.

Egan looked down.

The crew held a fishing net tight underneath him, prepared for him to fall.

"All right boy?" Rudgar called out.

"All right," Egan yelled.

At the helm, Captain Andover was watching him. When their eyes met, the captain nodded in encouragement.

Egan looked across the wooden beam. No one threatened him from below. No needles pierced his feet. No smoke clouded his path. Surrounded by the crisp ocean wind, there was no need to search for the sky.

Egan stepped around the rigging, bent down, and shimmied across the beam. He reached the leech edge, wrapped his feet together under the yard, and sat up. Pulling on the edge of the sail, Egan wrestled with the wind as he loosened and re-knotted the figure-of-eight.

"That right?" Egan called to the sailors below.

"Aye," Rudgar yelled. "Now look before comin' down."

"Wot?"

"Look o'er the water!"

Egan lifted his eyes. Surrounded by a vast expanse of water, the ship rocked along the endless line of waves that crested and crashed into the sea below. Egan was a wee seed pearl compared to the ocean that stretched out before him, but he was part of it. He was part of it, and his heart could hear its call. It was just as Da had said. Egan was at home among the water.

Egan looked towards the stern of the ship where a splinter of land was fading into the distance. The brisk wind that pressed against the sails caused his eyes to water, but the tears held no grief. They merely washed the remaining soot away.

Epilogue

"Now step I forth to whip hypocrisy."

-William Shakespeare, Love's Labour's Lost

In 1788, British Parliament passed *The Act for the Better Regulation of Chimney Sweepers and their Apprentices*, which prohibited the use of children under the age of eight years to clean chimneys. The act was not enforced.

In 1834, British Parliament passed *The Chimney Sweeps Act*, which prohibited the use of any child under the age of ten years to clean chimneys. The act was not enforced.

In 1840, British Parliament passed another chimney sweeps act, prohibiting the cleaning, sweeping, or coring of any chimney or flue by a person younger than twenty-one years of age. The act was not enforced.

In 1875, British Parliament required businesses to obtain police authorization to provide chimney-sweeping services; children could be used if the police monitored the sweeping activities. The act was not enforced.

The use of children to clean chimneys ended only with the advancement of central heating systems.

Historical Notes

Infants of the Brush: A Chimney Sweep's Story is based on the court case *Armory v. Delamirie*, which was an action in trover decided by Chief Justice Pratt of the King's Bench in 1722. Trover is a common law action to recover personal property that was wrongfully taken. Paul de Lamerie's name was misspelled as "Delamirie" in the court record. The following is the full text of the case:

ARMORY v. DELAMIRIE, 1 Strange 505 (K.B. 1722)

In Middlesex coram Pratt C.J.

The plaintiff being a chimney sweeper's boy found a jewel and carried it to the defendant's shop (who was a goldsmith) to know what it was, and delivered it into the hands of the apprentice, who under the pretense of weighing it, took out the stones, and calling to the master to let him know it came to three halfpence, the master offered the boy the money, who refused to take it, and insisted on having the thing again; whereupon the apprentice delivered him back the socket without the stones. And now in trover against the master these points were ruled:

1. That the finder of a jewel, though he does not by such finding acquire an absolute property or ownership, yet he has such a property as will enable him to keep it against all but the rightful owner, and consequently may maintain trover.

2. That the action well lay against the master, who gives credit to his apprentice, and is answerable for his neglect.

3. As to the value of the jewel several of the trade were examined to prove what a jewel of the finest water that would fit into the socket would be worth; and the Chief Justice directed the jury, that unless the defendant did produce the jewel, and shew it not to be of the finest water, they should presume the strongest against him, and make the value of the best jewels the measure of their damages: which they accordingly did.

A basic principle of property law was established by the holding in *Armory v. Delamirie* – a person who finds something has a right to keep it against all but the rightful owner (i.e. "finders keepers").

Armory v. Delamirie was one of a number of cases that began a complex discussion on the definition and scope of property rights that continues 300 years later. The principle of property ownership – that person who owns property has a right to keep that property against the whole world except from a person with a better right to that property – is ingrained in Western society and allows people to keep and defend their property against trespassers, thieves, arsonists, and others who would try to take or assert a right to that property.

Child ownership was an established point of law in the 1700s. The chimney sweeper's boy named as the plaintiff in *Armory v. Delamirie* most likely would not have had the right to bring a claim to the King's Bench. The case would have been brought by the boy's master and in the master's name. Therefore, I inferred that "Armory" was the name of the boy's master and not the name of the boy. In consideration of the cultural context of the case, it is unlikely that the chimney sweeper's boy benefited in any way from the value of the jewel or the decision of the court.

Armory v. Delamirie is one of the first cases to establish the doctrine of respondeat superior, which holds a master (or employer) legally liable for the wrongful act of his or her servant (or employee) if the servant performs such act in the course of the servant's duties for the master. The doctrine is based on two theories of equitability. First, it was unjust to hold a servant responsible to pay for a wrongful act that was done on behalf of his or her master. Second, the wronged person could recover damages from the master when the servant did not have the money to pay for his or her wrongful act, and, if appropriate, the master could recover such damages through the labor of his or her servant. In *Armory v. Delamirie*, Justice Pratt held Lamerie personally responsible for the acts of the apprentice on the basis of respondeat superior – Lamerie was answerable for his apprentice's neglect because the apprentice acted on his behalf.

The doctrine of respondeat superior was part of the common law adopted by the English colonies in America, and thereafter became part of the common law in the United States.

Despite the court decision against him, or maybe because of the decision, Paul de Lamerie became one of the greatest silversmiths of the 18th century. While his early record is fraught with indiscretions, his record is clean and noteworthy following the *Armory v. Delamirie* decision. Lamerie is known for his Rococo style, and many of his works are on display at the Victoria and Albert Museum in London. A two-handled silver cup and cover Lamerie hallmarked in 1720, was among the wedding gifts when Queen Elizabeth II married Prince Philip, Duke of Edinburgh in 1947.

Charles Greville is a character of my own imagination. Paul de Lamerie indentured David Eymars of Westminster in 1718 and Bennett Bradshaw of Leicestershire in 1721. I could not find any reliable evidence that either one of these young men was the apprentice involved in the case *Armory v. Delamirie*. To avoid incorrectly attributing the events of the case to either apprentice, I created the character of Charles Greville.

As for the rest of the story, I tried to remain true to historical accounts and find inspiration in newspapers, journals, and other primary accounts of the time.

Although a few climbing boys were children apprenticing with their parents, most were kidnapped, taken from the workhouse, or purchased from poor families. Commentators at the time called the use of climbing boys "thinly disguised slavery."

Chimney sweeping was an unforgiving trade. Masters forced boys (and girls) to climb up flues by poking their legs with needles or lighting a fire in the hearth underneath them. The idiom "light a fire under someone" has its origins in this cruel practice.

In 1828, Joseph Glass designed a chimney-cleaning machine that was capable of cleaning any flue; it was inexpensive at just £4 per unit. Master sweeps still preferred to use climbing boys because the machine required two people to operate it while a child could sweep a chimney unaided.

There are numerous records of climbing boys being malnourished, beaten, deformed, diseased, and crippled by "accidents." In 1831, John Pasey climbed a chimney in a coffee house. The brickwork was so decayed that when he reached the top, the whole chimney collapsed. He was found beneath the bricks, his skull crushed.

The Society for Superseding the Necessity of Climbing Boys reported in 1839 that a boy named William Wilson was ordered to clean a flue that was still hot from a fire that had recently been extinguished. He was grievously burned and hospitalized for weeks. His caregiver described him as a "meek, gentle, little creature…the tears started in his eyes when he was spoken kindly to."

The resilience of children amazes me. Around 1840, a picture was taken of a group of children who were used to excavate coal. Standing in the front is a young boy with a large grin; he looks thrilled to have his picture taken. It may have been the proudest moment of his life. In the darkest of circumstances, children will dance in the rain, play games with a clump of dried mud, and laugh when someone farts.

Egan, Pitt, and the other broomers in this story are fictional characters. While I gave them names and words on a page, their spirit comes from the child laborers who endured unspeakable cruelty and still found a reason to smile.

Appendix A
British Currency

British Coin	Common Name(s)	Value (In 1720)
Quarter Pence	Farthing	¼ Pence
Half Pence	Haypenny	½ Pence
Pence	Penny, pee	1 Pence
Twopence	Tuppence, copper, two penny bit	2 Pence
Sixpence	Tanner, six penny bit, six pee	6 Pence
Shilling	Bob, twelve pee	12 Pence
Half Crown	Half-a-crown	2 Shillings and a Sixpence
Crown		5 Shillings
Pound		20 Shillings (240 Pence)
Guinea	Gentlemen's pound	21 Shillings (252 Pence)

Appendix B
Definitions and Translations

A ghrá mo chroí – Gaelic greeting translated "love of my heart."

An tiarna déan trócaire a anam – Gaelic phrase translated "the Lord have mercy on his soul."

Gardy-loo – English form of the French term "garde à l'eau" translated "watch out for the water." The phrase was called out before the contents of a chamber pot were thrown out the window into the street. In British have since shortened the term to just "loo," the English word for toilet.

Jacke – A shortened form of "jackeen."

Jackeen – A contemptuous designation for a self-assertive worthless fellow.

Slán – Gaelic word meaning "safe." A shortened form of "goodbye."

Slán abhaile – Gaelic phrase meaning "safe home." It is used to say "goodbye."

Squib – a small firecracker.

Twig – Cockney word meaning "understand" or "okay."

Acknowledgements

I first read the case *Amory v. Delamirie* in 2006, preparing for my first class of Property Law at the University of Denver, Sturm College of Law. I then spent the next eleven years researching and writing *Infants of the Brush, A Chimney Sweep's Story*. It was a challenging project, and thankfully, I was not alone.

I owe a debt of gratitude to Seth Watson, my writing apprentice and cover model; Carrie Knoles for the inspired cover design; my astute father, James Watson, and adventurous mother, Sarah Watson (I would be lost without you); my little big brother, Adam Watson; dear friends Renee Motter, Debra Mazza, Pamela Nicol, Amie Adams, Corrie McClure, J. A. Van Denack, Stacey Stitt, and Will and Patrice Hubbell, who collectively spent countless hours reading drafts and agonizing with me over various details of this story; and my grandfather, A. Carlton Cockey, who scoured each book in his extensive library to help me with my research – I miss you each day that passes.

Gwendolyn Ashbaugh, thank you for your brilliant advice and the precious time you invested in my aspirations. I wish I could repay those hours.

Stephen Parolini, editor extraordinaire, thank you for your efforts and insight.

Finally, I would be remiss without saying a special thank you to my brothers, nephews, and former students who inspired each grin, prank, and yarn in this book.

ABOUT THE AUTHOR

A. M. Watson is a teacher, attorney, and author whose soul awakens when visiting libraries, museums, and historic sites. She will always consider Victor, Colorado home.

Infants of the Brush: A Chimney Sweep's Story is A. M. Watson's debut novel.

CPSIA information can be obtained
at www.ICGtesting.com
Printed in the USA
BVHW021326200223
658851BV00024B/220